Whoever it was chuckled.

"I do not believe this is the time to reveal my identity to you," the raspy voice said. "But I do see your pretty pearls down here. Would you like to get them back?"

"Yes," Clara cried, though her hands were shivering, her mouth felt dry. "Yes, please," she repeated in a slightly less high-pitched voice. A fortune down there, a goddamn fortune!

"That can be accomplished," the stranger in the well replied, "on certain conditions..."

"Which are?"

"That I shall eat by your table and sleep in your bed."

Clara was speechless. Was he making fun of her?

"What is your answer?" It sounded from the well.

He was definitely messing with her.

"Pearls first," she said, in a voice that didn't quite carry.

The person down there chuckled again. "You do not trust me, then? Very well. I will come to your house with the pearls this night. And then you will have to let me in."

"Wait!" A wave of fear made her feel slightly sick. She definitely did not want a demanding madman at her door. "You don't know where I live!"

He didn't reply at first, then the answer came faintly, as if he was far away: "Of course I know where the witches dwell."

Also recommended...

You may also like these other works published by ForbiddenFiction:

Touched by Death, a ForbiddenFiction Special Collection
An anthology of erotic encounters with death that balances sexy and horror in a way that makes readers squirm.

Unattainable love has always been one of the favorite themes of romance. Who could be more unattainable than the dead? Here are ten erotic tales of love and loss, terror and hope, and of course desires that cannot or perhaps should not be fulfilled. Here is the "little death" alongside the big Death. Here are people dying—and killing—for love.

Touched by Death is a erotic horror collection of stories filled with the living and the dying, the dead and the ones who come back. Within you'll find attempts at reviving lost love, new views on courting death, and evidence that obsessive vampire stalkers are not always romantic—though zombies sometimes are.

http://forbidden-fiction.com/library/collection/SPC-1.100001

The Charming by J.A. Jaken
Clayton MacAllister had it all, but the shadow of a past love blinded him until life was slipping through his fingers. Just as Clay is ready to give up on the idea that he might ever be happy, a charming stranger steps into his life like a blessing—or a curse. (M/M+)

http://forbidden-fiction.com/library/story/JAJ-1.000046

Wicked Fairy Tales

a ForbiddenFiction Special Collection

edited by D.M. Atkins

ForbiddenFiction
www.forbiddenfiction.com

an imprint of

Fantastic Fiction Publishing
www.fantasticfictionpublishing.com

WICKED FAIRY TALES
A Forbidden Fiction book

Fantastic Fiction Publishing
Hayward, California

© D.M. Atkins, 2012

CREDITS
Editors: D.M. Atkins, Rylan Hunter, Lon Sarver
Cover Design: Siolnatine
Cover art: Rainbowchaser at Dreamstime.com; KrisCole at Pixmac
Internal cover art: Jennie Harbour, Ben Newman, Siolnatine,
cynoclub and Fotosmurf at Pixmac, Leucrotta, Arthur Rackham,
Giuseppe Parisi and Konstantynov at Dreamstime
Internal cover design: D.M. Atkins, Siolnatine
Production Editor: Erika L Firanc
Proofreading: JhP323, Jae Knight, Aislinn, Kailin Morgan, Todd
Michaels

SKU: SPC-100002-02 FFP
ISBN: 978-1-62234-079-8

Published in the United States of America

DISCLAIMER

This book contains works of fiction which include explicit erotic content; it is intended for mature readers. Do not read this if it's not legal for you.

All the characters, locations and events herein are fictional. While elements of existing locations or historical characters or events may be used fictitiously, any resemblance to actual people, places or events is coincidental.

Some of these stories depict fictional BDSM; they are not intended to be used as an instruction manual. This book contains descriptions of erotic acts that may be immoral, illegal, or unsafe. The characters are not models for the Safe, Sane and Consensual forms embraced by most current practitioners of BDSM. The authors take license with the use of BDSM for dramatic effect. Do not take the events in this story as proof of the plausibility or safety of any particular practice.

If you enjoy this collection, you can sign up for a free membership at ForbiddenFiction.com and discuss it with other readers and the authors at the Wicked Fairy Tales story page at
http://forbiddenfiction.com/library/collection/SPC-1.100002

We do our best to proof all our work, but if you spot a text error we missed, please let us know via our website Contact Form at
http://forbiddenfiction.com/contact

For those of us who want more from our stories than happily ever after.

Contents

Milk

Claryssa Berg

In the mirror lives a secret the Wicked Queen cherishes above all else. Snow White is an apple begging to be devoured. In order to save the one, the Queen must rule the other, body and soul.

Milk

They always held a fascination for me, the arts of pleasure and pain. Even as a young princess I cared little for hearts, broken or whole — but I cared for this: the craving of the flesh, the hunger in a kiss, the power and thrills of ecstasy...

I first met my mistress when I was a child, appearing to me as an old woman with withered skin and ragged hair who looked out on me from the swirling depths of a mirror, brought to me as a gift from afar. A land of sun and desert, they told me, where the princesses lived in tents of brightly colored silk.

I used to look at her in the glass, and her ice yellow eyes were measuring me in return. Then she started to come out when I was alone, slithering across the gilded, jewelled frame as a white serpent and curling up in my lap. She told me her name was Zela, and that she had been imprisoned by magicians — tall men in embroidered robes who had cursed her for her wicked deeds. The silvery looking-glass was her prison — her coffin.

I was never afraid of my scaled friend. And as I grew older, she told me secrets — like who was planning to poison whom at my father's court and — more importantly — the secrets of the body, and who was doing whom behind closed doors. Her serpent tongue taught me much. She was my mistress in all, and for all the secrets she taught me, I gave her my affection in return. And she changed: in the mirror the old woman was gone and in her place was a goddess: white diamond skin, her hair a waterfall of white silk. I thought her so beautiful, every glimmering inch of her, down to the tips of her fangs, gleaming like polished ivory. To keep her that way, my confidant told me I would have to feed her my blood or my pleasure. I chose pleasure. Hiking my skirts up every night before the mirror, bringing myself over the edge with lust, I fed her all my passion. When she slithered out from behind the frame I gave her my milk, coaxed from my core. She licked it from my fingers, and when back behind the glass — she smiled.

When I was quite grown up, at the height of my beauty, Zela gave me the most precious gift of all: power to defy age, eternal youth in exchange for my services. To show her my gratitude, I had a rod made of quartz crystal with a carved serpent's head at the top in her honor. It became my steady companion in my explorations of pleasure, pain and the realms in between. Dripping with carnal wine, pleasure for her to feast upon, it was my gift for her, a token of our alliance... I am no fool; I know what Zela is, and what she wants — ever since she first approached me, I have known... But she is as useful to me as I am to her — ours is a perfect match...

I brought my first lovers to her, enjoying them in front of the mirror. It looked at those times as just a silvery slate in an ornate frame, but I knew better. Zela was in there, watching me at play: big men chained on the floor, spears erect and eager; me, a waif maid with red-golden hair, bringing my whip down on them. I rode them till they burst, and fed my serpent its spoils from my fingers. Those were happy days for us. But for a little while I feared they would be over. It was a marriage; of course, I was to marry a king. I did not know him at all, had only met him once and did not remember much of it. But I was a princess of some value, politically and economically, and I would have to face my fate as all maidens of my standing must. The fact that the king in question was old and probably all dried up did nothing to inspire me. And I feared for my nights — they had always been mine to do with as I pleased. Perhaps with an old husband it would be different. Maybe my nights had to be spent with ointments and teas of bitter herbs just to make him work as he ought to? My fears were many, my future looked grave, but that was before I met *her*.

I had heard of her, of course, she was renowned for her beauty already then. Skin like snow, they said, lips like blood and hair the color of ebony. They called her Snow White, though her real name was something quite different. I liked it though, as snow is the purest slate, so easy to taint — and tainting it soon became my greatest desire.

I was to be her queen, her stepmother, but she was just a few years younger than me, a woman just come into her bloom; her petals slowly opening to reveal the temptation inside. To men, the temptation was toxic, leaving them with bleeding hearts; to me, it was a challenge. I could meet her with temptation of my own.

True, she was a beauty, a beauty with hungry eyes. There was always a restlessness about her, even when she stood still. She reeked of her desire, yet unfulfilled, a passionate young woman, ready to be picked. As she first saw me at the reception in her father's great hall, her gaze lingered at my cleavage, her nostrils flared when her shiny, black gaze caressed my neck, my hair, my waist... Her fingers shivered slightly when she greeted me.

"You may kiss my ring," I dared her. The girl only smiled, and did it.

As dull as the father was, exciting was the daughter.

I could not help but tease her: touch her whenever I could, a brief hug, a hand on her wrist, her shoulder... she felt so soft, supple, pliant... And she blushed so prettily, little hands trembling, whenever she came in touch with my skin.

As I was the new queen she was expected to wait upon me with the rest of the ladies at court, and I picked her — always her, to help me undress, get dressed. I revelled in the heat I saw rising in her when she saw my naked body. Her gaze was always drawn, as by an invincible force, to the coppery hair at my crotch, the swell of my breasts — nipples puckered and hardened before her eyes.

I had Snow White watch while the maids oiled my skin, spoke to her about everyday things: dinners, hunting parties, weather, cakes, and smiled inwardly each time she lost the thread, licked her lips, shifted on the floor beside me. Then I let her lace my dress.

"How beautiful you are," she said in her sing-song voice. "You hair is so red, your eyes are so green... like emeralds, almost." She smiled her lovely smile.

Snow White was so kind, they said. Good-hearted and compassionate. A pleasant and well-behaved queen-to-be. And, yes. She was. But no one but me seemed to notice how it pleased *her* to do those kind deeds. How it ignited her fire to serve and obey. Her eyes lit up, her body relaxed and a heat rose in her cheeks every time I asked her to redo the lacings, comb through my hair again, adjust the ribbons on my shoes... Her lips would part slightly then, when she knelt before me on the floor, and she would wet them with the tip of her tongue, her bosom heaving beneath the exclusive fabrics of her dresses, while she adjusted the silly ribbons, one by one, and then once over again.

I wondered what lived in her heart... How much darkness, how much light. How much pleasure and how much pain... Would she be willing to let me have my way?

Zela coiled up in my lap, her fangs affectionately nibbling the skin on my hands. "As beautiful as you are, my queen," she teased me, "the girl is prettier still. I think we would want her milk."

Snow White was quite ripe for picking when I decided the time was right. I had been teasing her for weeks and her old father had already grown tired of his new bride, preferring to spend his night drinking wine and playing chess with the lords instead of trying to please me in bed.

I asked her to help me get ready for sleep, told all my other maids to leave. And as my dress of heavy, green silk came off she said, quite out of the blue:

"My father has been married twice before. I will never regard you as my mother."

It could have been haughty, even insulting, but I got her meaning at once.

"And I," I told her, "have never seen you as a daughter."

Our gazes met in Zela's mirror. For a minute we just stood there, looking at each other. Then she broke off the stare and I said: "Why don't you take off your dress as well?"

She gave me a shy glance and then she did as she was told, as I expected her to do. Off came the blue gown, down to the floor. She was quite naked underneath. I closed my arms around her neck, skin like expensive velvet, and we kissed, soft at first, then passion began to rise in me and I pried her lips open with my tongue. Kissed her sweet, open mouth. Licked the moist cave with my tongue. I caressed her breast with my open palm, and felt her eager hand upon my own as I tugged at the nipple, weighing the breast in my hand. I pulled her closer and inhaled the scent of her: sweet like flowers with something else underneath; spices and fur, sweat and fresh juices.

I turned her to face the mirror, told her not to be shy... She knelt between my thighs and arched her head backwards. Lips like blood, tongue like a snake. Her hot, moist breath was on my skin. My fingers in her hair, ebony tendrils of silk around my wrists...

You may say that I was cruel... but *she* was surely wicked. She licked me like a queen with her sugar mouth and honey tongue. Swirling, playing, eager, so eager... and then, tasting, licking my milk. Drops of salt and pleasure. Her fingers slipped inside of me. She was good at it, knew exactly what to do, coaxing it out of me, a harsh cry and then—I clenched around her hand, pressed her face to my crotch and she lapped it up eagerly, every drop of milk I gave... She was a good girl, Snow White. Good girl, indeed.

How bruised her lips looked afterwards, her eyes were glazed with heat. I said, "Bend over!" And she did, balanced on all fours before me—legs spread. I picked up a supple twig of willow from my bed and smacked it across her bum, that delicious white apple of meat spread out before me, once, twice... I could smell her sex; sweet apple milk. Another smack and she sighed. Her breasts in the mirror swung with the impact. Strawberry nipples and supple flesh. Yes, I hit her hard. Red swells, ridges of passion. I put the twig down, picked up my crystal rod and pushed it inside of her, crouched down behind her and worked her hard from behind. She sighed, moaned. I reached for one of her breasts and squeezed it in my palm. Pinched the strawberry peak with two fingers until she cried. Worked her even harder with the rod, let her nipple go to smack her bottom with my hand. Hard. Unable to restrain myself, my head dipped down and I bit her

—where I'd hit her, drew blood from one of her delicious cheeks. She came then, with a cry.

Afterwards I cleaned her with my tongue, licked the sweetness from her crotch. She watched me in the mirror... awed.

You may say that I was wicked, but she came to me almost every night after that. Wanted me to tie her up and slap her hot and wet. She was my precious princess, and took such pleasure in my games. Kneeling obediently at my feet, offering me her breasts, her behind, to do with as I pleased. All that creamy snow white skin was entirely at my disposal. I savoured every inch of it. The flowing juices of her sweetest meat, I dutifully offered to Zela. She was pleased. Grew even more brilliant, more beautiful in her prison.

I gifted my raven-haired princess a bead of polished onyx for each time she made me come. Her reward, her naughty gems. She had a rosary made of them and brought them to mass, praying her wicked wishes before the altar. Sometimes I caught her smiling, eyes closed, while she caressed the black pearls in her lap. I could see her blush: pale pink roses in her cheeks, and I knew she was aroused. Knew she would come and see me then, naked under her gown, and beg me to treat her like a naughty child: fingers inside of her, slaps on her bum, punishments performed by her tongue... Keep her on a leash of braided silk, silver clasps on her nipples—it was an art; to keep her satisfied took all of my cunning. To master her I had to be perfect in my demands. To rule a future queen, one must be mighty as a goddess. A constant challenge... and how she loved me...

The rosary is in the coffin with her now, clutched between her fingers. My dark angel of wicked wishes is lying there on display. It was another marriage, of course, that put an end to our games. Snow White was to marry a prince who lived far, far away...

She cried in my arms on the night that her father told her; my plump, juicy apple wanted to remain my slave. And I—I told her it would never happen, promised her we would never be apart... but after she had left me, I almost cried as well: Zela's plan had gone so well, I could not bear to have it ruined by an insignificant prince. Zela herself watched me from the mirror. She had a cunning expression on her beautiful face.

"Do not fret, my girl, it is time," she said. "I am strong now, have taken so much from her... I am sure it can be done." Then she came slithering out from the mirror.

The next night, when Snow White came and undressed by my bed, I sat up to my knees and offered her my breast, squeezed it between my fingers. A few drops of milky white appeared on my dark red nipple.

"Drink it," I urged her.

For the first time I saw hesitation in her gaze when she looked at me.

"Drink it!" I bid her again. "Think of my breast as a candied apple," I told her with a smile laced with promises of pleasure. "Suck at it as you would a piece of sugar; swallow it down like wine."

And she did it: drank and swallowed Zela's toxic milk, suckled me almost dry—before she fell to the floor, deathly pale. Gone.

Dead now, she is in the dungeons among her forefathers, in a coffin made entirely of glass. The spirits of seven departed knights are keeping watch at my command, making sure that no one but me touches her body. The fair skin, perfectly preserved, the ebony hair... and the lips as red as blood...

And when the day comes that my sordid husband is dead, and the power in this realm belongs to me, I shall go down there. I shall bite my lip until it bleeds and kiss her cold, red mouth. She will open her dark eyes and smile at me then. A goddess freed from the glass at last. Never again shall we be apart, separated by cold frames and reflective windows. She shall be my goddess for real then, dressed in the prettiest flesh we could find. No more a snake in my lap, or a dream, caught in the swirling mists of a mirror. Zela shall be my princess. And I—I shall kneel before the only one worthy of my love, and ask her, pleadingly, to let the red and blue tokens of her affection rain down on me from above.

If you enjoyed this story, you can discuss it with other readers and the author at the *Milk* story page at http://forbiddenfiction.com/library/story/CB1-1000013.

Geppetto Falls Off the Wagon

Matthew Nadelhaft

The great woodcutter Geppetto, envious of his creation Pinocchio's wild sex life, builds himself a female companion while on an alcohol-fueled bender. She comes to life hot and willing and Geppetto gets the ultimate sexual experience.

Geppetto Falls Off the Wagon

Snow White was sitting on Pinocchio's face, grinding her hips like a pestle and grunting, "Tell a lie! Tell the truth! Tell a lie!" Geppetto permitted himself one long, lustful survey of her porcelain buttocks, impaled on Pinocchio's nose, before closing the door in disgust. *The little bastard,* he thought. I make the boy out of nothing but an armload of planks, give him the gift of life, and what does he do? He whores his novelty nose to a train of slutty princesses and blushing damsels.

First there had been Little Red Riding Hood, that jailbait minx with her tote bag full of goodies and her thighs scissored around the lad's pencil neck for hours at a time. She had stamina; Geppetto had been kept awake entire nights by her wolfish howls. Then Briar Rose, who had woken up with years of repressed libido bursting her breast: far too much for that staid prince and his chaste good-morning smooches. She'd wanted it all, had ordered the boy through cowgirl, reverse cowgirl, missionary, and doggy-style nosejobs along with positions Geppetto couldn't have identified with the aid of the *Kama Sutra*. Their affair had reached a level of kinkiness Geppetto had never imagined. Briar Rose had nearly flooded him out of his room when they'd experimented with watersports, and afterwards the brat had the nerve to ask Geppetto for weatherproofing.

After that energetic fling had come Cinderella, with her shy-girl act, ragged Emo wardrobe, and pumpkin-sized hooters. She had almost turned the casual sex into a relationship. Then, one day, Cinderella had squealed to a stop outside the house in her mouse-powered sports car and climbed though Pinocchio's window to find him giving a throbbing snoot-ride to her fairy godmother. Pinocchio had tried to weasel his way out of it, but the same feature that kept him up to his eyebrows in muff had proved his undoing. By the time he had finished explaining, his nose had been so swollen even Alice, with her talent for making holes stretch, couldn't have fit it anywhere.

And now Snow White, the hottest disenfranchised princess in all of Fairyland. God damn. According to Sleazy, whose foul mouth and vivid imagination had gotten him banned from all the storybooks, Snow White could take all eight dwarves in a night and still have enough energy for three rounds behind closed doors with a Rampant Rabbit. But Sleazy had been known to lie almost as much as Pinocchio; according to the woodsman, Snow White never touched those dwarves. The one thing Geppetto knew for sure was that she gave Pinocchio's face regular and thorough workouts.

Aw fuck it, Geppetto thought. He knew the score: he was jealous. The last time he'd lubed his crankshaft, Rapunzel had been wearing a bob. And look at her now: Geppetto couldn't help remembering the time he'd been working on the fence in the front yard and glanced in the window to spy her mounting Pinocchio. Her blond hair had cascaded over the two of them like a shifting blanket and her completely shaved snatch gleamed with dew. It was almost more than he could bear to think about. Just listening to the wooden brat reaming his way through the Fairyland phone book was the closest Geppetto'd come to a sex life in decades. If he weren't so disgusted by the lad's antics he'd probably have been whacking off with his ear to the wall, imagining that it was his own lined face plumbing all those pink and puckered girl-parts. Maybe he could drill a hole in the wall…Too late to find out if the rumours were true about Little Red Riding Hood taking it in the butt, though, unless she came back for another round.

Geppetto rummaged noisily in his cabinets, hoping to remind the kid he was still alive but knowing Pinocchio wouldn't be able to hear anything with Snow White's thighs clapped over his ears. He emerged with a bottle of apricot brandy and a chipped mug. He'd given up drinking years ago, hoping to make himself a role-model for Pinocchio, and look where it had got him. Why deny himself any longer? Life had to hold some pleasures. The bottle had been in his cupboard for ages; the three bears had presented it to Geppetto in appreciation after he made them a wooden cage for that thieving Goldilocks. Goldilocks: even she'd be grown up by now. Wouldn't be a surprise to find her getting the nasal probing one of these days. The right combination of fibs and part-truths and Pinocchio's face-mounted dildo would probably be just right.

With a sigh like an asthmatic tea-kettle, Geppetto plunked his tired ass onto the workbench and poured himself a generous shot, then another. He kept knocking them back until the bottle was empty. Shit, was that all he had? He tossed aside work gloves and sketchbooks until he found several dusty bottles of cheap vodka and whiskey. Not the good stuff, but it would do for an all-night bender. If he wanted to restock on quality hooch, he'd better make something else for those bears. Or maybe the three little pigs had a stash. Those talking pork chops always needed something built, the way they went through houses.

Make something — yeah, that's what he should do. No more wallowing in self-pity. He was Geppetto, the finest damn woodcutter in the land. Who needed the ungrateful brat? He could build a new and better marionette, one that didn't fuck off with half the neighbourhood. Geppetto grabbed his toolbox and staggered towards the woodpile. Not just a surrogate son, this time, or a pathetic little buddy — a broad. Why should Pinocchio be the only one around here getting laid?

Geppetto assembled several blocks of wood — torso, arms, legs, head, and a short connecting plank for the neck. It took all of his willpower to start carving at the head, the way he normally did. This wasn't going to be a block of wood with two holes and a pair of tits, he told himself. It would be a masterpiece, like the boy. *Better* than the boy. Geppetto worked with maniacal energy. "Busy as a beaver," he cackled to himself as he chipped and shaped his wood. The cliché turned into a chant: "busy as a beaver, as a beaver, a beaver, beaver, bea-ver, BEA-VER…" Woodchips rained onto the floor and sawdust coated Geppetto's beard. His wrists ached but he drove himself onward, stopping only long enough to gulp the occasional mouthful of booze. His mallet rose and fell in a rhythmic blur, the chisel penetrating and shaping wood with urgent but tender ease. Geppetto worked without fatigue, fuelled by lust and alcohol. Hammering sounds drowned out Snow White's frantic grunting, then later Pinocchio's satisfied snores.

Geppetto stepped back to study his progress so far. The creature taking shape under his hands was beyond beautiful, her wide eyes framed by lashes like flowerbeds, her full lips a dark rosewood colour. The cheekbones sculpted her face into a luscious pear shape framed by a torrent of sandalwood hair. The limbs were smooth and delicate, yet muscular. He had modelled the legs after Gretel's: strong thighs and calves from tireless walking, supple, with elegant feet. The torso was proportioned but unfinished: Geppetto had saved it for last so he could concentrate on it exclusively, make it his finest work.

After two deep, mind-clearing slugs of whiskey he was ready for the challenge. Geppetto chose his best carving knives and started with a perfectly round but discreet indentation for the belly button. Then he set to work shaping the breasts into buoyant half-globes, like grapefruits lifting their faces towards the sun to say hello. He teased them into peaks topped by nipples alert with passion and promise. Not as prominent as Cinderella's eye-popping rack, but subtler. Geppetto was convinced Cinderella was magically enhanced, anyway.

Geppetto switched to a fine whittling knife for the details of the pubis. He was decorating the cleft with a cloud of curving hairs when a wicked thought struck him: he'd give her a landing strip! That would be far sexier and more womanly than Rapunzel's little-girl look. Then the labia. Geppetto was sweating as he incised a delicate slit between the legs before feathering it into lacy folds and crinkles and topping it off with a budding clitoris: the cherry atop the sundae.

Before he could get too entranced by his own creation Geppetto flipped it over and shaped the ass into ripe mounds. Using his hammer and chisel with deftness a pointillist painter would have envied, he split it with a deep, straight crack, then canted the edges. Probing to the bottom of the crack with his thinnest awl, working by touch alone, Geppetto produced a ring of tiny creases, even and symmetrical, radiating like petals from the pistil of a tantalizing flower. Geppetto stood for a second and gawked, slack-jawed. The ass was stunning: it possessed its own gravity. The woman herself was an orrery, a perfectly aligned set of spheres: breasts, mound, buttocks.

Geppetto mopped his brow. His heart thudded and his cock strained against his woodworking apron. What would he name her? Julietta. That had the right ring to it. Geppetto was ready for action. He groped under the workbench for the bag of magic dust gifted him long ago by good-witch Glenda, the dust he had used once on Pinocchio and then never again. He scooped a handful and sprinkled it over the mannequin, then waited, holding his breath, while she stirred.

The wooden woman turned over and sat up, blinking and looking around her. Geppetto was transfixed by the movement of her breasts as she breathed. Her dusky nipples hardened in the cool of the workshop's night air. So like flesh: she was far more realistic than Pinocchio! As the doll pivoted to dangle her feet over the edge of the table, Geppetto stared at her cunt. Had he really sculpted that? A neat arrangement of downy pubic hair framed the soft bulge of labia majora and those slim inner lips, just barely protruding in a teasing display of pink. Julietta shifted, taking in Geppetto and her surroundings, and her thighs parted, pulling the labia apart into a vibrant, gleaming vista that reminded Geppetto of a glorious dawn.

Introductions and explanations would have to wait, because Geppetto could not. He stripped off his leather apron and yanked his belt free, letting his trousers tumble into an ankle-deep canvas pool. Under the workbench he kept a pot of grease—that would do the trick. He slathered a dollop over his glans and a handful over Julietta's crotch and levered her upper body back onto the table. Then he parted her legs by shuffling forward, trousers snagging at his feet, until he was between her thighs, pressed up against the warmth of her belly.

One smooth thrust and Geppetto's modest (at best) dick was embedded to the balls in Julietta's crevice. Julietta gasped with surprise and delight, her fingers digging into Geppetto's shoulders. Geppetto moaned. The tunnel was so deep and tight; it gripped his cock with fierce strength. He eased himself back out and then plunged in again. He clasped Julietta's hips and lifted them off the table as he began a frenzied thrusting.

"Oh yeah, oh yeah baby," Geppetto grunted as his cock hammered in and out of Julietta's virgin hole. "Who's your daddy? Huh, doll? Who's your daddy!" Geppetto built to a frantic rhythm, his buttocks clenching with each deep stroke. He released Julietta's hips with one hand and rummaged for the grease again, coating his fingers. While his prick soaked in the warmth of Julietta's pussy, he reached beneath her trembling hips and fondled her ass until his fingers had wormed between the cheeks. He rubbed his gooey fingers in circles around the firm ring of her anus, spreading lubrication. His forefinger dipped inside and Geppetto wiggled it, trying to match the urgent quiverings of his cock in Julietta's quim.

Julietta was panting, tossing her head from side to side. Geppetto struggled not to come. "You want wood, baby? I'll give you wood!" He spun Julietta over and slipped out of her oozing vagina. Taking her ass in a fierce grip he rubbed his greasy cock between the smooth mounds of her buttocks, exploring the deep cleft like a snake probing the burrow of its prey. The engorged head of his prick nestled against her puckered rosebud and he pushed. Julietta made a shocked yipping noise, arched her back, and shimmied her ass towards Geppetto, engulfing his entire penis. Their moans mingled with the creaking of the table as they rocked themselves together. Dear God, her ass was tight! It reminded Geppetto of that drunken night years ago when he had tried to fuck his wood vice.

Geppetto's balls were slapping against Julietta's slick pussy lips and swollen clit as he drove himself harder and faster into the depths of her asshole. He released his grip with one hand to slap her ass, keeping time with Julietta's pants and contractions. He could feel the climax building within him; the need to come was almost intolerable. His cock burned. With a guttural howl Geppetto exploded into climax, pumping gout after gout of thick semen into Julietta's ass. The relief was minimal; Geppetto's penis still throbbed with a pleasure so intense it bordered on pain. No, it was pain! Geppetto felt as though he had thrust himself into a wasps' nest. He looked down as he slid out of Juliette's anal grasp and screamed.

When Pinocchio and Snow White tip-toed out for breakfast, they found Geppetto curled in a pool of blood at the feet of a sobbing, exquisite woman made of wood. While Snow White draped a blanket over the woman's shoulders, Pinocchio looked down at his creator with pity and a touch of scorn. The poor fool—had he never noticed Pinocchio sanding and varnishing his nose twice a day? Now the old man was dead of the worst case of splinters Fairyland had ever seen.

If you enjoyed this story, you can discuss it with other readers and the author at the *Geppetto Falls Off the Wagon* story page at http://forbiddenfiction.com/library/story/MN1-1.000033.

Forever After

Kailin Morgan

Dan is trying to live an ordinary life, well as ordinary as you can in the Kingdom. He has a good job working in the Library of Stories, even if his boss is a little flat — he is a magic mirror, after all. Then one day, Dan slips up and utters two little words — five tiny little letters — that are about to spin his story around and fill it with colour and laughter — and a Fairy Godmother. Who is a man. A man who sparkles.

Chapter 1

Once Upon a Time

"Once upon a time..."

Yeah, right. I put the book back on the shelf, lip curling in amused disgust. That's how they all start, and at the end the girl becomes a princess or a queen and they all live happily ever after. That's what you know, right?

Well, when did you ever think about the boys? I mean half of them don't even get named, and out of those that do... let's see...

Hansel, the boy that went off into the forest with his sister and got caught by the witch. She fattened him up and his sister poked a twig through the bars instead, so guess who had to eat all the extra food that the witch gave them? That's right, Hansel. Gretel came out, got a modelling contract and a job presenting some stupid reality show. Poor Hansel got a desk job and early onset diabetes.

Let's see, who else was there? Oh yeah, Rumplestiltskin. Oh man, that tied up the legal system for years, whilst they tried to decide whether his death was suicide or whether he was murdered. So no luck there. Jack? The dude grew a giant plant and stole a bird. He's not exactly a hero, you know?

Then you have the Princes. They don't even get their names in the book. Do you really think his mother named him Charming? Well, she didn't. His name was Lorenzo. At least that's a remotely romantic name. Me, my name's Dan. Not Daniel or Daniil. That's going to get me far.

So here I am, dusting and shelving books in the Library of Stories. They're all here — Cinderella, Snow White, the three little pigs have a whole shelf. Me, I'll be lucky to make a foot-note. But on I go. It's just sometimes I wish...

"Hey! You totally said the magic words. So what's up, butter-cup?"

The voice comes from behind me and I spin round, almost drop-ping the third volume of '*The History of Lupine Anti-heroes in Classical Literature.*' I catch it at the last minute and straighten up to come face-to-face with...

Colour is my first thought. Bright blue denims cling to his slender legs, his feet are encased in purple and blue high-top sneakers. A yel-low vest displays the muscles in his chest and abdomen, a green shirt hanging unbuttoned over the top. His dark hair falls in a wave over one eye, the other is a bright, sparkling blue — the colour of the sea in those adverts for holidays.

I blink and rub my eyes with the hand not clutching the book. I peek through my fingers, nope he's still there. He's bouncing lightly on his toes, blue eye looking me up and down. I frown, despondency making me droop slightly. I know what he sees; I see it every day in the mirror I have to report to for work.

I'm nothing special, just like my name. Slim, no muscles to speak of. My hair is brown, not golden or flaxen or dark as night, just brown, like the leaves that drop from the trees when the weather turns. My eyes are an indeterminate, muddy mix of brown and green, like the edge of a pond. I'm dressed in the uniform they give me; khaki trou-sers, with pockets to hold spare gloves and a tunic top with my name badge affixed to the undyed linen. I look like I escaped from a sepia photograph.

"C'm'on, doll-face. You said 'I wish'. Now you have to tell me what it is you wish for. That's the way these things work. You should know, working here and all."

"You're a..." I bite off the words before they come out, swallowing down the feminine term. He laughs at my discomfort, a tinkling sound that seems to fill the library silence with cascades of ringing bells, the image of water burbling brightly over time-smoothed pebbles.

"You can say it. I don't mind, I know what I am." He twirls proud-ly and clicks his fingers, a bright blue wand appearing in his hand. Streamers dangle from the star at the top, glittering with sequins and rhinestones. He grins again, bright and happy. I can only continue to stare mutely at him. This is way outside my comfort zone.

He sighs and his mouth turns down a little at the corners. I feel like I broke Baby Bear's chair, guilty that I caused his dismay, dimmed his enthusiasm, and I try a smile. It feels odd and awkward as I force my mouth to curve upwards, but it must look okay as he begins to glow again.

I turn away, carefully shelving the book, avoiding his eyes as I say, "Look, I really don't know why you're here. I mean it's not like I really made a wish or anything. Why don't you just write this one off and, you know, go find somebody really story-worthy?"

"But... don't you want your wish, or wishes? You know it depends on what you wish for... you can keep going for ages with the small things. It's a power deal, not a specific number of wishes. You know how they say size matters? Same with wishes. Too big and it's not as fun as you think. Keep it a bit smaller and you can go on and on and on." He smirks and I just stare blankly. He sighs and waves a hand, dismissively. "Here, why don't you read this and have a think about it and I'll come back later."

He thrusts a leaflet into my hand and disappears in a rainbow of glittering sparkles that fade before they hit the floor. I stare down at the folded paper, clutched in my fingers, and read the tagline.

"So you have a Fairy Godmother! — How does it all work? A guide to wishing."

I stuff the gaudy pamphlet into my pocket and return to work.

Later, on my lunch break, I pull it out, tucking it inside my copy of *Bookbinders Quarterly*. No point in providing fuel for gossip. I unfold it and skim the contents. Basically, it says that my Fairy Godmother can grant almost anything I wish for until a certain level is reached. Anything I wish for, that they can't create, has to come from somewhere, so if I wish for a mountain of gold, somewhere in the world gold disappears.

It has a list of Do's-and-Don'ts at the back. I read through them.

Do consider and word your wishes carefully. Wishes are non-refundable and if you slip up it's your fault.

Do be polite to your Fairy Godmother. Remember, they are just doing their job.

Don't wish for someone to love you. We can't create feelings. We can put you in a situation where you can meet people, but we can't make them like you.

Don't wish for more wishes. This wish will make all preceding wishes null and void and will result in you being blacklisted as greedy.

Do remember that your Fairy Godmother has been specially selected to work with you. Please feel free to ask them for advice.

I fold the leaflet back up and shove it back into my pocket. I finish the rest of my cheese sandwich and wash my hands thoroughly before pulling on a fresh set of gloves and heading back to work. The remainder of the day passes quietly and soon enough I am walking past the Mirror on my way home.

I turn to look into the Mirror, waiting for it to acknowledge me. My slender reflection stares back at me, hair curling round my ears, flicking up in back from having had my fingers run through it. I wonder if I have always looked so solemn. I go to try a smile, but just then my image swirls and the Mirror appears, the large face frowning down at me.

"Dan. Leaving the premises?" it asks.

"Yes. I completed sections five-six-seven point nine through to five-ninety."

"It has been so noted. Fare well." The face fades away again leaving just me. I don't bother with the smile, just head towards my small home.

I'm quite lucky really. Working for The Library means I get to live in the main Kingdom. I get a small, stone house, with a white trellis fence and a square of garden. I let myself in, rubbing the gargoyle knocker between its curled, brass ears. It lets out a soft purr of pleasure. I sigh and slump onto the small sofa that provides the only seating in the house.

I think about rising again to make myself a late dinner, but apathy assails me. I wish... There is a soft chiming noise behind me and I bite off the wish before it has a chance to form.

"Oh darn!" comes the voice of my Fairy Godmother. He advances around the sofa, dropping onto the coffee table to sit in front of me. He's still brightly dressed, although his green shirt is now buttoned. He smiles brightly at me, eyes creasing slightly at the corners. I can feel my own mouth curving slightly in reaction, but I try to ignore it.

"Come on, sweet-cheeks, make that wish. What do you want? Pizza? Maybe something more adventurous, like a Thai green curry? No?" He deflates a little again but then notices the pamphlet next to him on the coffee table where I had thrown it when I got home.

He picks it up and waves it at me. "So did you read it then? It's good, isn't it, even if I say so myself. Very informative, and so eye-catching." I should have guessed that he would have had something to do with it. Only he would have thought that yellow lettering was the way to go. He waits expectantly, one perfectly curved eyebrow raised in silent enquiry.

"Yes, I read it." I sigh. It seems mean to keep him waiting. He's just so... enthusiastic. He squeaks happily (and no, I'm not making that up) and almost vibrates where he sits. I drag myself up from my slump and head towards the small kitchen. Since it looks like he may be here for a while, it's only polite to offer him a drink.

I put the kettle on and call through, "Can I get you a drink? I'm making tea."

"Why didn't you just wish for one?" The voice comes from close behind me and I jerk, startled, almost dropping the jar of tea. I spin round and glower at him. He smiles back, unrepentant, questioning.

"Why would I wish for tea? It only takes a few minutes to make. And how do I know that the wish would get it right? I don't want to end up with Darjeeling when I wanted Earl Grey." I screw up my nose in mild disgust at the thought and he stares, fascinated. I can feel a blush rising up my throat and I turn back to the kettle until my skin cools.

Once the tea is brewing, I set the pot and two cups onto a small tray along with sugar and milk and bring the whole lot over to the table. This of course makes my Fairy Godmother shift to the sofa, sitting beside me, watching avidly as I go through the small ritual of pouring tea.

I realise that I can't keep calling him Fairy Godmother. "So, since it seems you're going to be here until I wish for something, do you have a name?" I realise immediately how ungracious that sounded but the words are already out. I try adding a smile to the question, going for friendly, sure it's coming out more as serial-killer.

He gives me a soft look, slightly bemused, a whole lot of something else that I can't identify. "You know, no-one ever asked me that before. Hi, Dan, my name's Camael. Yeah, a bit more of a mouthful than Dan, but then my mother was a whack-job, so who knows what she was on when I was born."

I blink hard at him, not knowing where to go with that info-dump. My mouth opens though before I can really rein it back and I end up blurting, "So, wait, Fairy Godpeople have mothers?" I go to clap my palm over my face in shame at my own stupidity but realise that I'm still holding my teacup and only narrowly avoid a nasty cup/nose interaction. I put the tea cup down, the small clink of the china hidden by the amused peals of laughter coming from the man next to me. I think in the few minutes he's been with me he's laughed more than I have in my entire life. I wish I could... I snap the thought off before it forms and clamp my lips together, sucking in a noisy breath through my nose.

Once I'm sure I can control my mind and my misbehaving mouth, I say, "Look, Camael, I'm sorry. I didn't really mean to make a wish. Just now I'm pretty hungry and tired and really, you can just go do whatever else it is you do and I'll give you a shout if I think of a wish, okay."

His face falls and his shoulders droop, his whole body stilling. I want to take the words back, but I can't, I won't. I'm just a boring library drone and the sooner everyone realises that and just leaves me alone the better. He tries to smile at me, but it's small and doesn't quite make his eyes sparkle as much as they usually do. And what am I doing noticing how his eyes sparkle?

"Okay. I'll go. Maybe I'll see you tomorrow?"

"Yeah, sure, maybe. Okay?" His smile brightens a little and he disappears in fainter shower of sparkles; these ones seem sadder, shades of blue and pale, washed out magenta. I feel awful.

I make myself a sandwich and curl up on the sofa. I know I should eat better, but it's hard to get excited about cooking for yourself. The sky outside continues to fade into night with its usual display of coruscating colours. Sometimes I just think it would be nice if it got dark without all the fanfare. I pull off my work clothes and slip on my pale blue pyjamas. Curling up in my bed, my mind drifts back to that moment when I turned around and met that brilliant blue gaze. For a moment I think about wishing but sleep swirls over me, tangles me in its net and drags me under.

Chapter 2
Breakfast for Two

I awake the next morning, curiously unsettled. I can't quite put my finger on it until I roll over and come nose to nose with Camael. I make a strange hiccuping noise, definitely not a girlish scream, and he blinks those deep azure eyes at me in amusement.

"Morning, cutie-pie! I know I said I would wait until you wished, but I just had the thought that you would be totally adorable when you woke up, and yay, I was right."

I frown at him, despite knowing that it makes my nose scrunch up. I'm pretty sure I have a case of epic bed-head as well, but I manfully resist the urge to lift my hands and pat at it. I sigh instead and close my eyes again. I know he's still there; the soft fragrance of neroli and cedarwood gives him away. Also, I can feel him staring at me. I bite back another sigh and open my eyes again.

"Hi," he chirps. "Yep, still here. You know you have the most amazing eyes. I can't quite decide if they're green or brown. Maybe they change with your mood. That would be so cool if they did." He bounces up into a seated position and claps his hands together.

"What are you feeling right now? Then I need to change your mood. Do you like pancakes? I love pancakes. Would pancakes make you feel different?" The words come out in a blur and I just decide to ignore most of them.

I turn away, getting up and wandering into the bathroom, shutting the door firmly behind myself. Fifteen minutes, one shower and two bitten off wishes later, I re-emerge, feeling more human, but in dire need of coffee. Camael is sitting cross-legged in the middle of the bed, flicking through 'Birds and Their Roles and Associated Rituals in

Modern and Historical Tales.' His brow is ever so slightly furrowed, his tongue poking from between his soft, pink lips.

He looks up and blinks at me. "That's what you're wearing?" I look down at myself; plain black trousers today, as I'm not working, and a grey, fine-knit pullover.

"Yes?" I wonder why it came out with a question mark at the end. "Not all of us can dress like, like..." I don't finish the sentence, knowing it is going to sound rude whatever I say. Still, my gaze lingers as he slides slowly off the bed; his slender legs are clad in warm red denim, a white belt matching his white and red high-tops. A red, short-sleeved t-shirt sits snugly over a white, long-sleeved undershirt. It should look stupidly festive, but instead it looks...

I cut that thought off in a hurry. I don't know exactly how the mind reading thing that seems to happen occasionally works, but until I do, my mind is on lock-down. He smiles and twirls, hand on hip, unperturbed. "I know. It does take special skills to pull this kind of look off, but I think I manage." He flips the long fringe of hair away from his eyes and I muffle the sudden burst of jealousy as his hair sits perfectly to the side, framing the sharp curve of his cheekbone.

He pushes past me into the small kitchen area and starts raking through the cupboards and the fridge. Once he's made a small pile on the counter, he begins humming softly to himself, mixing things together in a large bowl that I had forgotten I had. I squeeze past him and put the kettle on again. I have a feeling that this day is going to require more coffee.

"Milk, two sugars please," he carols at me cheerily as he heats up a skillet over the small cooker. I fetch another cup and make coffee. Soon the air fills with the delicious scent of pancakes, as he pours spoonfuls of batter into the pan, flipping them with ease until a small stack builds up on the plate.

He twirls past me, placing two plates on the table along with butter and cutlery. I bring over the coffee and then Camael brings over the pile of softly steaming pancakes. We both sit at the table and Camael takes a long, appreciative sip of the coffee.

"Perfect," he smiles at me and helps himself to some pancakes before waving his fork at the remaining heap. "Go on, I swear they're perfectly edible, although it would be nice if we had syrup..." He bats absurdly long eyelashes at me, looking at me from under that dark fall of hair.

"Oh all right then, I wish we had a bottle of maple syrup, not too big though, just ordinary sized." Surely that wish can't go wrong. Camael grins and clicks his fingers, although I'm positive that's just for show. A bottle of syrup appears and he lunges for it, pouring a large dose of the sticky liquid all over his plate. He forks up a mouthful of syrup smothered pancake and makes a decadent moan, eyelashes fluttering again as his tongue flickers over his glistening lips.

I don't notice that, not at all. I bend my head to my own plate. The pancakes are good, soft and fluffy, and I push a piece around in the yellow pool of melted butter on my plate before letting it slide over my tongue. There will be no pornographic moaning on my end though. Not even a little.

Pancakes finished, he bounces back to his feet, leaning against the counter, hips canted forwards, hands on the edge of the worktop behind him. "So, cupcake, what do you for fun round here?"

I frown, and swallow down the last bite, savouring the taste. Suddenly he pushes away from the counter and I find myself almost cross-eyed as he pushes his face close to mine, staring into my eyes. I can feel the soft huffs of his breath on my face as I swallow nervously. He grins and nods to himself, smiling happily before settling back against the counter.

"So, fun? You do know what that is, right?"

"Yes, I know what fun is," I snap back, taking the dishes and beginning to wash up. *I just don't have it.* The thought slips unbidden through my mind and I nibble at my lower lip.

"Oh." There is a long pause and then he continues, "Well, what do you usually do at the weekend?"

"Shop, clean, sometimes I read. And before you ask, I don't want to wish for a self-cleaning house or anything like that. I've read the Fantasia warnings; we all know how that turned out. Plus, cleaning can be therapeutic sometimes, putting things in order."

"But that's your job as well," he pouts slightly, looking confused.

"Yes, well. Maybe I like things to be nice and orderly. Everything in its place and a reason for everything." *Chaos and spontaneity are painful and only lead to tears and trouble.* I blink away the dark thought. "And

I like to shop too—that way I can see what the best choice is." Camael doesn't need to know that I nearly always buy the same things, week after week.

"You can come with me if you want," I offer ungraciously and he beams happily at me, all sparkling blue eyes and shiny, syrup-glossed mouth.

Shopping does not go as I planned. I come home with an extra bag, filled with chocolate cereal, cookies, a stripy cheese that Camael had found at the delicatessen and other small bits and pieces that had somehow found their way into my shopping basket.

"That was fun." He claps his hands together, gleeful, the air around him almost gleaming in sympathy with his joy. "I can see why you don't wish for food, it's so much more fun to go and smell and feel everything. I never knew that there were so many different types of biscuit." He's still munching on a packet he had opened on the way home.

"You'll make yourself sick you know, eating like that."

He makes a raspberry noise and flaps a hand at me. "Nuh-uh. Never been sick a day in my life." He shoves another cookie into his mouth and gives me a crumb-filled smirk. He disappears through to the living room with the remainder of the pack. I unpack my shopping and clean the kitchen, shaking the crumbs from the toaster out on to the small bird-table outside.

I wipe my hands once I've finished and wander through to check on Camael. Most of me hopes that he has gotten bored and disappeared back to wherever Fairy Godpeople come from. A small part of me hopes desperately that he is still there. The small part wins and glows gently inside me. I try to shove it in a mental box.

The soft swell of happiness inside dims once I see his face. His default almost smile has gone, the corners of his soft pink lips curved down, the usually plush bottom one pulled tight and pale, dimpled with the imprint of teeth. He looks up at me, his eyes darker and filled with worry.

"Something is wrong with me. I have this terrible pain. I think I have something inside of me." His bottom lip pushes out in a pout as his hands clutch around his abdomen. A low groan comes out of him followed by a burp and a hiccup. He reaches for me, hands clutching tight around my forearms, eyes wide and filling with tears.

"I'm sorry. I don't think I'm going to be able to help you with your wishes. I think I'm dying. You should have someone check for curses, just to be safe." He groans again, rocking forwards slightly around the distended swell of his belly.

I pry his fingers loose and fetch a basin from the kitchen just in case. I come back through to find him still looking wretched and pained. Placing the basin next to the couch, I shift him into the middle of the seat before dropping to the floor and removing his shoes. His socks are red too and I bite back a smile. I lift up onto my knees and push at him until he is lying down on his left side, legs curled up onto the sofa.

Trying not to watch my hands too closely I unfasten his belt and then the button and zipper on his jeans. A soft moan of relief comes from above my head and my hand rubs gently at the slightly distended bulge. I stare at it, surprised by how daring it is.

"So, what do you think it is? Am I dying?" I turn to face him, something inside me twisting slightly at the despairing look on his face. I think it might be sympathetic indigestion.

"Unless you can give birth to a Gingerbread baby, I think you just ate too much, too quickly. I did tell you not to eat the whole packet." I brandish the crumpled wrapper in censure.

"So, can you cure it? Please, I don't like feeling like this. I don't like this pain thing at all."

"Well, you can be sick. Preferably in the bathroom, although if you can't make it..." I wave my hand at the basin beside me. "Or you can just wait until your digestive system struggles through the sugar overload you just gave it."

"I don't think I want to be sick. That doesn't sound at all pleasant. Would you sit with me? Please?" I shift up onto the sofa, lifting his upper body and settling in behind him, resting his head on my thighs. He lets out a soft sigh and curls up his legs, one hand rubbing over his stomach. I let my hand rest against the dark tumble of hair, fingers brushing it away from his eyes. Those long lashes drift closed and another sigh shudders its way out of him.

Quiet fills the room and I find my head lolling back against the cushions behind me, my own lashes fluttering down. I can't remember the last time I ever took a nap, but the warmth of Camael's body against my hip and thigh, the soft sounds of the birds outside as they peck at the crumbs conspire against me and I drift off.

A faint noise brings me awake and I freeze, confused and disorientated. Why am I sleeping on my sofa? And what is that weight on my... Oh dancing princesses! My face flames and I swallow down the moan that rolls up my throat, teeth sinking into my lower lip so hard I'm surprised I don't taste blood.

I tilt my head down slowly and take in the view that presents itself. At some point Camael had rolled over and his right cheek is pressed into my thigh, lips slightly parted, lashes casting dark shadows across those gorgeous cheekbones. That is not the most worrying thing. Camael's hands had come up as well and his left arm drapes across his body, hand curled around the edge of my hip, fingers just tucked under the hem of my pullover. This is still not the most worrying thing. His right arm is curled up in front of his body, and the back of his hand is pressed against the soft bulge that is starting to ruin the line of my black slacks.

His breath gusts out across my thigh and his hand twitches, rubbing over me, making me jerk slightly. I try to run the Dewey system in my head, but the warm scent of the man curled up against me, the weight of his body on mine, has my thoughts in a tumble. I close my eyes, scrunching them tight, wondering if I can somehow wish this moment away. This kind of thing just doesn't happen to me. It doesn't happen ever actually.

"Well now, this is new." The words are drawled softly against my hip, tone sleepy and honey-thick. Colour burns up my face once more and I wonder that I have any blood left to make my brain function. Clearly I don't, as I can't even manage to stutter an apology or pull away. Instead I just blink stupidly down at Camael as he presses his hand harder against the rising length of my shaft. His left hands slides over the warm skin at my hip, fingers working further up under the grey knit, pushing into me as he lifts himself up a little, blue eyes wide and fixated on the distorted material at my groin. He rotates his wrist and cups my flesh gently, thumb rubbing in a line along the length of me.

Finally, the spell, or whatever it is, breaks and I jerk up, spilling Camael onto the floor in a pile of waving limbs as I leap over him and run for the bedroom and sanctuary. I slam the door behind me, collapsing, knees buckling beneath me as I slide down the cool wood. I squeeze my eyes shut and desperately try to keep my mind blank, determined not to wish for something that would make this whole situation so much worse than it already is.

I hear Camael call my name from the other side of the door, his voice bewildered and a little frightened. I blink back tears. I did that to him. Me and my oddities, my perversion. I try not to wish him away, instead I just hope that he will go away and leave me alone, that he will realise that I don't deserve a wish. Finally, I hear the faint chime that signals his departure.

I sit, leaning against the uncaring support of the door, for a long while. Eventually, I pull myself up, tears a sticky trail on my face. I wash myself off and make myself dinner, determinedly ignoring the strange additions to my cupboards. I force myself through my normal evening activities and go to bed, curling up in the dark, alone and cold. I stare into the blackness of my room, eyes burning, but I cannot close them for fear of seeing an azure gaze, darkened with fear and disgust.

We've all read the books, we all know the stories and nowhere, not in any single one of them, is it okay for a man to love another man. It just never happens.

Chapter 3
Three Wishes

Sleep must claim me again at some point because I awake to bright sunlight, my head aching. I roll over but the bed is empty beside me and a small part of my soul shrivels further. I berate it for being so stupidly hopeful. I garden and clean the rest of the small house until it gleams, pushing my body through the actions, trying to dull my mind. The day passes with no signs of glitter or smiles or sparkling blue eyes. I don't miss them at all.

The week begins and I focus on my job, making sure every painstaking little detail is completed to the best of my ability. I run after work, until my legs ache and my lungs heave, then collapse, exhausted, into bed every night. I don't dream about laughter and bright, dimpled smiles, long legs and slim hips. For the first time that I can remember, I don't dream at all.

Friday comes and I drag my leaden body along to the Mirror to make my weekly report. I think I should feel horrified at the image that greets me, but I don't seem to have the energy. My usually wavy brown hair is lying limp around my face, the ends barely curling. The dark shadows under my eyes are threatening to bleed down my cheekbones, making my skin look paler than usual. My cheekbones stand out, the line of my jaw almost as sharp. I try to remember eating lunch, but come up blank. That must explain the hollow pit inside me — it's hunger, plain and simple, not the absence of anything else.

The Mirror frowns at me and dismisses my report. "You will return to your residence until you have recovered from your malady. Please keep us updated on your progress," it intones. I wave a limp hand in acknowledgement and wonder what I will do if I can't distract myself with work.

Once home, I force myself to eat, the salad leaves tasteless and dry on my tongue. Unbidden, the thought runs through my mind before I can stop it.

I wish I had some salad dressing.

It's the most banal and ridiculous wish, but my breath seizes in my lungs as a soft chime sounds from behind me. A hand appears from over my shoulder, the wrist adorned with a single plastic bangle and a woven bracelet. The skin gleams faintly and the soft aroma of neroli drifts past my nose. My lungs finally agree to work and allow me to suck in a neroli-scented breath as I watch the hand place a small, not too large, bottle of dressing on the table next to me.

The arm pulls back and I can hear the faintest sound of footsteps moving away. Without thinking I find myself pushing away from the table, my chair clattering hard against the floor as it tumbles over. I leap over the legs with grace I would never be able to repeat and take the three steps that have me in front of Camael, fingers wrapped hard around the firm flesh of his upper arms.

I stare at him for a long, silent minute, taking in the dark blue pants, the washed out purple shirt. It's the dullest I've seen him, his hair drooping over his eyes, the one visible one staring down at the floor between my bare feet. The silence drags out and I'm frozen, desperately wanting to move but unable to take the next step, terror holding me tight.

His head tilts just enough to let that single azure eye meet my dark hazel. His lips part as if he is about to speak and I lunge at him, cutting off the words before they form, crushing my mouth to his in what may be the worst first kiss in the history of kisses. I can always check the books later.

Our noses bump and I catch his lip with my teeth, making him squeak with either surprise or pain. I turn my head and get a mouthful of hair as he tries to move as well. I gag and stumble backwards, the hands that are still clamped around his arms causing him to step forwards as well, the weight of him sending me sprawling backwards onto the floor, head cracking against a leg of the up-turned chair. Tears spring to my eyes as I bite my own tongue.

Mute and hurting, I gaze up at him, stunned by my own actions.

His chest is heaving, with what I can't tell as his eyes are hidden behind the hair that has drifted across that exquisite face. I must have gone mad, that's what has happened. I watch, trapped like Sleeping Beauty's courtiers, a fly in amber, caught in time, as he lifts a slender hand and brushes his hair away from his face.

Time starts again and the words blurt out of me in a disjointed babble. "Oh toads and apples, I'm so sorry! I don't know what... I mean, there's no excuse for it... but I didn't think you'd come back and then there you were and you looked... and Oh I just wish it hadn't happened." I clap my hand over my mouth, hazel eyes wide. I can feel the faint sting of mortified tears threaten at the back of them.

"No. No! You don't get to unwish that. I won't. You can't make me."

"But, but why?" I stutter, confused by his defiant tone.

"Because..." He drops to his knees between my spread thighs and leans in to place his lips gently against my own. They caress softly over the dip and arch of my cupid's bow before dropping to suck gently at my bitten, bruised lower lip, soothing away the hurt. He pulls back and I watch as colour flames up his cheeks, flushing him a beautiful rose pink. The brief thought floats through my mind that I really must stop dipping into the romance section of the library, before my inner voice gets any sappier than it is.

"Because if you wish it away, I would never have had the nerve to do that." His voice is faint, barely audible but it makes my heart hiccup in my chest and my eyes widen before I lean up, returning that faint kiss. My lashes flutter down as he presses into the touch and I part my lips, letting my tongue slide out to discover the taste of him. He's sweet, not like syrup, better, warm and rich, like clover honey cake fresh from the oven. His mouth opens slightly and I feel the gentle brush of his tongue tip as it meets mine.

We hold that awkward position, nothing touching but our mouths until my arms ache and I drop back, gaze taking in the reddened curve of his mouth, the soft blush that must match my own.

A tiny giggle bursts from that delicious mouth and I startle slightly before my own lips curve in response. He giggles again, sitting back on his heels as laughter swells, pealing out of him in bubbling gasps. I give him a minute before I push at his arm, mock pouting.

"Hey, it wasn't that bad!" I state indignantly. He stops laughing and grins.

"Oh it was. Worst first kiss in the history of forever. But..." He leans in and presses a kiss to the tip of my nose. "The second one was awesome." I slump back, all the tension flooding out of me. My head makes contact with the chair again and I yelp, rubbing at the small lump forming on the back of my head. He tips me forward, pushing my head towards my knees, fingers gently probing through my hair.

"You'll live," he states happily, before he adds, "but you really need to shower."

I want to frown at him, but I know he's right, my personal hygiene routine has suffered along with my eating habits. I push myself up and hold out a hand, helping him up as well. He pushes me in the direction of the bathroom before turning to right the chair.

"Go, scrub. I'll make us something to eat, if you have anything in the cupboards that is." He flaps his hands at me and I back out of the room, not wanting to look away in case I have been imagining it all.

I shower and shave, looking up to the mirror to find a soft smile curving my lips. It looks good on me and I resolve to try and do it more often. Maybe I can persuade Camael to help me with that. I pull on my blue pyjamas, the only coloured clothes I own and wander back down to the kitchen.

I barely recognise the figure bustling around the small space. Gone are the dark blue and purple, replaced by buttercup yellow jeans and a white vest. His feet are bare and he has a bright green apron tied around his middle. He turns around and I spot the message emblazoned across the front in orange letters. "Kiss the cook."

I step forward and obey the apron, brushing my lips over Camael's smile, daring a slight suck to the small pout of his lower lip. He sighs happily before he turns back to the cooker. Five minutes later we sit down to a small meal of pasta with broccoli and cheese, the limp salad from earlier discarded. A slender vase sits in the middle of the table, a selection of flowers from the garden filling it, adding a splash of bright colour to the plain furniture. I think there may be a metaphor in there somewhere.

I wash up afterwards and then follow Camael through to my living room, where he pours me another glass of wine. He curls up next to me on the sofa and leans his head on my arm. We sit in silence for a little while, before he pushes away and turns to face me, curling his legs up in front of him.

"So, do you have your wish yet?"

"I know what I would like to wish for but Rule three says I can't," I murmur softly, almost afraid to meet that clever cerulean stare.

"I don't think you need to wish for that anyway," he says just as gently, colour staining his cheeks once more.

"Oh," I say, disappointed for a brief moment before I catch his meaning. "Oh!"

"But if we're talking about rules, you could always consider the last one."

I try to picture the pamphlet in my mind. What was it... oh... your Fairy Godmother has been picked just for you, ask your Fairy God-mother for advice. I tilt his chin up and kiss him quick and hard. "So what do you think I should wish for?"

"Well, since we've been sticking to the small wishes," he leans forward and whispers into my ear. All the blood in my body seems to shoot in two opposite directions, half making my face flame a bril-liant red, the other half pushing my cock out hard against my pyjama bottoms. I groan and cover my face with my hands, mortified at my reaction. A soft laugh fills the air and then there is the faint sound of fingers clicking followed by the sound of a small bottle being placed on the table.

"Cherry flavoured? I like the way you wish." Camael pulls my hands away from my face and wraps them around his hips. I flex my fingers against the bone of his pelvis and hide my face in his neck instead, licking at the warm skin, sucking small kisses into the curve, listening intently to each gasp and soft cry of pleasure, memorising and cataloguing each one.

His fingers work at the buttons of my pyjama top, exposing my stomach and then further up. His hands rub over the exposed flesh and quickly find the hardened peaks of my nipples, pressing over them in slow circles before the fingers pluck and tease at each small nub, making me writhe against him. My head falls back against the arm of the sofa and I fight to hide the small wince of pain. There is no way I want to distract Camael from his current activity.

For my own health though I pull his mouth away from my collar-bone and press a small kiss on to the slick temptation it offers. "Bedroom?"

"Mmm, did I already say that I like the way you think?" He eases himself up and pulls his vest off as he stands. I stare at the smooth expanse of chest, the skin glowing softly with his excitement, nipples dark and pebbled. My gaze drops lower, finds the small trail of dark hair that directs my eyes further down to the soft bulge, blatantly obvious in the figure-hugging canary jeans. It twitches under my avid look and I moan, low and pained, before I grab his arm and drag him to the bedroom. He pulls back and stretches towards the table, grabbing the small bottle with a wicked grin.

We tumble onto the bed, a tangle of arms and legs that quickly sorts itself. I end up sprawled on my back, legs wide, Camael cradled between them, his groin pressing deliciously down against my eager erection. I wrap my fingers around the line of his jaw and neck and pull him down into another kiss.

This one is different yet again, hot and wet, full of tongue and breath as we rock into one another. I let my tongue delve deeper into the damp cavern of his mouth, discovering the sharp ridges of his teeth, the textures of his palate, the way his tongue curls and entwines around mine, pushing back into my own mouth. After long, heady minutes he pulls away, leaving me struggling for breath, my tongue licking away the taste of him from my own lips.

His mouth moves down, making slick circles around my nipples, teeth scraping at the surprisingly sensitive buds. My skin contracts and I can feel my pyjama bottoms dampen with the increasing evidence of my arousal. I push up against Camael's stomach, searching for something more. His hands clamp around my hips, holding them to the bed as his mouth moves lower still, tongue flickering over the indent of my navel, then sucking a hard kiss into the dip of my pelvis, just above the waistband of my pyjamas. He repeats this on the other hip and then pulls away, hands going to the button of his jeans.

Camael pauses for a moment and fixes me with both blue eyes, the colour now dark as the night sky, just as the sun dips below the horizon. I just answer his unspoken question with a smile, hands pushing at my own clothing, shucking them to my knees, before I kick free of them, lying naked and exposed to his gaze.

His stare drops straight to my groin and I fight the urge to cover myself with my hands, hiding nothing from him. His eyes widen further and his tongue licks out over kiss-swollen lips as his fingers fumble at his own clothing. All too soon and not soon enough he crawls back over me and lowers himself down so that we touch, knees to nipples, heated skin to burning flesh.

He shifts his weight slightly causing the hard line of his shaft to rub along the side of mine and I jerk up into him. We both moan and sink into another kiss, slow and gentle as we rock and rub and rut, trying to drag the moment out.

"Not enough, I need... I want... Will you?"

Will I what? My puzzlement must show on my face and he pushes up and blinks down at me. "You haven't," he waves a hand at both of us, "done any of this before? I'm your first?" I nod as much as I can from my prone position and he lights up, grin blindingly happy.

"Okay, I'll do it this time, but in future I think you're gonna want to help with this part as well, but baby steps and all that." He grabs the small bottle and pours some into his palm. My erection twitches with anticipation, wetting my stomach as I watch him slick his fingers. Instead of wrapping them around me though, his hand moves behind his hips and he leans forwards over me, face contracting slightly as he cries out and then moans deeply.

His arm moves back and forth and I puzzle briefly over the movement before I realise that if I lean to the left slightly I will be able to see our reflections in the mirror. I lean up and kiss his shoulder and stare down the length of his spine, meeting my own dark eyes in the mirror. My skin is flushed, eyes sparkling, lips swollen and red. It hardly looks like me at all. I look further down and muffle my groan in the meat of Camael's shoulder as I realise what he is doing.

I watch entranced as a slick finger works in and out of his body, flexing and curving before it pulls out and he presses two fingers to the small entrance to his body. They slip inside on a gleam of slick, his hips pushing out to meet them and he twists his hand. Suddenly I have to know how he feels and I reach for the small bottle, lubing up my own fingers. I reach in between us and curve my hand along the length of his shaft, feeling it pulse against my arm as my hand moves lower still, behind the soft velvet of his sac.

I watch in the mirror as my fingers circle around his, adding a deeper gleam to his flesh. I prod at the furl of muscle and he moans in affirmation as I press harder, my finger easing in beside his. The position of our bodies means I can only curve the top of my finger in, but the feel of his muscles fluttering, the heated silk of his flesh hugging mine has me dropping prone to the bed, wiggling down so I can push further in, twisting and stroking at his inner walls, until he writhes above me, the air filled with the scent of him, the sound of his soft cries and pleas.

He jerks his fingers out with a harsh gasp and pulls my hand away as well, shifting me back up the bed with one sharp tug. He straddles my hips and wraps a firm hand around me, slicking up my erection with the remaining lube. With his fingers still wrapped around the base of me, he rises up and slowly, slowly takes me inside of him. My mind shorts out and the next few minutes disappear in a haze of heat and grinding pushes and then Camael is bouncing on top of me, his hand caressing furiously over the hard length of his own erection until his head tips back, a gasp stuttering out of him. His groin pushes down hard, his body contracts in waves around me and my hips jerk and push up hard, once, twice and the world splinters as I pulse deep inside him, feeling Camael's release coat my twitching stomach muscles.

I come back to myself, sticky and overheated, Camael's body a limp weight over mine, his breath huffing over the curve of my arm, head resting over the slowing drumbeat of my heart. I feel his mouth curve against my chest and he lets out a soft breath of laughter.

"Now that is what some people call a 'Happy Ending'." He laughs again at his own joke and I pet happily at his hair, content and blissed out. A brief worry flutters through me.

"But we don't just get the one?" I ask stupidly. He laughs again, the movement making delicious things happen lower down in his body.

"Oh no, you can wish for as many happy endings as you like." He kisses me soundly and drops his head back to my chest. "Just give me ten minutes."

I smile into his hair, thinking that I'd be happy to give him all of forever after.

If you enjoyed this story, you can discuss it with other readers
and the author at the *Forever After* story page at
http://forbiddenfiction.com/library/story/KM1-1.000105.

Demon in the Well

Claryssa Berg

Clara inherits her old aunts' house and with it the responsibility to feed "the demon" in the well. Clara doesn't believe in demons, or witches, or magic of any kind — until she drops her pearl necklace into the well and, to her astonishment, a voice from the deep says that she can have them back if he can eat by her table and sleep in her bed.

Demon in the Well

"Come closer, dear." She still remembered the scene, just as vivid as the day it happened. "Come closer... have a look." Aunt Laura's yellow rubber gloves were covered in slime and frog's blood.

"It's nothing to be afraid of," Aunt Mabel chimed in. It wriggled and moved in the sack by her feet. In her hand she held a knife with a mother of pearl handle; it shimmered softly in the moonlight.

"No." Nine year old Clara refused, shivering and cold in her nightgown. "I think I'll stay here." She stood by the trees that marked the entrance to the clearing. She wished she had never snuck out of bed, but stayed inside where it was warm and safe.

"One day this will be your job. You might as well come now and see how it's done," said tall and dry Aunt Laura.

"We won't be around forever, dear." Chubby, little Mabel squeezed a dead frog over the dark opening of the well. When the blood had run dry, she shook the frog lightly and tossed it aside, on top of a growing pile of amphibians. Mabel's gloves had large blue flowers on them. It was the same pair she used when gardening.

"When this place is yours," Aunt Laura picked up the thread, "you must always remember to feed the demon. If you don't, he will come loose."

Little Clara wrinkled her nose with disgust. Catching the frogs by the lake with Aunt Mabel had been fun. She had counted them for her — one hundred frogs. But watching them die like this, cut and squeezed, was no fun. And their talk about the demon... Surely the aunts didn't think it was for real? Clara had assumed they were just teasing her, making up a story to scare her — they often did that, the aunts... Told her how bats could attack and tangle in her hair, impossible to get out... that ravens on the roof top was an omen of death, and that the old scrolls and bottles in the attic were stuff to do magic with... It wasn't real, any of it. But nevertheless there they were, cutting and squeezing and feeding the frogs' blood to the demon in the well.

Grown-up Clara shrugged off the memory and entered the night-shrouded clearing. She approached the well: just a circle, a round hole in the ground. Strange women, that's what the aunts had been. They had kept to themselves, mostly. Her father's aunts really, but they had adopted Clara as their beloved niece, and left her everything, as they had promised to do... It was an unexpected blessing. The recent divorce had left Clara beyond broke; she desperately needed the money from the old farm and money from the treasures the sisters had gathered over the years. The most precious one was wrought around Clara's neck: pearls—rows upon rows of them, slightly yellow with age. Perfect orbs. Worth a fortune. That sale alone would clear most of her debts.

Clara turned around and left the clearing behind. Walked through the garden and went back inside the cosy kitchen for a late night snack and a glass of good wine. She went to bed with the pearls around her neck, clutching a fistful of them in her hand, mingled with strands of her long, white-blonde hair. Salvation at last.

She wished she could mourn her aunts more.

The next day Clara went back to the well, just to see it in daylight. No path led there; the aunts hadn't been visiting much, probably just when they fed it—their demon.

The lawyer who'd been reading her Mabel's will had given Clara a peculiar look when he read the words: *Feed the demon in well once a year with the blood of a hundred healthy frogs. Pearl-handled knife in the cupboard over the kitchen sink.* No one in their right mind could possibly hold it against her if she didn't...

The clearing didn't look much different from the night before, it was still gloomy; the old trees with their gnarled roots raised their leafy branches towards the sky and blocked out most of the sunlight. Dark green foliage, almost black. Clara approached the well; nothing to see but a hole in the ground. She bent down to take a closer look, fondling the precious pearls as she did it, and accidentally snapped the old string. The pearls fell into the well, a shower of small, gleaming balls. Clara cried out and tried to catch them, but was too late. She could hear them hit the water.

"Damn!" she cursed. "Stupid well from fucking hell!" She slumped down on the ground and hit her fist against the ground. "God," she wiped tears from eyes, "how am I going to get them back?"

"That depends," a raspy voice answered from the well, "on what you are willing to give."

Startled, she rose to her feet in an instant, her gaze fixed on the well. Her heart pounded hard and fast in her chest and cool perspiration poured out on her skin.

"Who is that?" In her mind she imagined pictures of hidden passages, mines. Some weirdo wandering around down there. A homeless person perhaps or the local madman...

Whoever it was chuckled. "I do not believe this is the time to reveal my identity to you," the raspy voice said. "But I do see your pretty pearls down here. Would you like to get them back?"

"Yes," Clara cried, though her hands were shivering, her mouth felt dry. "Yes, please," she repeated in a slightly less high-pitched voice. A fortune down there, a goddamn fortune!

"That can be accomplished," the stranger in the well replied, "on certain conditions..."

"Which are?"

"That I shall eat by your table and sleep in your bed."

Clara was speechless. Was he making fun of her?

"What is your answer?" It sounded from the well.

He was definitely messing with her.

"Pearls first," she said, in a voice that didn't quite carry.

The person down there chuckled again. "You do not trust me, then? Very well. I will come to your house with the pearls this night. And then you will have to let me in."

"Wait!" A wave of fear made her feel slightly sick. She definitely did not want a demanding madman at her door. "You don't know where I live!"

He didn't reply at first, then the answer came faintly, as if he was far away: "Of course I know where the witches dwell."

"I'm not a witch!" Clara yelled down the well, but this time she got no answer.

Clara felt nervous and edgy. She aimlessly wandered through the familiar rooms, looking at the overstuffed chairs and cushions, the embroidered throw pillows and the dusty rugs on the floor. Should she call the police? Was the man in the well dangerous? And how was she to get her pearls back? Maybe she could hire a diver? She had a can of pepper spray in her purse, and the knife was in the cupboard above the sink. With a sudden resolution she went to get both, just in case....

Night came, slow as molasses, or so it felt in her nervous state. Nothing happened. For hours she waited, with the knife in her hand, gaze fixed on the door. At last she put it down and went to take a shower to unwind. Outside the window she heard frogs calling. That was strange. They usually didn't leave the lake. It had to be their mating season.

She stepped out of the shower and put on a robe, fuzzy and pink, and walked back downstairs. It was almost midnight. Almost safe. She poured herself some water. The frogs sang outside, loud and out of tune. There came a knock on the door.

Clara startled and cursed loudly before cautiously approaching the window. Lace curtains — useless, she could see right through them. And there he was, standing in the darkness. She couldn't make out his features, but he was big. Massive. His hands were cradled in front of his chest. What was there? Was it the pearls he so protectively cupped, or did he just want her to think so? Clara took a deep breath, stepped back from the window and tried to calm her racing heart. She grabbed the pepper spray and the knife from the counter and slipped them into the pockets of her robe.

"Yes?" She threw the door wide open, almost hitting him with it. Then, instead of standing firmly in the doorway blocking the entrance as she had planned, she gave him one glance, then stumbled backwards and didn't stop until her back hit the kitchen table.

"Who are *you*?" She asked in a whisper as he crossed the threshold and entered the house.

"Who *are* you?" she repeated when he approached her with his hands outstretched, the white of her precious pearls shimmering against his deep green skin.

He stopped right in front of her; his yellow eyes had vertical pupils, like slits. His hair was long, black. He had no ears. No ears! Clara almost started laughing from the sheer insanity of it all, but bit her tongue.

"You really do not know?" he asked, sounding amused.

"How would I— How..." she stumbled through the words, her mouth felt dry.

"I am the Prince in the well, of course. Your prisoner." He took a step to the left and let the pearls drizzle from his fingers, down on the aunts' flowery table cloth.

"I have no prisoner." Quite mad. He had to be quite mad. But then he wasn't quite human either... "The demon in the well," she spoke it out loud.

"I beg your pardon?" The yellow eyes met hers. He blinked; he had more than one set of eye-lids, she noticed, sliding across his pupils. His eye-lashes were black and slightly curved, his eye-brows dramatically arched. "I am certainly not that," he said in his raspy voice, "I used to be the prince of these lands, and well-respected at that. They were marshes then, until the witch came by and imprisoned me in that well. She wanted the lands, you see, but as I am tied to them she could not let me die. She cursed me instead, changed my form and tied me to the well, feeding me each year with frog's blood." He uttered the last words with disgust. His expression suddenly filled with rage and Clara took a few steps away from him. She was scared. Could think of nothing to say. The scene was surreal, as if cut from a nightmare—but the creature was there; flesh and blood, standing on her kitchen floor. "But this year," he continued triumphantly, "there has been no blood and so I am free to leave the well. And if I can break the curse, I will be truly free..."

"What happens then?" Clara managed to ask in a dry whisper.

He looked at her sternly. "I will become myself again, of course. I will have my body back—and my lands, if you help me."

"Me? How?" A new explosion of fear in her gut? Would he hurt her?

"I have already told you," the demon-prince replied. "My conditions: Eat at your table and sleep in your bed."

"Only that?" This time she was laughing, loud and hysterical. "But why me?!"

For the first time he almost smiled, a slight twitch of his green lips. "Because you are the witch."

"But I am not—"

"—but you *are*. I can smell it!"

Was it true then...? Had to be so.... The demon in the well was real enough and the cutting and squeezing of frogs was real too... A family farm so old no one could remember how long it had been theirs. The attic filled with parchments and scrolls, bottles filled with liquids and powders. Gods, what had they done? Her foremothers... Her aunts!

She swallowed hard, repressed the fear. "If you swear not to hurt me—in any way, I will help you." What else could she do? He had after all given back her pearls.

He smiled for real then, blinked again and unsettled her with his many eye-lids. "Thank you," he said simply.

Clara crossed the floor on shaky legs, babbling. "What do you want to eat, then? A sandwich? Cake? Please, sit down," she managed, and he did. Stark naked on the white painted seat of the chair, shamelessly displaying his cock. It was the biggest she had ever seen, outside the pages of glossy magazines, dark green in colour. Clara blushed. Suddenly the prominent maleness of the creature felt more awkward than the terror and surrealism of the situation. She began roaming through the cupboards.

"I will eat anything, as long as it is by your table," he answered her question, watched her calmly as she roamed.

Clara settled for chocolate and gave him a piece. She leaned in on the sink and watched him eat, his teeth looked sharp. "Quite good," he said with a nod. His legs looked extremely long, his thighs uncommonly thick. He was fit, all sinews and muscles under the skin. She wondered what he'd looked like as a prince. His voice was raspy and hoarse, but his words were from another time. It was lovely....

"How long have you been down there?" she asked him.

"Too long," he promptly replied and licked his padded finger-tips with a very long, pink tongue.

The next part of the bargain was harder. Clara switched off the kitchen lights, pearls on the table all forgotten. She felt nervous, yet strangely light-headed, when she led him upstairs and opened the door to her bedroom.

"Do I have to sleep in here as well?" she asked.

"Yes." He confidently stepped inside the room. "That is a part of the bargain."

She walked in after him and closed the door. She was suddenly aware that she didn't wear anything under her robe, just a pair of pant-ies. A flimsy, stupid thing of silk and ribbons...Then again, *he* wasn't exactly dressed either. Clara looked at his backside as he eased into her bed. His tangled, black hair against the whiteness of her pillow. Firm buttocks, strong thighs. He turned to face her and she blushed.

His eyes were watching her while she undressed, slid the robe down to the floor. She tried not to notice—he wasn't there for *that*, was he? The deal was to share her bed, not her body, wasn't it? She lay down beside him, as close to the edge of the bed as she could while stubbornly refusing to check if he still watched her, utterly self-con-scious of her bare breasts, nipples puckered in the cool air. She pulled the covers over them both, left the bedside light on.

"Sleep, then," she said hoarsely.

"Yes," he replied and closed his eyes. Clara let out of a sigh of relief, turned over on her side, away from him—and then she couldn't sleep. She should have been able to; there had been a lot to deal with, wrap her mind around—yet sleep escaped her every time she closed her eyes and tried. She turned around again and watched him instead, listened to his breathing. It had been a while since she slept with a man beside her. She could smell him in the air: fresh water, rich soil, musk... she shifted on the bed. She wondered if she could touch herself without him noticing. The thin cover did nothing but outline his massive chest, the long legs, the bulge of his cock.... She shifted again, looked at it. Could almost see it grow under the crispy white linen. The longer she looked, the bigger it appeared. Straighter, fuller. She glanced at his face and met his gaze. Yellow and strange. There was a smile on his lips. "Fuck me," she whispered and wondered if he'd understand.

He was upon her in an instant. She yelped with surprise when he straddled her hips with cool, smooth thighs. His hands grabbed her breasts and squeezed them with strong fingers. Clara's heart beat faster in her chest. What had she done? Excitement and fear fought within her as she looked up at him, reached out her arms and let them slide around his neck. She pulled him down for a kiss, licked his lips, dark as black cherries, tasted his long, slick tongue. Water. His yellow eyes shone strangely in the dim light. It excited her.

Bravely, she freed one of her hands and let it go exploring, down his chest, the stomach, between his legs. She closed her eyes for a moment, enjoying the bliss of finding him perfectly erect, large and throbbing against her hand. He startled when she touched him, made a grunting noise. She took hold of him, squeezed him, stroked his length slowly, up and down. Moaned herself, just to feel it in her hand, in anticipation of what it would do to her. Warm and wet between her thighs now. She wondered if he could smell it.

She dared to look at his face again. He was breathing fast, his nostrils were flaring. For a second she experienced fear again, then he lowered his head and bit lightly into her skin, just below her ear, licked her neck, sniffed her. She let his cock go and grabbed his shoulders, held on to them and arched towards him while his tongue, his unbelievably long tongue, licked a trail from her neck to her breast. The rough tip rubbed her nipple, made it pucker and shape like a raspberry. Clara moaned, she lifted her hips off the mattress and rubbed herself against the hard, green flesh. No more fear then, just want.

"Fuck me," she repeated her plea. She could feel her own moisture leaking from her slit, slicking the skin on the insides of her thighs. "Fuck me," she said again and clung to his shoulders, let her own tongue taste his skin—no salt there, just water, plain and pure.

The membranes half covered his eyes. His hands on her skin caressed her roughly. "Beautiful witch," he murmured. Then his palm
slapped her hip with a smacking sound. Not hard enough to sting,
just to have her moan. A smile curved his lips. "Turn around," his
raspy voice sounded while he moved off her body and Clara did what
she was told; rolled over with her back, and her rear, to him. She rose
to her fours, changed her mind and held on to the headboard instead,
licked her lips as she spread her legs as wide as she possibly could.
Didn't care about the shamelessness of the position, didn't mind the
vulnerability in showing herself to him like that, all open and wet.
Her breathing came hard and she held on to the wood as she braced
herself for what was to come.

A finger first, probing at her; she heard his breathing too, shallow
and fast. One knuckle sunk inside of her, then another, suction, his
finger felt almost like a kiss, like a mouth. She felt no revulsion for the
inhuman touch. It turned her on.

"Good," she uttered, "feels good." Another finger then, another
sucking sensation. And another one, not inside, but at the tip of her clit,
sucking hard. Clara screamed and clutched at the headboard, rode the
violent sensations when an orgasm hit without warning and made her
body shake with release. Magic, pure magic, in that touch. She gasped
for air; her forehead was slick with sweat. He gave a satisfied grunt
behind her back and withdrew his hand from between her thighs.

"You smell good," she heard his voice, "taste good." She turned
her head just in time to see him lick the last of her juices from his fingers. "Now you shall feel good," he stated with a confident smile and
positioned himself, at last, between her thighs. The tip of his erection
probed against her opening. Clara moaned with anticipation and then
he pushed all the way inside of her. Then he fucked her. Clara held on
to the headboard and pushed her rear against him. His hands held her
hips in a hard grip, guiding her, keeping her in place. Clara's rhythmic moans mingled with his. He filled every inch of her; hit all her
sensitive spots with every thrust. He moved steadily faster, slammed
into her, with increasing force. Trapping her in the pleasure with his
cock and his hands, until at last she couldn't take more but gave in to
an orgasm that made her muscles tighten hard around him, milk him
with her waves. It made him come as well. He gave a deep sigh of re-

lief, buckled on top of her and dragged her with him down on the bed. She landed on top of him, lay there gasping while the last few waves coursed through her body. Her warm skin was covered in salt, his cooler one in scentless moisture. A rich amount of clear liquid came seeping out from between her legs and down on his green skin.

"Lovely," she uttered when she regained her voice.

"You too," answered the demon beneath her, circling her waist with his arms.

She had him three more times that night, always from behind, until she taught him otherwise. At last they fell asleep in a heap of rumpled sheets and juices. The next morning, she swore to herself before dozing off, she'd show him how good it could be when *she* was on top....

The next morning, however, arrived with a surprise: instead of finding her alluring demon beside her, she found something that looked like the trunk of a tree. Clara jumped out of bed, grabbed her robe and covered herself up while staring at the thing, as if it had eyes and could see her. Its edges were rounded, the surface rough-looking. There was no sign of her demon anywhere. Then it dawned on her, that *it*, the thing might in fact, be him.

Slowly she climbed back in bed, reached out a hand and touched it. It didn't move. It just lay there, looking wooden. Felt rough, not warm, nor cold. Was he inside?

"Hello?" She tried to talk to the trunk but received no answer. This was not supposed to happen, was it? He was supposed to become a prince again, wasn't he? Her frustration grew as she patted and knocked on the thing. Was this all, then? One night of pleasure and then he was gone? That was most definitely not fair! She'd just rediscovered how nice it could be, having someone there — in her bed... She scratched at the thing with her fingernails, cursed at it, kissed it...

Finally she gave up and went downstairs. All day she was brooding, checking the thing in her bed every hour. What was she to do with it? Carry it outside? Bury it? Put it back in the well?

As dusk approached, however, something *did* happen upstairs: tiny cracks appeared on the surface of the thing, criss-crossing the texture. Clara's heart raced again as she stood by the bed, unable to take her eyes off the thing. The Prince! Of course! This had to be it. He wasn't dead at all, he was just changing! She sat down beside it, staring, while the cracks widened and the thing began to fall apart. She wondered what he'd look like, her prince, when he arrived. Handsome, for sure! Exquisite! She pictured him in her mind; long legs, soft hair — hers.

The thing fell apart completely, bits of the shell rained down on the bed — then... He arrived: as long as her palm from wrist to fingertips, green as before, yet not so attractive. A frog jumped down on the floor and looked at her. Blinked once, twice, then it jumped out the door.

"Wait," Clara yelled and ran after it. "You cannot leave me now!"

But it did. It jumped down the stairs, across the kitchen floor, up on the window sill, and didn't even offer her another glance before it jumped down on the ground to join the choir of frogs in the grass.

The next night Clara went outside. She crossed the garden and entered the path to the lake. She scanned her surroundings as she walked: the land might be his again, but it hadn't changed. Looked just the same. She was armed with a flashlight and an empty glass jar; under her arm was a thick scroll, dusty and old, from the attic. On top of the page it said in ancient letters, written in an ink resembling faded blood: *How to curse a frog*.

If you enjoyed this story, you can discuss it with other readers and the author at the *Demon in the Well* story page at http://forbiddenfiction.com/library/story/CB1-1.000049.

A Little Night Swimming

Mina Kelly

Becky knows better than to be trapped by the tide at night, but it's funny how a bottle of cheap vodka can overcome an entire upbringing by the sea. She grew up with all the myths, too, but when her cute rescuer invites her into deep waters for a swim it's not so much the *mer* as the *maid* that makes Becky hesitate.

A Little Night Swimming

Becky wandered away from the party, an empty bottle of shop-brand alcopop still dangling from one hand. The music was tinny and barely audible beneath the sound of the waves, and she couldn't understand why they bothered. But then, most of them had never lived by the sea, not before they came to university.

That, she supposed, was the root of all this anti-climax. They were all moving away, going places. She'd never been anywhere, wasn't going anywhere. Just here, all along.

She kicked off her shoes and let the damp sand squidge between her toes. Someone—Mark—called her name, but she was just drunk enough not to care. The cliff rose from the sea wall on her right, intruding on the sand at irregular intervals to split it into little coves. Maybe it was the alcohol making her maudlin, but no matter how many coves she scrambled into, none seemed quite far enough or quite private enough for her peace of mind.

Somewhere around the fifth cove she had the presence of mind to put the bottle down. Somewhere around the sixth she put her shoes down too, and didn't realise until the eighth.

Somewhere long after she lost count, she realised the tide was coming in.

The waves lapped at her bare feet and she glanced back the way she'd come. The moon cast a false path across the water, all the way back to the main beach. She was more than halfway around the bay now, probably a mile from where she'd started. No wonder the tide was coming in.

It wasn't just a matter of paddling to get back, she knew. She'd have to swim if she wanted to rejoin the party, now little more than a bright spot in the distance where they'd lit their campfire.

She looked around the cove she was in. The tideline was only a metre or so up the cliff. She couldn't climb the whole way up, but she figured even half drunk she should be able to get above the tideline. It would be cold, and she'd get wet, but it was a whole heck of a lot less dangerous than trying to swim at this time of night.

A whole hell *of a lot*. Mark had always teased her when she said "heck" or "geez" or any other "baby swear." She got his point, she really did. If it wasn't for him she'd still be living with her parents. She liked her independence. Almost as much as she liked being walking distance from her parents' place on a Sunday lunch time. And the thing with Mark... the on and off thing...

It ought to be an "on" thing. She knew that. She wanted it to be that. She just didn't want it enough or something. She wasn't sure. He was nice, and sweet, and had a great sense of humour, and was built like an American movie star even if he was English, and her parents loved him. There was just something missing. When they'd been "off," she'd tried other guys. Tried bad boys, tried geeky boys, tried boring boys and exciting boys and all the different kind of boys her roommates matched her up with. All she seemed to have learned was even though boys could be pretty sweet about you changing your mind about sex, word still got around you were some kind of prick tease.

Maybe she was just waiting for "the one." Just that kind of girl, that had a "one."

Or maybe she was the other kind of girl.

She wished now she'd brought another drink with her.

Becky leant back against the cliff, and watched the sea creep closer to her perch. There were stars reflected in the rock pools, and the moon hung fat and low in the sky, so bright it was like someone had finally swapped out the old bulb for a new one. The swish of the waves was familiar, that regular six and then a larger seventh. The way they caught on each other, sometimes reinforcing, sometimes interrupting. Just repeating the same pattern, over and over, the inching of the tide barely noticeable.

Until it jumped. Becky blinked at it, cold water almost at her feet. She'd fallen asleep.

"Lucky" was the word that came to mind. She glanced behind her, judging how much space she had to scoot back and up the cliff. Not much. This wasn't a good place to —

The hand on her ankle was warmer than the water, though not by much.

Not sure she wanted to see, but knowing she had to look, Becky turned her head.

Her perch was such that immediately in front of her was a hollow in the rock, so though her feet were only just wet, inches away the water was several feet deep. Floating on the surface was a clump of seaweed, silver in the moonlight. In the darkness the water was almost opaque, but Becky could just make out a shape beneath the weeds.

A wave lifted the seaweed, but when it receded the weed didn't. From beneath the tangled knot a pair of dark eyes met Becky's.

"Um. Hi."

The hand withdrew from Becky's ankle. The eyes moved backwards. Into deeper water, Becky realised.

Becky slid down from her perch, until she stood a little over waist deep in the hollow the other girl had just vacated. The water didn't feel so cold now, not against the hot flush of her skin.

She tried to tell herself it was one of the other partygoers, some-one foolhardy enough to swim all the way out here to see if she was okay, but the distant beach was empty and dark now, and besides, she knew better. She'd been raised here. She knew a mermaid when she met one.

The mermaid bobbed a little higher in the water, her strong tail holding her vertical. What Becky had taken for weeds was a kind of short hair, spiky and asymmetric. The mermaid's face was round, eyes large and nose small, mouth drawn up in a small smile.

The mermaid pointed at herself. "Sheaar," she said, her voice soft and almost purring, like the sea on a stone beach. She pointed at Becky.

"Becky," she said. "Hi."

"Hhhhh," Sheaar said, and beckoned to her.

The water lapped at the underside of Becky's breasts, her nipples tightening at its caress. Sheaar was cute. Really cute. There was some-thing tomboyish about her Becky liked.

She swallowed and pushed away from the rock beneath her feet. Treading water now, she let the rocking of the waves pull her closer to Sheaar. Becky was a strong swimmer, like anyone who grew up beside the sea, though a little voice at the back of her head was screaming at her now. The thing was, it wasn't the little voice that warned her against doing dangerous things, no. It wasn't the voice that could cut through any drunken haze when she was considering climbing that wall or jumping that gap or swimming in that water. It sounded a lot more like the little voice that warned her against doing unfeminine things, that warned her not to dwell on certain dreams and not to spend time with certain girls.

It definitely didn't like this girl, that was for certain.

Sheaar took Becky's arm and pulled her closer. She had no fear of drowning in the night. Becky looked for gills, but the rise and fall of the waves told her not to bother. Sheaar was a mammal. Six nipples stood out brown against her torso. Not six breasts, or at least not six large ones, but Becky wanted to put her hands to them and compare them with her own. Let Sheaar do the same. Not sexually, she told the little voice. Experimentally.

Sheaar's hands were large, her fingers odd proportions, but her grip on Becky was secure. The tide tried to push them back towards the cliffs, but as Becky's toes touched smooth rock Sheaar's strong tail thrust them away from the cliff, into the deeper water between the stone outcrops. Instinctively, Becky grabbed the mermaid's waist. The mermaid's powerful tail could support them both with far less effort than it would take Becky to tread water, and the further they were from the cliffs the safer they were. Well, in one sense.

Those dark eyes were so much closer now, the reflection of the sea in them, and the sea reflecting the starlight. Becky felt if she looked up she'd see the eyes reflected in the sky, like three mirrors had been placed at angles to each other and there'd be Beckies from here to infinity if she got between them.

Sheaar closed the distance between them.

Her lips were different to a human's. Smoother, a little harder, but parting against Becky's and persuading Becky's to part. Her tongue was smooth against the roof of Becky's mouth, stroking behind her teeth. Becky licked the bottom of Sheaar's tongue cautiously. Sheaar's hands tightened on Becky's arms.

Becky pulled back as far as she could without letting go of Sheaar. She was still drunk, had to be, though she didn't feel it as much. Or the mermaid was asserting some kind of influence over her, some kind of siren-esque magic.

Sheaar cocked her had to one side, small smile a little larger now. She let go of one of Becky's arms to run her fingers through Becky's hair, apparently interested in its completely different texture to her own. Becky swallowed hard. Sheaar's hand ran through her hair to her shoulder, and further down, to Becky's breast. Her hard nipples were visible through the wet material of her t-shirt, her bikini top beneath so thin she might as well not have bothered.

Sheaar reached for the hem of Becky's t-shirt. She met Becky's eyes, her expression quizzical. Becky nodded, and let go so Sheaar could lift the t-shirt over her head. She trod water, waiting to take hold of Sheaar again. To save herself the effort, of course. Not for any other reason. Like letting Sheaar strip her was some kind of scientific experiment.

Her excuses dissolved like salt in water. The little voice inside diluted so far it was silenced. That kiss had been...

She was more embarrassed than ashamed; embarrassed not to have figured this out about herself sooner. It didn't seem worth denying now, not with an opportunity like this presenting itself.

Her t-shirt still half over her head, covering her eyes, Becky felt Sheaar's breath against her cheek. Their lips met again. Maybe being blindfolded made her braver, but this time Becky deepened the kiss almost immediately, her tongue eagerly pushing between Sheaar's lips. Sheaar pressed against her, warm and firm against Becky's bare skin. Sheaar's nipples were as hard as Becky's.

Sheaar gave the t-shirt a final tug, and Becky could see her again. Her lips were swollen with the kiss, her eyes hooded. Becky's breath caught in her chest, her breasts heaving against Sheaar's.

Becky put a hand to one of Sheaar's lower breasts, covering it with her hand. Sheaar's nipple quivered against her palm. She'd got drunk once, at a party, and agreed to a dare a bit like this. Mark had been watching, but not as enthusiastically as the other guys. Becky wondered if he'd known, even then, before she had.

Sheaar reached behind Becky's head to untie her bikini. The strings around her neck slipped free, and it floated between them like a French maid's apron. Becky placed her other hand on another of Sheaar's breasts, reaching this time for her nipple. She rolled it between her fingers. Sheaar moaned; a fluting, high-pitched noise that reminded Becky of dolphins. Emboldened, Becky risked a gentle pinch. Sheaar's head fell back, her moan louder and longer.

Becky moved between Sheaar's breasts, experimenting with each of them. Stroking, squeezing, pinching, pressing, and when she worked up the nerve, sucking. Sheaar's skin tasted of salt, unsurprisingly, but it was smooth under the tongue. She was warmer than the sea around them. Hot-blooded, Becky thought and smiled. Sheaar squirmed at the sensation, Becky's lips obviously ticklish against her skin.

Sheaar was lying almost horizontal now, her body designed to be reasonably buoyant. Becky rested on top of her, her legs in the water on either side. To kiss Sheaar's chest she had to risk getting a faceful of the occasional wave, but years of snorkelling had taught her how to judge her breathing so well it was instinctive. She barely noticed when she had to hold her breath for a couple of extra seconds, and besides, she was far too busy to care.

Becky kissed her way up Sheaar's torso, zig-zagging back and forth to kiss the tip of each of her nipples. As she neared the top she decided to try something different, and instead of a gentle peck she took Sheaar's top-right nipple into her mouth. She rolled it between her lips, flicked it with her tongue.

Sheaar moaned, her body writhing beneath Becky. Becky's breasts rubbed against Sheaar's middle pair, Sheaar's hard nipples teasing Becky's own.

Becky's cold, wet shorts clung tightly to her behind, making the damp heat between her legs all the more obvious. She never got wet like this with a guy; she and Mark had had to resort to lube most times, when she could work up the enthusiasm.

Sheaar was wet too; Becky could feel it against her stomach. It occurred to her that without legs Sheaar's slit must be somewhere on the front of her body. She wondered if the mermaid had a clitoris.

There was only one way to find out.

While her nerve still held, Becky worked her way back down Sheaar's body. Sheaar's hands found Becky's hair, tangled by the sea into a mess even Sheaar's long fingers couldn't penetrate. Sheaar's body was basically hairless and Becky slid down it easily. She rested on Sheaar's tail, her legs wrapped around the end of it and her hands on Sheaar's hips. Sheaar managed to get a loose grip on the back of Becky's head, guiding her to where Sheaar needed her to be.

Sheaar's slit was just that on the surface. It would be invisible when she was swimming, but now, as turned on as she was, it was a little swollen, the edges parting to reveal a glimpse of the lips beneath. They were pink against the grey skin, even in the moonlight, and Becky was relieved to see they were as familiar as her own. She hadn't known what to expect. At least Sheaar was all mammal rather than half fish.

Becky suspected if she let go of Sheaar's hips she would be in danger of sliding off altogether, so the only avenue of exploration open to her was her tongue. She'd never done this before, wasn't sure quite what to do. Mark had only... this wasn't the time to be thinking about Mark, she realised. It wasn't like he'd ever got her off this way.

Becky pressed her mouth to Sheaar's slit in a gentle kiss. Sheaar sighed, just audible above the waves. Becky tried another kiss, a little more passionate. Her tongue slipped between her lips and parted Sheaar's, moving between the folds. She traced patterns up and down with the rhythm of the waves, seeking Sheaar's clitoris, if she had one.

She did, and Becky knew she'd found it because Sheaar bucked, her tail jerking so powerfully Becky was lifted clean out of the water. The cold air was sudden, Becky breaking out all over in goosebumps. She tightened her legs around Sheaar's tail, and resolved to get the same reaction again.

Now she'd found Sheaar's clitoris it was easier. She teased it with her tongue, always in time with the waves, back and forth. Sheaar mewled. She didn't move as much now, obviously making a conscious effort to stay still. Her self-control teased Becky, waved a red flag in front of her, and she wanted to break it. God knew she'd wanted someone to break hers in the past.

Becky managed to cross her legs at the ankle on the other side of

Sheaar's tail. Sheaar's hands tightened in her hair, and when Becky risked moving a hand from Sheaar's hip she found herself still reasonably secure. She walked her fingers across Sheaar's body, eliciting a series of shivers. She moved her mouth a little to make room for them, dragging her bottom lip across Sheaar's folds until her lips were pursed against Sheaar's clitoris. Her first two fingers traced the smooth edges of Sheaar's slit, then inside the ruffled edges of her lips.

She slid both fingers into Sheaar's passage, so much warmer than the sea around them and almost wetter, if that were possible. She glanced up Sheaar's body; her head was so far back it was under water, and her six nipples stood proud like standing stones on a headland.

Becky scissored her fingers inside Sheaar. A few feet away a stream of bubbles broke the surface of the ocean, and Sheaar's head reappeared, gasping. Becky met her eyes and Sheaar gazed at her, a loose smile and wild eyes begging Becky to keep going. Her hands tightened on Becky's hair.

Becky did. She lowered her head to Sheaar's slit again, mindful of the waves breaking across Sheaar's body. Pushing her fingers deeper inside Sheaar, she pressed her tongue hard against Sheaar's clitoris. She'd been able to roll her tongue since childhood, and Sheaar appreciated her practice. She crooked her fingers, beckoning to Sheaar's oncoming orgasm. Crooked them again, rolled and swirled her tongue again, and Sheaar's whole body spasmed. Becky clung on, withdrawing her fingers so she could lick Sheaar through her orgasm, taste every drop of that hot liquor.

Sheaar submerged completely. Becky was forced to let go and surface for air.

She felt light-headed; she'd been holding her breath longer than she realised. Her feet pedalled slowly, hands circling in the water. Her bikini top was still tethered around her waist, moving just below the surface of the water.

She'd never done that before. Still, she couldn't have done that badly. Becky's lips quirked into a smile. She couldn't see Sheaar, but she could feel her movements beneath the water, the cold sea moving around and between her own legs. She was aching, she realised. She'd never needed sex so badly.

Still a little smug from Sheaar's orgasm, Becky reached for the button of her shorts and pushed them down her legs so she could kick them off.

There was no sign of Sheaar. Even the swirling of the water around her — counter to the waves, proof of Sheaar's nearness — stopped. For a terrified moment Becky thought she'd misunderstood altogether, but then there were hands on her thighs, easing the shorts down her legs, caressing as they pushed.

Becky watched her shorts float to the surface. Sheaar remained submerged. Her hands remained on Becky's legs. Becky's heart refused to remain anything, stuttering and leaping like a grasshopper with fleas.

The seconds stretched, waiting for something to happen. What would Sheaar do? Fingers? Mouth? What would she focus on first?

Something touched Becky's back. Something smooth against her butt. She jerked forward. And there was a mouth on her cunt. She registered hot and wet, and her body held firm between the two diverse muscles of tongue and tail.

Becky could feel Sheaar's hips beneath her feet. Becky parted her legs, and as Sheaar settled into a more comfortable position Becky wrapped her legs around Sheaar's upper body, ankles crossed beneath her back.

Sheaar's mouth was wide and warm. Her lips were thin but they formed a perfect seal around Becky's slit. It was a strange feeling, but Becky appreciated it as the cold sea water was gradually displaced with Sheaar's warm saliva. Sheaar ran the tip of her tongue along the inner curve of Becky's labia, teasing the ruffles of her inner lips and tasting Becky's own wetness. It was gentle, exploratory, and Becky wanted so much more.

She got it. Sheaar's tongue — nimbler and more dexterous than Becky's own — found her clitoris and tapped it. Little staccato taps, arrhythmic enough to drive Becky wild. Sheaar's hands edged up Becky's thighs until her long fingers wound all the way from Becky's buttocks to the crease where her legs met her pubic curve. Her tail came up to support Becky's upper back, keeping her head well clear of the waves. Becky was open and aching, desperate for something to push her over the edge.

Sheaar lifted her mouth from Becky's slit and let the cold sea flood in. The shock was so powerful Becky couldn't see if it was good or bad, just that it made her arch her back and tighten her legs around Sheaar's chest. She was glad of Sheaar's tail, and even more of Sheaar's ability to hold her breath as Sheaar's tongue thrust inside her, chasing the cold away again. Heat built inside Becky until it overflowed within her; she came in a white-hot weightless moment.

As Becky surfaced from her orgasm so did Sheaar from the sea.

The mermaid was flushed, smiling, but she kept a little distance between herself and Becky. Becky felt somehow shy now, unsure of what to say. If Sheaar could even understand her; they hadn't exactly relied on words to communicate so far, had they? She had a strange urge to say thank you — she *was* grateful, in so many ways — but it didn't seem right. They couldn't curl up and go to sleep. Becky had always supposed this was what it would feel like after a one night stand, but she didn't want this to be a one night stand. She had no clue how to convey this, though.

Sheaar held something out to Becky, a light blush dusting her cheeks too. It was Becky's bikini briefs. She almost laughed, realising she still wore the tissue-thin top. Well, it would save walking home naked, anyway.

The cold was insidious, and if she didn't get out of the water soon she'd be in real trouble. They'd drifted a little further from shore, but not so far that Becky couldn't make it back to the cliffs. But what then? She couldn't climb then, and she couldn't stay in the water. Sit there until the tide went out again, nothing between her and the night but a wet bikini?

Sheaar said something in her hissing language, head cocked to one side. Becky could do nothing but shrug, knowing her expression must convey her lack of understanding. Sheaar said something else, swam towards Becky with a single push of her tail, and wrapped both arms around her in a tight hug.

Becky cuddled into her strong arms. Sheaar cupped a hand under Becky' chin. When Becky was looking into her eyes, Sheaar pointed at Becky and then herself. *We'll meet again*, Becky thought. She began to hum. Sheaar grinned, obviously delighted, and joined in. Not quite a siren, but still a lover of songs.

There was an odd noise overhead. It took Becky a moment to recognise it over the sound of the waves, its rhythm out of time with theirs. Sheaar pressed a quick kiss to her lips, too quick for Becky to respond, and disappeared beneath her. Becky's world lit up, painfully bright. Something dropped into the water beside her.

"If you can, hold onto the ladder and we'll pull you up."

The words were shouted over the thwopthwop of the helicopter blades. Becky could barely see the ladder, still blinded by the spotlight, but she managed to grab hold of it. She was going to have little enough dignity left by the time she'd thought up some lie to tell them, so fuck them pulling her up like some half-drowned, half-drunk student; she started to climb. She'd gone to school with half the guys in that helicopter — a peril of being a local — and she wasn't going to let them think a little night swim had worn her out.

Halfway up, she glanced down. The light didn't penetrate the sea far, most of it reflected by the choppy waves, but she could just make out a shadow beneath her. Long and slender, it looped through the water with a combination of grace and power Becky knew would get her wet every time she thought of it. The shadow waved, and Becky blew her a kiss.

The lifeguards hauled Becky into the helicopter. Its bright colours were garish after the dark beauty of the ocean at night. She let herself be wrapped in a towel, accepted the plastic mug of tea, and tried to keep her explanation as vague as she could. Her mind wasn't really on what she was saying. Above the young woman opposite, the one with the Thermos flask poised to top Becky's mug up again, was a piece of paper taped to the wall. Tomorrow's high tide would be 11pm, Becky read. Perfect.

If you enjoyed this story, you can discuss it with other readers and the author at the *A Little Night Swimming* story page at http://forbiddenfiction.com/library/story/MK1-1.000069.

Little Henna Hair

R.W. Whitefield

A werewolf sees a sexy redhead dancing in his nightclub, and he follows her into an alley. He doesn't expect her to take on the big, bad wolf, but Little Henna Hair is more than able—she's willing.

Little Henna Hair

Little Henna Hair can dance all night long, if she likes. Gleaming black spirals crayoned across her cheeks, fishnets torn just so, big green eyes flitting from face to face. Vintage vinyl purse packed full of goodies stolen from Grandma's medicine cabinet. Strutting, whirling, throwing her head back and laughing from sheer giddy love on the dance floor, letting the blue and purple lights spill over her face like fairies.

She can't see me, not in the crush of squirrel-boys with sincere stripy shirts shaking their bony asses. I'm hiding tonight anyway, watching the kids dance from my little perch on the second floor, right behind the lights. I'd like to say they remind me of my own youth, the vitality ebbed away over the years, but the truth is I'm stronger and more alive than any of them will ever be.

"Sir?" Movement in the shadows, and I whirl around to see a waitress standing behind me.

"Don't sneak up on me like that. Move slowly around me. I told you, I don't like sudden movements." This isn't the whim of a decrepit nightclub owner, just a precaution. If I see something flash past the corner of my eye, I'm likely to pounce, no matter what skin I wear. I don't want to have police come around to investigate a disemboweled waitress.

"Closing time, sir. 4 AM." She sidles up to me, running a candy-red fingernail along the cuff of my suit. "Do you want me to escort you home?" Tempting. I can smell her arousal. But tonight is for Little Henna Hair down there, in the middle of the dance floor.

"I'll walk." I pat her on the ass. "Go close down."

The lights turn off, the kids file out the door, whispering and moaning and giggling to each other. I've slipped out the back door already, watching them break off in twos and threes. I hope Little Henna Hair came here alone. Friends make it harder to follow. One of them always notices a shadow or a sound, panics, runs, and then you either have to make yourself give up chase, or you have the police on your tail.

Ah, here she comes, swinging her bag. Does a little dance step, a little twirl, traipsing down the sidewalk. Alone. I can smell her perfume from here, something sweet and heavy, flowers wilted and burnt.

I let her get half a block away from me before I turn. More room for the chase; it's no fun if you catch them right away. Concentrate, close my eyes, I shed my skin. Gone is the distinguished older man, iron-grey hair, pinstriped suit, ice-blue eyes that warn of spankings and canings if a frivolous young thing gets out of line. Here are sharp teeth, a red tongue, claws and fur, and a nose that can smell a sweet little puppy a mile away.

Her scent's stronger now, almost overwhelming. I run silent, swift, a grey shadow through the alleyways, following the twists and turns she takes. Little Henna Hair, didn't your mother tell you to stay out of alleyways?

Ah, and there she is, a red blur atop a swirl of black leather and pale skin. I can't help myself; I start panting. A little reflex left over from my human form.

The legs stop.

"Who's there?" She glances over her shoulder, but I've slipped back into the shadows. All she'll see are my eyes gleaming, if that. "Come on out." She backs away, right into a brick wall. No more chase? Maybe she's tired. "I mean it. Logan? Mel? Is that one of you, playing a joke?" I growl, just a little. Her head whips around. "Please." I can smell her fear. Good enough.

I slink out of the shadows, into the moonlight. Full moon tonight. She backs away, green eyes widening.

"Oh. A doggie!" Doggie? Has the girl never seen a nature show? Does she think I'm some lost pup? I snarl, show my teeth.

She crouches.

"Come here," she whispers. "Come here." The fear's gone, that tangy smell in my mouth. A strange little smile grows on her face. "My, what big teeth you have."

I tense my legs and pounce on the girl, bowling her over onto the pavement. The vinyl purse flies out of her hand, and I have her pinned to the ground, my paws on her shoulders, breathing hot onto her face.

She's laughing, laughing, the girl is *laughing;* why isn't she scared that I'm going to tear her throat out?

"Nice doggie," she whispers, "nice wolf, sweet boy." Her pale hands bury themselves in my fur, gripping handfuls of it. "So soft, so soft." They're everywhere, somehow, stroking my belly, trailing down the smooth path of fur on my head.

What's wrong with this picture? Predator, prey, Little Henna Hair and the Big Bad Wolf. Where's the fear I smelled a moment ago? I growl again, licking my chops. The better to eat you with, my dear!

"I know you," she whispers, "I've seen you around. Skulking in the alleys after my friends. I saw you change, in the shadows." Her hand trails down my nose.

A chill runs down my back. I will myself to shift again, slowly twisting my bones into the form of the man I show the world. I see her eyes widen.

It's one thing to be nuzzling a wild animal in an urban alley. That's exotic, exciting, something to tell your friends the next day if you get out of it alive.

Being pinned to the ground by a naked man in an alley is something quite, quite different, especially if you're a delicate Goth flower like Little Henna Hair. My hands tighten around her shoulders.

"Very clever, my dear," I murmur. "Clever girl. You've been watching me? For how long?"

She swallows.

"A few weeks. Ever since I started coming. You don't..." Her voice is wavering, and she sounds less sure of herself. "I know you don't eat them. Not like wolves do." Her hands reach up to stroke the back of my neck. "I saw them come back, after all."

"Quite right." I bend my head and kiss her, catching her lower lip in my teeth.

She twists her head to the side, breaking the kiss.

"No."

I growl, and I know it sounds the same.

"No? No?"

"I mean..." Her hands bury themselves in my hair. "Wolf. I want to you be a wolf." She smiles and runs her tongue over her lips. "That's what I led you here for."

I laugh, and change, and the moonlight is sweet. In my human form, I'm weaker than I'd like to be, my muscles puny even at the height of their strength. But as my form changes beneath me, I can feel energy and power ripple through my body, unlimited and unbound. The moonlight washes over me like a warm bath, cleansing and hot, making everything easy, simple. This girl is mine and that's all I need to know.

Little Henna Hair's eyes widen, so beautiful and blue. She twines her milk-white arms around me and buries her head in my shoulder. My hair must tickle her nose, but she's breathing in my musk. I try to hide it when I'm in human form, slather on cologne and aftershave so humans won't catch a whiff of me and scare off like mice. But when I'm a wolf I can't help it; the scent comes out of my skin.

She loves it. I can tell. I can hear her breathing, the hitch in her voice like a gasp. Her hands are twisting in the hair on my back, movement without meaning, burning off her own energy, her excitement, everything she's feeling.

"Pretty," she says, the sounds of her red mouth muffled through my hair, but now my sensitive ears can hear it all. I can hear her heart beating faster. Being scared is exciting to humans, arousing. Adrenaline pumps through the blood, the sinews stiffen.

I like what we look like in my mind's eye, the moonlight picking highlights out of Little Henna Hair's hair, twinkling in her blue eyes, her pale skin like milk. Her legs are long, shapely, splayed out under me like the broken legs of a doll. And I, a grey hulking beast on top of her. I sink my teeth slowly into the curve of her neck, not hard enough to tear, just hard enough to make it ache good, like she wants. Anyone who saw us now would think I was eating her, about to tear her delicate body apart.

Maybe she likes that. Maybe she dreams about this, being torn apart by a wild animal, her last breath a fatal orgasm. I won't do it, no, because she's too precious to waste—but it's tempting. She tastes good, sweet and earthy, sweat and perfume.

Little Henna Hair pushes me away, and I growl, the sound coming from deep within me. Does she think she can push me away so easily? She's mine, mine, and I'll fight for her.

She lifts her hand, and I think she's going to hit me, bop me on the nose like I was a disobedient pup. But her hand rests on my head.

"Easy," she whispers, "I'm just taking off my clothes. You want me naked, don't you?" She puts her hands on her shirt, lifts it to reveal two perky, soft, white, perfect breasts. Pale and round like the moon. Her nipples are red and hard. The scent from her skin is stronger now, and I can hear each beat of her heart, pumping her sweat into the air.

I stick out my tongue and lick her, long and slow, tasting the skin between her breasts. She laughs, and the sound multiplies in my ears like bells.

"Good boy," she says, "good pup, that tickles." I know my tongue is rough and wet, it leaves a thick, sloppy mark on her so unlike the neat, thin saliva of a human boy. I drag my tongue over her nipples, lapping and licking, and she buries her hand in my hair and pulls, making wordless sounds, sounds that are closer to howls than anything human she's said.

And that's what gets my wolf body going, what makes arousal and want, need, lust rush through me like strength, like moonlight, like bones and flesh that twist and change. Before, it was the man who wanted her. Now, it's truly the wolf.

Her skirt is flimsy, tears off with barely a nibble, and she's not wearing anything underneath. Just her cunt, and the scent is driving me wild, making me want to hop around like a puppy. When she laughs again and spreads her legs, I nuzzle her soft thighs. They're so vulnerable, so fragile. I could rip her skin off with a bite if I wanted. But I won't tear her apart, won't hurt her. I sink my teeth slowly into her legs, just enough to mark her, to hurt just a little. By the time we're done, she'll have my teeth marks all over her body, red marks on that soft white skin.

She slips her hand down her flat stomach, down into the cleft of her cunt, getting that wonderful smell all over her fingers, her hand. Her pubic hair is curly and wiry, hiding the slickness of her clit, the soft folds of her vaginal lips. I dip my tongue into her cleft, lapping up her juices, the slick and viscous fluid smells of her, of sex. My rough tongue must feel so harsh on her clitoris, so unique, not like the flat, smooth tongues of most men. I know it is because she's making harsh, rough sounds in the back of her throat.

Her long white legs wrap around my neck and torso, resting in my thick fur, clinging to me like a monkey's legs. She's so limber, this one, and I'm so strong. Her hips are pistoning forwards, her cunt getting wetter by the moment, and I want to make her come.

"No," she murmurs into my fur, "no. Not yet." She unwraps her long legs from me and sits up. I growl, wanting to bury my nose in her again, taste and smell her sex. But she shakes her head. "I want you in me."

I've never fucked a human in this shape. Wolves fuck wolves, humans fuck humans—it's how it's done. No woman wants a great, hairy wolf over her, thrusting into her. But Little Henna Hair does, is eager for it. I start to doubt her. Is she a human at all? Is she some kind of fae, or another like me?

She kneels and takes my face in her hands, her green, green eyes looking into mine, and I forget my concerns, forget my fears and my doubts.

"Good boy," she whispers, and my only desire now is pleasing her, making her come. In my fog of arousal, I think I could be tame for her, could be her wild thing enslaved if she wanted. She's so beautiful, the most beautiful thing I've ever seen. The idea of fawning over her is almost erotic, an animalistic fetish.

I'm panting for her, drooling, slavering. She smiles at me and pats me on the head—if it were anyone else, I'd bite her hand off. But I just open my mouth and loll out my tongue, watching as she rises to her feet and turns around.

"It'll be easier this way," she says.

She wrestles off her coat and spreads it on the ground, gets on her knees, showing her tight, pert white ass to me, and spreads her legs open. Her cunt looks so wet, glistening in the moonlight. She wiggles her ass, inviting me in, asking me to mount her.

I charge forward, raising my body up and laying it down on hers, that slim white frame pinned under my muscular, hairy body. I can feel my cock engorging, ready to plunge into her, ready to fuck her and fill her with my seed. The urge rises within me. I want to mate, I need to, and she's waiting for me.

Little Henna Hair moans under me, and I slide my hard cock into her soft, wet cunt. She feels so tight around me, like silk. She gasps and moans, and I can feel her cunt constrict around my cock.

"You're so big. Good boy. Good boy."

I try to slow my thrusts so I don't hurt her, that delicate human body, but she smells so good, I can't hold back. I want to bury myself in her, stay inside of her. My conscious mind is almost gone, dissolved inside my lust for her. I can barely control the way my wolf body is thrusting into her cunt. I can hear her squeaking underneath me, her body rocking with my thrusts.

I feel powerful again, wild and in control. She's so small beneath me, and my cock is inside of her, controlling the way her body is rocking back and forth. I fuck faster, harder, feeling the wet walls of her cunt contract and expand with her pleasure. I feel the knot at the base of my cock swelling, feel my body preparing to come inside her soon. She's too tight for me to push my knot inside her, be locked together like a puzzle piece, but I'm responding to her as though she's a bitch in heat.

Little Henna Hair splays her fingers out on her coat, moaning as her hands curl into something like claws. She moves her body against me, riding out my thrusts, using her body to push my cock deeper into her than ever before. It's putting me on the edge, feeling how hot, how tight she is inside. I'd expected her to not be able to take what I have to give, but her cunt is even swallowing up my knot.

"Fuck—fuck—fuck—" Her vulgar chanting sounds like a howl, like something musical, worthy of being my mate. I know what it means, know her desire, her order, her warning. She's about to come.

Power surges through my body as I slam my cock into her. I throw back my head and howl, a declaration and a boast. She is mine, I am her's, and I am making her come. I am shooting my seed into her, marking her in a way that goes deeper than scent, deeper than red tooth marks on pale skin.

The full moon, riding high in the sky, is the only witness to our shared orgasm. I pull out of her and wince as I change back into my human form, using my suddenly soft hand to steady myself against the rough brick wall as my legs wobble upright. The roughness of the brick against my palm makes me think of how my rough skin, my tongue, must have felt against the most delicate parts of her body.

Little Henna Hair is still splayed on the ground, but she's staring up at me now with green eyes, her expression unreadable, her perfect hair askew and mussed. I grin, perhaps a little uneasily. She's the first woman who's ever had this kind of effect on me, who's made me want to cede that kind of control to her, even for a moment.

To be her dog? Her pup? *What was I thinking?*

I'm a predator, an alpha. I take women, I don't get taken by them — no matter how easily they come to me, how much pleasure they take from me. I stalked her, I took her, and she capitulated, drawn by my strength and power. Perhaps I was just overcome, pleased she'd let me in so easily. That's got to be it. I smile more confidently now, showing my teeth.

"So, darling," I say, "was it good for you?"

She cocks her head to the side, purses her lips, rolls up her eyes as though she's thinking, and then she shrugs.

"It could have been better."

"Better?" I growl, and she laughs and extends her hand.

"Help me up," she says, "and I'll show you." I pull her up, and she brushes off her skirt before looking into my eyes. Her legs are shaking a little, but she manages to stay upright, not even wobbling into me.

I'd expected her to be nearly wrecked afterwards — shaking, scraped up, out of breath. Little Henna Hair seems to be barely affected, possessed of some supernatural poise, that slim frame far stronger than it seems. Her eyes are so, so blue, and they scare me.

Her slim hand darts forward and she puts a finger under my chin. My mouth opens in shock, and before I can growl again to warn her off, she tugs me forward and kisses me on the mouth. It's a hard, biting kiss, but she laughs into my mouth before she lets me go.

Little Henna Hair saunters off into the night, and even if I traced the scent of her sweat and come, I don't think I could find her again. But I know she'll find me. Her last words, her parting shot over her shoulder, told me so.

"Good boy. Next time, I'll bring a collar for you."

I shift back into wolf form. I'd rather run home. Maybe I'll catch her again, and we'll see who's going to wear that collar she promised.

If you enjoyed this story, you can discuss it with other readers and the author at the *Little Henna Hair* story page at http://forbiddenfiction.com/library/story/RWW-1.000076.

To Market

Elizabeth A. Schechter

Do not seek the Goblin Market. Do not barter with those you find there. And above all, do not taste of the goblin's seed... To save his childhood sweetheart, Conn dares the dangers of the Goblin Market only to fall under the spell of the goblin himself. Will love save everything or destroy their lives?

Chapter 1
The Goblin Market

"We must not look at goblin men,
We must not buy their fruits"

My name is Conn, and I am no man's son. My mother claimed to have gotten me from one of the Gentry. I don't know the truth of that, if my father was indeed one of the Sidhe, or if he was simply a silver-tongued peddler who never thought again of the girl he left behind him in Hunter's Dell. All I know is that for my whole life, it was just my Ma and me in our little hut by the edge of the forest. Ma... well, the folks in the village called her Wise Meg, or Uncanny Meg, or Meg the Witch, and they came to her for their charms and simples and all the things that made the parson look down his long nose at us when we came to market. Ma told their fortunes and read their palms, made their love charms and uncrossed their cows, and before she died, she taught me her art. Now the village comes to me. That was how it all began.

I had been in my garden that morning, trying to convince the small patch of stubborn dirt that I needed radishes more than I needed rocks. When I saw the rider coming up the road, I knew that he was coming to see me. I leaned on my hoe and waited, and was surprised to see that it was Patrick Grady who was riding up to my gate. The richest man in the village, Grady looked down at me from atop his tall horse like I was something he'd rather not have found under his boot. Then he swallowed his pride, nodded a curt greeting, and cleared his throat, "I've need of an uncrossing."

I nodded. "Is it a cow or a horse you're asking for?"

The expression on his face wouldn't have been out of place if he'd swallowed a live toad. "Neither. 'Tis my daughter."

I dropped my hoe. "Something's happened to Bess?"

He didn't answer, turning his horse back down the road. "Will you come?"

He must have known that I wouldn't have said no, that I would never turn my back on Bess. She was my childhood playmate, a bold, headstrong girl who'd been willing to defy her father because she wanted the village bastard for a friend. She'd wanted to have me as something more, too; the night of her sixteenth birthday, she'd brought me into the hayloft of her father's barn. Grady and his men found us there, both of us half-dressed; Grady dragged his daughter off to the house, leaving his loyal pack of rowdies with instructions to "deal with the bastard." They did, hanging me by my wrists from the hayloft and laying my back open with a horsewhip, then leaving me there until one of the stable-boys took pity on me, cut me down and took me home. A few days later, Grady had ridden up to our gate, and told my mother that if he ever caught me near his girl again, he'd kill me himself.

Since that day, I'd avoided the market, avoided going into the village. I couldn't bear the thought of seeing Bess and not being able to go up to her, talk to her, share everything with her the way we had since we were small. But I never stopped thinking of her, dreaming of her, recalling the few precious moments that we'd had in the hayloft before we'd been found.

What in heaven's name must have happened to her that could bring Grady to look for *my* help?

Grady's house was the finest in the village, and every time Bess had brought me here, she'd brought me in through the front hall to sit in the drawing room like an honored guest. This time, I went to the kitchen door, and found a familiar face there. Moira, Bess' old nurse, met me at the door, wringing her hands as she escorted me into the house and up the servants' stairs.

"Conn, you can help her?" she asked, her voice cracking with fear.

"I don't know, Moira. I will try," I answered, trying to keep my own voice steady. "Where are we going?"

"Miss Bess' bedchamber." Moira led me to the second floor, and down the hall. Grady himself was waiting outside a door, and as I reached it, he opened the door and gestured me inside. I walked in and stopped, stunned at what I saw. Bess lay in the center of the wide, curtained bed, writhing and moaning like a woman possessed. Her fair hair was dirty and matted, and her fine gown was filthy, tattered and torn. Worst of all, her arms were spread wide, her wrists lashed to the bedposts.

I turned to Grady, "What happened here?"

At the sound of my voice, Bess turned. She saw me standing in the doorway, smiled with delight, and called my name. I'd heard her say my name like that once before, and it had made my blood race. Now, the heat in her voice and the wildness in her eyes horrified me. I couldn't imagine what could have caused this. Grady gestured for me to join him in the corridor, closing the door firmly behind me.

"Tell me what happened," I said, trying to ignore the fact that I could still hear Bess through the door, whimpering and crying, calling my name.

Grady shook his head, not meeting my eyes. "We don't know. She went for a walk one evening, and didn't come home. The next morning, we found her wandering in the sheep pasture on the east side of the village, looking like she'd lost her wits. The doctor has been here, and the parson. She attacked the parson, tried to get out of the house. That's why she's bound." Grady stared at the door. "It's been three days, and she only gets worse."

I nodded. He was lying about something, but what, I had no idea. "Let me back in," I said. "I need to look at her, see if I can see anything."

Grady pushed me none-too-gently towards Bess' door. "Moira, go with him," he growled. Then he turned and stalked down the hall.

Moira held the door open for me, then followed me into the room. Once she had closed the door, I turned to face her. "What is he not telling me?" I demanded.

She looked at me and whispered, "He'll have me out on the streets if he finds out I've told you anything."

I met her eyes. "Moira, tell me what I need to save her."

She stared for a moment at the struggling girl on the bed, then nodded. "The Master has arranged a marriage for Miss Bess. To Lord Faraday."

I hissed at the name. Lord Faraday was our liege lord, but that didn't mean I had to like the man. He was a heavy-handed man, I'd heard, and he'd buried four wives that I knew about. Moira nodded again.

"When he told Miss Bess, she refused. She told him..." she paused and then looked at me. "Conn, she told her father that if he forced her, she'd go to the goblins. They didn't find her in the sheep meadow. They found her at Hunter's Oak."

I turned and stared at the bed in shock. She had gone to the goblin market?

If you were to wander in the gloaming towards the hollow where the tree that the old folks called the Hunter's Oak had once stood, you would hear the goblins, calling to the unwary: "Who will buy? Come and buy!" No one knew for certain when they had first come to Hunter's Dell. There were some, my mother told me, who were foolish enough to go into the hollow and take what the goblins offered. But when they returned to the hollow, seeking more of the same, they found it empty; the goblins never came twice to someone who had tasted their wares. All of those poor souls had died horribly within a few days, refusing food and drink, pining for whatever they had found in the hollow. Ma had told me once that she thought there might have been a way to save them, if there had been someone brave enough to try it. I wasn't brave, but I cared for Bess, and I was bound to try and save her.

I crossed to Bess' bedside and sat down next to her; she leaned towards me as much as her bonds would allow, whimpering softly.

"Conn," she moaned. "Touch me, please." Her eyes met mine, and I was stricken to not see joy that usually shone from behind her eyes. There was only need there, and want, only what the goblins had thrust upon her. I cupped her cheek and leaned forward to kiss her forehead.

"I'll bring you what you need, Bess," I whispered. "I swear it."

Then I pulled back, reaching into the satchel I wore over my shoulder and pulling out a small, brown bottle that I handed to Moira, "Give her this, a full dram mixed into some milk. It will make her sleep. I should be back before she wakes, or very shortly after."

Moira looked at me in horror. "Conn, what are you going to do?"

I looked back at Bess, who was crying and calling for me to come back. It near broke my heart to turn away and leave her.

"I'm going to the goblins."

I took a long breath, gathered my courage, and walked down the hill into the hollow. I could hear the goblins calling from somewhere down near the stream, but until I came up to the remains of the oak, I couldn't see them. And once I did, I had to stop and stare.

Ma had never told me that goblins were beautiful. I'd been expecting monsters. Instead, I was facing angels. They were tall and thin, taller than any man, and covered from head to heels in sleek, glistening fur that reminded me of the otters that played in the forest pool. They were dressed solely in long, beaded loincloths that swayed in the evening breeze, and they moved with a fluid grace that made them look like they were gliding on air. When one of them turned to look at me, I could see its eyes were golden, and slitted like a cat's. It came closer, the setting sun turning its mottled gray and black fur into flame, and when it reached me, it crouched slightly so that it was closer to my height.

"Welcome to the goblin market, young mortal. Will you come and see our wares?"

I nodded, too awestruck to say a word, letting the goblin take me by the hand and lead me into their market. There were carts and baskets full to overflowing with fruit, most of it impossible to find this early in the spring—there were apples piled up next to peaches, full bunches of grapes lying next to cherries and figs, strawberries in baskets with pears and quince. The goblin escorted me from one end of the market to the other, and when we reached the end, it waved one arm expansively. "What will you have, young mortal?"

I shook off the spell that the goblin's beauty cast over me. I was here for a reason. "There was a girl, a few nights past. What did she choose?" I asked.

The goblin laughed, "The golden girl! Yes, she came to me, and greatly enjoyed her choice. You wish to have what she had?"

I nodded slowly, not sure what I was agreeing to. The goblin took my arm and led me off; I could feel its sharp claws pricking me through my sleeve.

It led me away from the market, into a copse of young willows that grew along the banks of the stream. In the center of the copse there was a clearing, and it was there that the goblin stopped, turned towards me and smiled again.

"Take off your clothing, pretty mortal," it said, running long fingers through my hair.

I whispered Bess' name like a prayer as I unslung my satchel and took off my shirt and breeches; the goblin must have heard me, because it cocked its head to the side and studied me for a long moment.

"The golden girl, she is your lover?" The cat eyes narrowed. "No, not a lover. But beloved, none-the-less. Why have you come?"

"Because I love her," I answered.

It laughed, resting one long hand on my back between my shoulders, "Intriguing. Come here, mortal, and see what your golden girl bought at the goblin market."

The goblin led me to a mossy bank, guided me gently down onto my back and then stretched out next to me. It said not a word to me, arranging my arms and legs as if I were a doll, until I lay there with my arms flung over my head and my legs slightly apart. It nodded, seemingly satisfied, and then sat up and made a long, low trilling sound. Immediately, I felt something cold curling around my wrists and my ankles; I tried to jump up but was held fast to the turf as slender green vines rose from the moss, wrapping around my body and holding me fast. The goblin laughed, moving so that it was again lying next to me, soft fur rubbing against my side as I struggled against the vines.

"Pretty mortal," it crooned, and smiled, showing all of its sharp, white teeth. Then, to my shock, it kissed me.

When I was twelve, a minor lord who had sought my mother's

aid rewarded her with a flagon of fine brandy. Ma had let me taste the wine, and I had always remembered the smooth warmth, oak mixed with wood smoke and peat and apples. The goblin's lips tasted like that, like brandy, heat and desire; I found myself drunk on that taste, forgetting my fear. When the goblin pulled back, I strained up, wanting more, and heard the creature laugh.

"Patience, little one. Patience." It stood, and loosened the belt around its hips, letting the loincloth fall to the ground, revealing to me finally that this goblin was male. His cock was erect, long and curved, and as thick around as my wrist. He looked down at himself, running one hand down his length. "So, you see now what goblin fruit your little golden girl enjoyed? Would you like a taste?" he asked, and laughed again as he lay back down, running his fingers over my skin in swirling patterns that left fire in their wake. I could feel myself responding to his touch, until I ached with desire. He laughed again, sliding down over my body until he lay over my legs, his breath warm on my cock.

"You are a virgin?" he asked. "You've never lain with a woman before, or a man?"

"I... yes. No." I was addled by his breath and his warmth, and wasn't sure what question I was answering. He trilled softly, sliding his hands under my ass.

"Untouched fruit is the sweetest. What payment do you offer, young mortal, for your taste of goblin fruit?"

Payment? I couldn't clear my head, couldn't think of anything but his kiss and his touch and his breath on my aching, throbbing cock. He ran one finger down my shaft, and I gasped at the sensation.

"Barter, perhaps? Will you give me seed for seed?" Without waiting for an answer, he lowered his mouth over my cock, swallowing me whole. It was like nothing I had ever felt before, and I howled as he caressed me with his rough tongue and slid one long, slender finger into my ass. I strained against the vines, trying to move, wanting *more*, even though I had no idea what more would be. I felt him laugh again, and he stopped and raised his head, sliding up to cover my body with his own and kiss me again.

"You taste magnificent," he murmured, licking my ear and then nibbling my neck with his sharp teeth. "Shall you have your taste now?" He got to his knees, shifted, turned around until his cock was suspended over my mouth. I heard him laugh again, "Do to me what I did to you. Do not bite." He took me into his mouth again, and lowered his hips so that his cock tapped against my lips. Uncertain, with only his direction to guide me, I lightly touched his cock with my tongue, feeling his hum of pleasure as a jolt through my own cock. Encouraged, I kept on, gently bathing him with my tongue until he groaned and shifted his hips lower, raising his head so that he could whisper, "Take me."

Obediently, I opened my mouth wide, and he slid his cock between my lips, filling my mouth and cutting off my voice. His cock tasted of honey, salt and something wonderful and exotic, and I eagerly swirled my tongue over the head, wanting more. The goblin moaned, increasing his own efforts until I was thrashing under him, moaning, sucking, licking, finally screaming as I spent. Laughing, he licked me clean and then trilled something; I felt the vines on my arms loosen and fall away.

"Touch me," the goblin said, and I could not tell if he was commanding or begging. I slid my hands up the fur of his thighs, luxuriating in the softness, hearing the goblin moan and trill as he started to slowly pump in and out of my mouth. Inspired by what he had done to me, I wrapped my arms around his hips and slid one hand over his ass, running my fingers down his cleft, seeking the hidden entrance there. The goblin yowled like a cat in heat when my fingers found their target; he went rigid, and I felt his cock pulsing, growing impossibly thicker. My mouth filled with warm liquid, thick, sweet-salt, honey and brandy; I swallowed, drinking deep, lost in pleasure. Then I lost myself in a soft, warm embrace as I fell asleep in the goblin's arms.

I woke feeling soft fur under my cheek and long fingers in my hair. For a moment, I was confused, then everything came back to me and I jumped up to see the goblin looking at me.

"You are truly magnificent," he murmured. "There is something to you, something different. You are not like the other mortals I have tasted. You are more like my own people."

I couldn't speak; I stared at him for a moment, then turned away. I'd failed. Worse, I'd condemned myself to the same fate as Bess.

A soft arm encircled my shoulders, "Whatever is wrong? Did I not please you?"

His voice sounded truly concerned. I looked up into his golden eyes and decided to trust. "I came here because I needed to bring the goblin seed back to Bess. To save her life. I failed her." I didn't add that I'd condemned myself, too.

The goblin cocked his head to one side, "I don't understand. Your golden girl is ill?"

I blinked, "You don't know? You don't know what happens when mortals come to the goblin market?"

"No," the goblin answered. "Among my own people, I am considered very young. I have had very few of your kind. "

I tried to gather my wits. "When a mortal comes to the goblin market, when we taste the goblin fruit, we... pine for it. And we die, in a matter of days. My mother, she thought that if we could get another taste, it would cure the need, but no one who has ever been here has ever been able to find you again."

The goblin reared back, and I could see horror in his eyes, "Die? The golden girl will *die* because she lay with me?" He reached out and touched my arm, "You will die?"

I nodded, surprised by the goblin's reaction, his obvious distress. He jerked to his feet, striding across the copse with none of his previous grace. Then he came back, throwing himself down onto his knees in front of me, "Mortal-beloved, please believe me. I did not know!"

Stunned, I nodded again. "I... believe you."

He curled himself into a small ball, his head resting on my knees, "We think of you as... fruit to be plucked. I came with the others because I am old enough to mate now. I would have taken your essence, and I would have gone to the mating fields of my home. I would have shared what I have taken from you and from the others with one that I desired, and if they found me worthy, they would have mated with me. No one told me that harvesting from you would mean your death." He raised his head, and I could see sorrow and regret, "I did not know it would hurt you. I did not know you were intelligent. I did not know that you knew love." He shook his head and stood, holding his hand out to me. "Come with me, mortal," he commanded.

"Where?"

"We will make the cure for your golden girl. And we will make a cure for you. Are you sure of this?"

I shook my head, "No."

He nodded, "Then we will try. And if it does not work... then we will find another way."

I followed the goblin, my head spinning, trying to understand what he had told me. "But, what about you?"

"So long as I return to my home before dawn, I will be fine," he said. "Come and sit with me." He sat down with his back to a tree, and I knelt down next to him. He smiled at me, and said sadly, "I wish you had not told me. I will not be able to bring myself to come again."

"I'm sorry." It seemed like a silly thing to say, but I was sorry that I'd caused this compassionate creature pain. He reached out and patted my leg.

"It is not your fault. Do you have something to carry the seed in?" I jumped up and ran back to my clothes, taking an empty bottle from my satchel and bringing it back. The goblin took it and set it aside, then looked at me and held out his arms, "Come and sit with me, mortal. Touch me and help me to save your life."

I moved into his embrace, resting my cheek against the soft fur of his chest. He guided me, telling me where to touch him and how, until I knew what gave him pleasure and could do it without coaching. So I coaxed him to fullness again, and lay across him to lick his cock until he cried out and spilled his seed into his own hands. When he poured it into the bottle, the straw-colored liquid barely filled a quarter of the bottle.

"Will it be enough?" he murmured.

"For one, I think," I answered. "I'll bring it to Bess. Then..."

"Then you will come back. I will be ready for you when you re-turn," the goblin said as he slid his arm around me. "I will not let you die. But you must be back here before dawn. If I do not return home, the way between your world and mine will be sealed, and the goblin market will never again come to this place." Gently, he pushed me away, "There is not much time."

I scrambled into my clothes, taking the bottle in my hand and turning to leave the willows; I stopped, looking back to see the goblin looking at me. Quickly, I went over to him, leaned down, and kissed him. "Thank you," I said quickly. Then I turned and ran.

I ran all the way back to Grady's house, the precious bottle clutched in my fist, feeling the goblin seed burning in my blood. I was gasping for breath as I reached the kitchen door, which opened immediately. Panting like a dog, I pushed past a shocked Moira and nearly collapsed onto the long table. She grabbed me and pushed me into a chair, then bustled away, returning with a cup that she shoved under my nose.

"Drink it," she commanded. I nodded, drinking and tasting brandy. The taste reminded me of the goblin's kiss, and I pushed the glass away with shaking hands.

"Moira, I have it," I said, holding up the bottle. She took it from me, looking at the liquid inside.

"What is it?" she asked.

"It... it's the cure." I got to my feet, painfully aware of Moira's curious look, not wanting to tell her just what was in the bottle, or how I had gotten it. I held my hand out and said, "There isn't much time."

Moira nodded, handing the bottle back to me. I stood up and wove an unsteady path to the stairs and up to Bess' room. I let myself in and closed the door behind me, then turned to see Bess watching me, hunger plain on her face.

"I've brought it for you, Bess," I said, crossing to sit on the edge of the bed. I held the bottle to her lips and let her drink, fighting to keep my hands steady. She gulped the liquid greedily, draining the bottle and then licking her lips; she shivered violently, whimpered once, then wailed, her body going stiff and jerking hard against her bonds. I jumped back, dropping the bottle, and then grabbed at the ropes, fumbling with the knots until she was free, laying limp in the middle of the bed. For a moment, I was afraid that the goblin had tricked me, until Bess moaned softly and opened her eyes. She looked up at me and smiled, "Conn."

Dizzy with relief, I pulled Bess into my arms, hugging her tightly, breathing in her scent. And it was her scent, my awareness of her as a woman, and my own growing need that pushed my restraint to the breaking point; I pushed her back down onto the bed, claiming her mouth in a possessive kiss and running my hands down her sides. She gasped in surprise, then giggled against my mouth and ran her hands up underneath my shirt.

Behind us, I heard the door crash open, then someone grabbed me by the back of the neck and dragged me from the bed. I heard Bess scream, then something came crashing down on the back of my head and I knew nothing else.

Chapter 2
The Fruit Forbidden

"Hug me, kiss me, suck my juices
Squeezed from goblin fruits for you"

I clawed my way out of a darkness that seemed to be filled with screaming, pain and need, and found myself on the floor of a strange room. I was alone and naked, with ropes digging into my wrists and ankles, and a foul tasting rag shoved in my mouth and tied there. I had no idea how I had gotten here, or what had happened; all I knew was that my head was pounding, and I ached with need, my cock hard and throbbing. The light slanting through the windows told me that I'd been unconscious for quite some time—it had still been dark when I reached Grady's house, with barely a glimmer of sunrise on the horizon. The shadows on the floor told me it was past midday, and any hope for me was long gone. The goblin would have returned to his world by now, and I would never see him or the market again.

I heard footsteps, and the two men who entered the room were two of Grady's rowdies: Fergus Durkin and his son, Hugh. I shivered when I saw Hugh, fear briefly overriding lust. I despised Hugh—he was a bully who fancied himself irresistible to either sex, and who abused his rank at every turn. He'd tried to coerce me into his bed once, and when I'd refused him, had haunted our gate for weeks, until my mother had threatened to turn him into a toad.

The older Durkin came over and grabbed my arm, hauling me to a sitting position.

"Nice of you to join us, bastard," he said. "I was starting to wonder if you'd ever wake up." I glared at him, and Durkin laughed. "We won't keep you for long, bastard. We're keeping you safe and sound and hidden away until Grady's girl is wedded and bedded. Tomorrow midday, you'll get your clothes back and you'll be free to go."

Hugh came over and leered down at me, and the cause of my shivering changed from fear to something else. "Grady said we could have a little fun with you while we waited, bastard. Looks like you need it." He rested his hand on his belt buckle, and I whimpered. No, not him... yes. Yes, please...

"I told you no, Hugh," Durkin snapped as he stood up. "The boy is a witch, like his ma. I won't have him cursing me and mine, so you leave him alone." Ignoring my muffled protests — let him stay! — Durkin herded his son out the door, and slammed it behind them. I heard the bolt shoot home, and then silence.

The hours passed in a kind of delirium of need and pain. In my madness, I dreamed of freeing myself from the gag, calling Hugh back into the room, inviting his touch. I dreamed of encouraging him to take me, if only so that I might find some ease for the pressure growing inside me. Desperate for some relief, unable even to touch myself, I struggled and fought against the ropes until my aching arms went numb, and I was screaming into the gag in frustration. Around me, the shadows grew longer and the room grew darker. When it was finally too dark to see, and I was too tired to move, I just lay where my struggles had left me, on my stomach in the middle of the floor.

It was there that Hugh found me. He came into the room with a lantern, walking on stocking feet to make no noise. He stood over me and laughed as I blinked in the sudden light.

"You wouldn't curse me for giving you what you want, now would you?" he asked, using one foot to flip me over onto my back. He prodded my cock with his toes, and I whimpered, making him laugh. "And you want this, don't you, bastard?"

There was a small part of me that wanted to refuse, but it was drowned out by the overwhelming waves of lust; I nodded, thrusting my hips up, moaning through the gag.

Hugh smirked down at me. "I knew it. You're a slut, just like your ma." He didn't bother to loosen the ropes that bound me, hauling me roughly over a bolster that he took from the bed. I squirmed against the cool satin of the bolster, hearing Hugh as he knelt behind me, kneading my ass with rough hands and laughing at my muffled whimpers of encouragement.

"Pretty boy," he whispered. "Been wanting this since we brought you up here, pretty boy." I heard him moving behind me, heard the door open. I expected and almost dreaded that I would hear Durkin's voice, chasing Hugh off before I'd found some kind of relief. Instead, there was a surprised gasp from Hugh; he collapsed over my legs and didn't move. I twisted, straining until I could see the door, and the figure standing there. Tall, taller than any man, and he had to stoop to get through the door. But there was no way he could be here...

The goblin glided across the floor and dropped to his knees next to me so that he could push Hugh off my legs, then tugged me off of the bolster and into a sitting position. Gently, the goblin pushed my head to the side and untied the gag, then held me tightly as I was taken with a coughing fit.

"Are you unhurt, beloved?" the goblin asked, leaning close so that he could look into my eyes.

I nodded, rubbing my cheek against his soft fur, "...touch me. Please..."

The goblin reached out to rest his long hand over my heart, "Mortal-beloved, I am here. I will make you well again."

His touch set fire to my skin, and I moaned, straining against the ropes, "It hurts..."

He leaned me back against the bolster and stood, raising his hands; I felt myself rising, moving through the air until I came to rest on the bed. My head hung over the edge, and I watched through half-lidded eyes as he removed his loincloth and came to stand at my head. He ran long fingers over my cheek and through my hair, "Open your mouth, beloved. Take what you need."

He slowly pressed his cock into my mouth, resting one hand on my chest and holding me in place. He wrapped his other hand around my cock, leaning forward to lay over me and take me into his mouth. Still bound, pinned under his weight, driven near-mad by his fur on my skin and the roughness of his tongue, I sucked and moaned and screamed under him, reaching the heights of pleasure time and time again. Finally I could take no more; I fell into darkness with the sounds of his moans ringing in my ears and the taste of honey and brandy on my tongue.

I woke with soft fur under my cheek, and opened my eyes to see the goblin smiling at me. I jumped, and his arms around me tightened.

"All is well. You are safe. I have kept watch. It is nearly dawn, and there is no one stirring," he said quietly. "Are you all right, mortal-beloved?"

I looked at my wrist and the livid rope-burns there, considered the question, "I ache all over, and I'm starving. But I think I'm all right. Do you think we can find any food?"

The goblin smiled, "We will find something. If necessary, I will hunt for you."

When I stood, I was so unsteady on my feet that the goblin had to carry me down the stairs; I looked around curiously. "Where are we?" I asked.

"The golden girl told me that this is Durkin's house," he answered.

"And Durkin?"

"Is fast asleep and will remain so," the goblin answered. "I can hold both men asleep until past dawn. We can eat, you can find clothing, and we can be away long before they wake."

He sat me down at the table in the kitchen and rummaged through the pantry, finding the remains of a good dinner. I fell to with good appetite, while the goblin nibbled at a piece of bread and then pushed it aside.

"Beloved, Conn," he said. "I... the golden girl, she is the one who sent me here."

I stopped eating, looking at him, "Bess sent you? Goblin, where is she?"

He looked down at the tabletop, "She... is not here. Conn... she is going away."

I frowned, "I don't understand. Gone where?"

The goblin wouldn't look at me, "She has gone to be married. I spoke to her last night, and she left just after dawn today. She will be married in the morning."

"Married?" I repeated, stunned. "She... but she didn't want to marry Lord Faraday! That was why she went to the market to begin with!"

"I know. She gave me something for you." He stood and disappeared up the stairs, returning a few moments later with his loincloth and a pouch. From the pouch he took a folded piece of parchment. "I do not know what it says," the goblin said, sounding apologetic. "I cannot read your writing."

I took the letter and opened it, seeing Bess' fine handwriting. She thanked me for being her friend, for caring for her. She wished me well, and would think of me fondly. She asked me to do the same. Not a word of love, or any mention of the goblin market.

I set the letter down and looked at the goblin, "I don't understand. I... thought she loved me. She told me she loved me."

He shook his head, "I asked her that. I told her that you loved her. And she said that you were children together, and that children must grow up. That children have fancies, and that you were hers. She said she was sorry that you did not understand that there was truly nothing between you." He stood up and came around the table, kneeling next to my chair. "Conn, I am sorry. I think, perhaps, that she is no longer the girl who came to the goblin market. She has been frightened, and badly. Now, she wants to forget. And she wants safety. This marriage gives her that." He shook his head. "All the same, I do not know how she cannot love you. She is a fool."

I let out a bark of laughter, "No. She's right. I'm the fool, for thinking that someone like her would be happy with a bastard like me." I turned, tossed the letter into the fireplace, and looked back at the goblin. "I need clothes. We'll have to hurry if we're to get you back to the goblin market before dawn."

Silence. The goblin stood up and walked over to a window, his back to me; he sighed and said sadly, "The goblin market is gone."

I frowned, and then remembered why that one statement was so important... and so horrifying. I jumped to my feet. "You were supposed to go home!"

He turned to me and answered quietly, "I did. When you did not return, I went home, and I confronted my sire. I demanded to know why he did not tell me that what we did killed your kind. He laughed

93

at me, called me a sentimental fool." He sighed. "He told me I was too young, and that..." he paused for a moment, then sighed again, " ...that I should not play with my food. He was going to ban me from coming back to the market. He said that I had proved I was not mature enough. But I begged, and he relented. I came back, because I was hoping you would try to find me. And when midnight came, and you did not appear, I went to look for you. I followed your scent to your home, and you were not there. I searched until I despaired of ever finding you. Then I thought of going to your Bess. She told me where you were. I did not return home, I stayed, and I hid myself here, and watched. When it was just the two men, I came for you."

I nodded, "And now you found me, and we're safe. For now. We can still get you back to the market."

"We cannot. There is not enough time to get there before dawn. The market will vanish and will never more come to this place."

"Then we need to get you out of here. Out of Hunter's Dell, before anyone sees you. They'll know what you are, and they won't let you live if they find you." I sat back down and leaned back in my chair. "We can go to my hut. I have food and clothes there, and a bit of money put by. We can leave through the forest so you're not seen. Then... I don't know. Maybe... maybe we can find the goblin market again, get you home."

"No. I will not return to the goblin market."

"Why not?" I asked. "Your home..."

The goblin came back to the table, knelt down next to me. "I could not have you, if I went home. You would not be welcome there," the goblin said. "You belong in this place no more than I. There is more of my kind than theirs in you, Conn. So come with me. I want to be with you. I know the way to other places, other worlds, where we might live and be happy. If you will come with me?"

I blinked, not sure I'd heard him properly, "You... you want me to come with you? But..."

He was quiet for a moment, then reached out and took my hand. "I want you to be with me, my mortal-beloved."

I blinked, "But, I'm a bastard!"

"I do not know what that means. But truly, does it matter?" he asked. "You love, you think, you are dear to me. Is that not enough?"

My head was spinning, "I..."

"Conn," he said my name and made it sound like a caress. "I will not refuse you. I will not turn my back on you. I will not leave you. When one of my kind mates, it forms a bond that will not be severed, will not break. When my kind mates, it is for life." He stood and tugged me to my feet. "I can show you, beloved. Join with me."

I let him lead me, and was surprised when we returned to the bedroom where I'd been held captive. "I don't understand."

"Love me. Let me love you."

I looked at him curiously. "What were we doing, then?"

The goblin laughed. "Among my people, what we have done are the games of children old enough to understand the mating process, but not old enough to mate. It is only with one's mate that one would offer their entire body." He held his arms out to me. "I am offering, Conn. If you will have me."

I looked up into his eyes, listened to my heart, and walked into his embrace. As he made to lead me to bed, I stopped him. "I don't even know your name."

He smiled, and trilled something. Then he laughed. "I doubt you could say it. We will decide later what you will call me."

I let him lay me down, and when he lay down with me, I rolled onto my side and reached out to stroke his fur. He purred like a cat, and I smiled. "What do we do?" I asked.

In answer, he rolled me over onto my stomach, moving to cover me with his body. "Trust me, my beloved. I will not hurt you."

I nodded. "I trust you."

He kissed the back of my neck, and I felt his hands slip between my legs and start playing with my balls; I moaned, and he laughed. "Relax, Conn. Let me play."

Play he did, toying with me until I was nearly as aroused as I'd been under the spell of the goblin market. He teased me with his fingers and tongue, then told me to spread my legs and slowly slid one finger into my ass. One finger became two, and two became three, doing arcane things inside of me until I was frantic with desire. I was near to howling when he took his fingers away; he drew me to my knees and I felt the head of his cock move to take the place of his fingers.

"I love you, Conn," he whispered, slowly pressing his way into my body. It was hard at first, and it hurt; but he stopped, touching me gently, whispering and trilling until I calmed and relaxed and let him try again, until at last he was inside, and I was stretched full and gasping in pleasure. He started to move, pumping slowly, working his way almost entirely out of me, and then sliding back in, letting me move with him, push back against him, demand more and more until neither of us could say a word for the gasping and moaning. I spent first, losing my balance and sprawling out on the bed. He fell on top of me, still pumping, wailing as his seed filled me. Afterwards, we lay curled around each other, my head on his chest, and I found myself feeling more at home than I ever had before. He was right. I didn't belong in Hunter's Dell. I never had. I had only been waiting for someone to show me the truth.

After a while, he raised his head and looked at me, "You have not answered me. Is it not enough that I love you?"

I smiled at him, raised myself up so that I might kiss him, reveling in the heady taste of his lips, "Yes. It's enough. More than enough. I love you, too."

By the time the sun had risen, we had left Hunter's Dell, taking forest paths that I had never before seen, following my golden-eyed lover wherever he would lead me. There were times when I wondered what they thought, back in Hunter's Dell, if they ever wondered where Conn the witch had gone, or what had happened to the goblin market. I wondered if Lady Faraday ever thought about me. Then my goblin would smile at me, or run his fingers through my hair, and none of it would matter. He loved me, and I loved him. That was all that mattered.

And we lived happily ever after.

If you enjoyed this story, you can discuss it with other readers and the author at the *To Market* story page. at http://forbiddenfiction.com/library/story/ES1-1.000035.

Elf Esteem

Nobilis Reed

When you're the only lesbian bondage slut in town, finding a partner isn't easy, especially when you've just broken up. But sometimes all it takes is a little magic to get back into the game.

Elf Esteem

I live alone, so hearing the sound of my computer booting up in the middle of the night is a little surreal. Add that to the fact I hadn't slept for at least twenty-four hours and you can understand why I wasn't in a completely normal state of mind. I put on some panties and a tee shirt so I'd be at least a little decent, and crept down the stairs.

When I saw my computer mouse moving around with nobody sitting in front of it, I was pretty sure I was either dreaming or hallucinating. When I got a little closer, and spotted the little creature pushing it about, I blinked, shook my head, and looked again.

I had a pretty good vantage point from the stairs, looking straight down at the coffee table where my keyboard and mouse sat next to an empty pizza box and the tablet computer I use when out of the house. Right there, both hands on the mouse, was an honest-to-god fairy, about six inches tall. She had pale skin, long hair that was so blonde it was yellow, and a dress that looked like it might have been made out of leaves. I sat down on the steps, rubbed my eyes, and looked again. Still there.

What the hell did a fairy want with my computer?

I looked up at my big HD screen on the wall. It was easy to see what she was bringing up, even from across the room.

Porn. She went straight into my bookmarks folder, down to the one marked "macramé," and pulled up one of my old favorites. "Furry Lady dot com" splashed across my screen. My login and password were already filled in and I watched in stunned silence as she entered the site and started browsing through the available videos.

I stormed down the steps and stood in front of her.

"Excuse me? What do you think you're doing?"

I'm used to making an impression when I confront someone, especially by surprise. I'm not short, and I'm not small. Maybe the impact was lessened a bit by the fact that my sizable tits were unrestrained by anything resembling a bra, but I was mad and the thought hadn't occurred to me to put on a robe.

"Oh!" Her voice was incredibly high-pitched. "Excuse me!" She had an odd accent, a cross between Scottish and Welsh, and sounded more surprised than scared. "I thought you'd be sleeping. I'll just be on my way, go ahead, don't mind me." She flew up into the air, did a quick loop-the-loop, and flitted backwards toward the kitchen area. She was flapping her little blue butterfly wings as fast as she could, but she was about as fast as a butterfly, too. Not very.

I spotted the open window behind her, ran across the room and slammed it shut.

"So you're the one who's been cutting holes in my screens!"

"Sorry!" She backed away again, landing on the back of my couch. "I didn't mean to rile ye. I was just curious about all the pretty lasses."

I slapped my forehead and blinked.

"What the fuck am I doing. I'm standing here shouting at a fairy." I sat down at my dining table and tried to get my head together. It didn't feel like a dream and I hadn't taken anything to make me hallucinate. I began to doubt my sanity.

There was a -thunk- on the table next to me, followed by a gently crinkling pop and a hiss. I looked up. There was a beer, freshly opened, a wisp of condensation floating from the mouth. Standing next to it was the fairy, with an apologetic smile on her face. Up close, I saw her dress wasn't made of the leaves and bark I originally thought, but was carefully folded out of crisp paper money. She was slim and athletic in build, like a dancer or a fencer.

"Thanks," I said, bringing the cold bottle to my lips.

"You're welcome!" I took a swallow then pulled it away with a grimace.

"Shit." I stood up, emptied the beer into the sink and dropped the bottle into the recycling.

"What's the matter?"

"It's an India pale ale. Those were for my ex."

"You miss her fiercely," said the fairy.

"Gee, how'd you guess?"

"You drank a hogshead o' beer and watched porn until the wee hours o' the night," she said, completely missing my sarcasm.

"So you're a peeping Tom, as well as a trespasser." Getting off the subject of Paula felt like a very good idea.

She scratched her head and shrugged. "I guess I am." She didn't seem in any way apologetic.

"Why?" I asked. "The wee folk aren't known for interest in computers."

"Just curious. I saw what you were watching. I wanted to see more."

"After six hours?"

"Well, that *was* three weeks ago, ye ken."

"Wait a minute...I've replaced that screen three times since them. How often have you been coming in and using my computer?"

"Every night." There was no shame in her voice, no blush to her pale complexion. She was totally unrepentant. "It would have been easier if you'd leave the chimney flue open once in a while."

"Shit."

"It's not as good as a real tumble, though," said the fairy, glancing over her shoulder at the screen.

"No, it's not."

"So why haven't you found another playmate? You're a fair lass! You've got hair the color o' roses, a bounteous bosom and plentiful posterior, and you have freckles enough for three leopards."

I groaned and shook my head. I definitely didn't need those last few attributes highlighted, and my hair color came out of a bottle.

"I'll never find anyone like Paula. What we had was special. You wouldn't understand."

"I'm smart," she said. "Probably the smartest fairy around here. Sharp enough to figure out yon computer. I'll wager I ken."

"In a small town like this, it's hard enough finding another dyke, much less one I can connect with like I did with her. Add to that..."

"That you like getting tied up?"

I scowled.

"I've seen you watch porn, and I know what you have in the box under the bed. I know what you like."

"Don't remind me."

"You're angry at me."

"Yes! Of course I'm angry at you! You broke into my house! Invaded my privacy! I think I have a right to be angry."

"Maybe I could help you relax?" She cocked her head to one side and gave me a sexy smile.

I laughed.

"You? You want to top *me*? Kiddo, I'm twenty-two stone. If I sat on you, I'd probably squash you flat."

"I'm not a kid. I'm a hundred and eighty years old. And I'm stronger than I look."

"I guess you'd have to be to get a beer out of the pantry. But being a top is about more than just what you see in porn. There's a relationship there. Trust. A common sense of purpose. How can I trust you?" I couldn't believe I was having this conversation with a fairy.

"You mortals. Always so afraid. And you think we're silly. Why not just try it and see? What have you got to lose?"

"If there's an emergency, I need to know you can get me free in a hurry, for one thing."

"That's fair. Go get a rope."

"You're going to cut it?"

"You'll see."

I went to the bedroom and got a big thick one, and dumped it onto the dining room table. She picked up the end and held it out to me.

"Tie a few loops around your thigh, as tight as you can."

I sat down at the dining room table and did as she said. I wasn't a rigger by any stretch of the imagination, but I had picked up a few tricks. I made several loops, knotting them together on each wrapping, to make a decorative sheath running halfway down my thigh.

"Ready?" she asked.

"Go for it." I leaned back in my chair.

She jumped from her spot on the table and flew down onto my thigh. She hardly weighed anything. When she shook her behind, glittery dust fell from her wings and the knots were gone. They hadn't broken or snapped, the ropes hadn't been cut or shredded, the knots were just *gone*. The rope hung from my thigh as if I'd just laid it there.

She turned and looked up at me, with her chin held up and fists propped on her hips.

"Okay," I said, becoming even more convinced I'd come unhinged. "I guess you can handle that part." I picked up the coil of rope and laid it back on the table.

"Anything else on your mind? Any other reservations?" she asked.

"I guess I'm just having trouble imagining how it would work. You're so small."

"That doesn't sound like a reason not to try it. That sounds like a reason to go for it."

"I think I at least need to know your name."

"'Mistress' will suffice."

I shrugged. "I guess."

"So is it a deal? Do you promise to do as I say, until you say your safeword?"

"Okay, as long as you don't gag me. I don't like being gagged."

"I won't put anything in your mouth," she said, with a sparkle in her eye. "Do you promise?"

"Yes."

Her face lit up with a broad smile, and she clapped her hands together.

"Marvelous! Bring your toy box out to the living room."

I got up from my chair, went to the bedroom where the big wooden box of rope and other toys was stored, and met her out where the computer was still running.

"Set them down here on the table, and push it out of the way. We're going to do this right on the floor." I did as she said, and stood in the middle of the room.

"Good! You're an obedient creature, I see." She fluttered around me then sat on the table I'd pushed aside. "Take off your clothes." When I opened my mouth to say something, she raised her hand and waggled a finger at me. "And don't speak unless it's to say your safeword!"

I nodded. I did not yet feel the warm excitement playing bondage games with my ex brought, but we had only gotten started. I figured I could play along until it either happened, or it was clear it wasn't going to. Mostly, I was curious about how she was going to manage it. Fairy dust or not, she just didn't seem to have the gravitas to be a real top.

Then again, she had gotten me to shut up. Paula had never managed that.

While I was stripping down, she sorted through my rope collection and set pieces aside. Even the biggest coils weren't too heavy for her, but several of them were awkward for her to handle. She piled those to one side. The ones she picked out were either thin, or short. These she tied knots in, occasionally giving me an appraising glance. I started to wonder what she had in store for me.

When I was naked, she had me sit in the middle of the floor, and gave me two pieces tied-off in loops about eight inches in diameter, which went loosely over my thighs. Then she handed me one of the smallest ropes in the collection. It was hardly more than a scrap, just a foot long or so and only four millimeters in diameter. She had me use it to tie my big toes together. The black twist contrasted with my pale skin in a way that always looked attractive to me, which was why all the rope in my collection was black.

Next came a yard-long piece of rope with a hard, fixed loop on one end, and a slip-knot loop on the other. The fixed loop went over my head, with the end trailing down my back.

At her command I bent forward, raised my knees, and slipped my arms down through the loops on my thighs, so that my shoulders and knees touched. She then moved behind me and had me put my hands through a loop of rope that ran through the slip knot, and tug it tight.

She'd tied the loops at just the right length to bind without cutting off my circulation. I wanted to ask how she had gotten them so perfect without having to measure, but I didn't want to break the atmosphere I felt building around us.

One moment I was completely free to move, and a few seconds later I was securely bound from knees to wrists. I took a deep breath-- or at least, as deep a breath as I could take, bent over the way I was — and took stock.

I wasn't completely immobilized, but all I could really do was squirm. I could shuffle around a little on my heels and my butt. As

I realized just how limited I was, I felt that shivering realization that yes, I was stuck, and yes, I really was at her mercy.

"There you go," she said. "Anything binding too much? Any problems?" She walked around me, tugging at the ropes to check the knots.

I shook my head.

"Excellent. You're doing quite well. Now do you believe this will work?"

I nodded.

"You may speak, if you like."

"Thank you, Mistress."

She clapped her hands and hopped into the air and hovered.

"Oh, wonderful! I've got a mortal subbie. We are going to have so much fun!" The gesture would have broken the mood if it weren't for the devilish look in her eye.

She stepped over my feet, into the space between my legs, under my torso. Her tiny hands caressed my breasts, making slow circles on the flesh hanging above her. My nipples stiffened, but she teased me, coming closer and closer but never quite touching.

"These are marvelous!" She said. "Oh, I could play with these all night." She looked up at me, that scary-cute smile broadening. "What do you think of that idea?"

"Please, mistress. I would like more than that."

"Oh, so you're a greedy wench, are you? Here we went to all the trouble to get you tied up and you want more?" she asked, still stroking and kneading my too-long neglected flesh.

"Yes. I am."

"Well then..." She flitted up to the toy box and pulled out the homemade nipple clamps. I made them myself, just a pair of springy clothespins with some twine strung between them. They hadn't been attached to me in years. With a bit of old clothesline looped over one shoulder, she flitted back to where she had been. She slapped each nipple lightly to get it good and hard, then squeezed the arms of a clothespin between both hands to get it to open and clamp down. When both were in place, she tugged lightly on the string, looking up into my face.

I didn't remember the sensation being that strong. They squeezed hard, and I winced with each tug on the string. It wasn't quite enough to make me cry out, but it was definitely having an effect.

She giggled and looped the clothesline over the string, causing more tugs on the clothespins.

"Now I want you to keep these here," she said. "I like the pink color they bring to your nipples. Such a lovely shade! It would be a shame to lose it."

"Yes, mistress."

She reached up and patted me on the cheek.

"That's the right attitude!" Then she shivered with glee and bent down on her hands and knees, pushing the clothesline down under my butt. Her wings fluttered briefly against my sex and I felt a tingle run up my spine.

I gasped, making her giggle again. I whimpered when she stopped.

"Aww, don't worry my pet. We'll be back there before too long." She zipped out and around behind me, and I craned my head to look over my shoulder. She fished the rope out from underneath me, making the soft cotton rub against me as it went.

"Head back," she said. "Look up at the ceiling." I obeyed, and there were more tugs on the clothespins, along with new ones on my hair. She was tying the ends to my ponytail, carefully arranging the clothesline to run between my labia, on either side of my clit. I could feel the soft cotton sheath of the ropes between the cheeks of my ass. My head wasn't pulled back at an extreme angle, but I wouldn't be able to move much without pulling off at least one of the clothespins, and I didn't want to do that.

Huh.

I didn't want to pull off the clothespins. I thought the feeling of not wanting to disappoint was something special for Paula, something that came from being in love with her, part of our special relationship.

The relationship that turned out not to be so special after all.

It felt good, there, the same as always. In fact, it was a little stronger than usual. The feeling was almost as strong as the first time Paula and I tried out that hunk of clothesline and discovered just how much I liked being tied up. A painful tug on my nipples told me I was letting my head fall too far forward. I pulled back, lifting my gaze from the floor.

There was a new image on the computer. My mistress had flown over to the keyboard and brought up a different site.

A bondage site, one I wasn't familiar with. This wasn't something from my usual bookmarks. She signed in, created a login and password, and picked out a video, obviously quite familiar with the process.

"Wait!" I exclaimed, "That's my credit card number!" I straightened up, which brought my head forward, which in turn yanked one of the clothespins off. A little "eep" escaped my lips both from the shock of the release, the rope rubbing against my clit, and the realization I had disobeyed two of my new mistress's commands.

She turned and put her little hands on her hips, and flew up so she was silhouetted against the screen. She clicked her tongue and shook her head.

"There you go, undoing all my hard work." She flitted down beneath me and put the clothespin back in place. "This definitely requires a response, don't you think so?"

I started to speak, and stopped myself. I nodded. The movement rubbed the rope against my clit some more and tugged the clothespins on my nipples; I gasped in pleasure.

She laughed and flew back to the toy box, clearing my field of view so I could see the video. The girl on the screen was getting tied to a spider web made of heavy chains, hanging upside-down with loops of rope all over her body. She had a really nice figure, soft boobs and well-padded thighs that took a dramatic imprint of the ropes against her body.

"What do you think?" she said, pulling a Ping-Pong paddle out of the box and giving it a few practice swings.

I nodded again, feeling a tingle of anticipation come to my ass. Once again, the rope transferred the movement to my nipples and clit, and I had to stifle a moan.

"Okay, now get on your knees," she said, as she flew over my back and behind me.

I scootched my feet in and rolled forward, landing clumsily on my knees. The movement pushed my forehead against the carpet, and made the ropes shift once again. The position was marvelously humbling, especially given the size of my mistress.

The experience was different from my sessions with Paula, I realized. She spent a lot of energy trying to out-butch me, metaphorically climbing on top, rather than giving me the challenge of dropping down and relaxing into the bottom role. With my new mistress, there was no question of who was stronger or tougher. I was. And it didn't matter; she was the top and that was all there was to it. There was no need to dominate physically, because she had the confidence and charm to make me do all the work.

"What do you think, would twenty strokes be enough?" she asked from behind me.

I couldn't turn my head to see, so I just nodded.

"Count 'em," she said, and the first blow landed on my ass. The paddle had a nubby rubber surface that did nothing to cushion the blow. What's more, even in the fairies' tiny hands, it landed with a definite bite.

"One," I said, my voice already becoming breathy and choked. Another stroke landed, on the other ass cheek. "Two." The pain was sharp and tingly, spreading warmth over my posterior as the blood rose to the surface. I knew I would already be turning red.

I could no longer see the video. There was a slapping noise coming from it, sounding like a flogger of some kind, and murmurs of pain and ecstasy. The sub had been gagged. I wished my mistress had gagged me; it was so much harder to stay quiet, to limit myself to counting off the numbers, without it.

I concentrated on counting and maintaining my composure. My world narrowed to just those numbers and the stinging slap of the paddle against my ass. Nothing else existed, nothing else mattered, nothing else could intrude. Work, family, and even the mourning of my relationship with Paula fell away.

After the last blow landed, I felt a gentle touch on my rump.

"Now then, feeling better?"

"Uh-huh."

"You can talk now, if you like."

"Thank you, mistress."

She walked around to my face, pushed up against the carpet, and kissed my cheek.

"I think you're due for a reward."

"Thank you, mistress."

I heard her wings flutter, but I wasn't paying attention to where she was anymore, or what she was doing. I was too far gone, too deep into the experience to care. When I felt her fiddling with the ropes running between my pussy lips, I didn't think, 'What is she doing?' I just accepted it. It was happening, it felt good, and that's all that mattered.

Something small, round, and hard nestled between the ropes and my inner lips, and then it started to buzz. As the sensation built, I recognized it as the variable-speed vibrating egg Paula surprised me with a year or so before. We left it in the bottom of the toy box after the first few tries because it seemed too weak, but placed where it was, on the surface instead of down inside, it was much more intense. I moaned out loud, desperate to arch my back, but every movement tugged on my nipples, reminding me to keep still. The effect increased the tension in my muscles, as I held myself as still as I could.

With the ropes holding it in place, my mistress shifted her attention to my clit. The ropes still ran on either side, and as I dealt with the effects of the vibrator, they rubbed against it in slight, uneven strokes. Then I felt her hands on it, kneading and caressing, far more delicate than even a tongue could be. The contrast between the heaviness of the ropes and the feather-light touch of her hands was like nothing I'd felt before. I struggled against the urgent need to thrash against my bonds.

Both clothespins popped off at once as I finally let go, spasms rocking my body so hard I thought I might fall over. I could hear my mistress's exultant, bubbly laughter all through it. When I was finally able to open my eyes again, I was greeted by the sight of a naked fairy standing about a foot in front of my face, hands on hips, dripping wet. I fought hard to stifle a chuckle but a bit of it got out.

"Will you just look at me?" she said. "You got me all wet."

"I'm sorry, mistress," I said, without much sincerity.

"I think you need to clean me off."

"Yes, mistress." I tried to slip back into the submissive role but it wasn't easy.

She walked over to my mouth and slapped my upper lip.

"Tongue," she said.

I stuck out my tongue. She used it like a bath towel, guiding it over her tiny body, while she ooh-ed and ah-ed and mm-ed. It was hard to identify which body parts I was licking, everything was so tiny and universally wet. After a few big slurps, I felt one leg swing over my tongue, and she began rubbing against it. Based on the glimpses I could see down below my nose, she seemed to be humping the side, so I made it as hard and flat as I could, which wasn't an easy task.

She didn't complain. After a minute or so of humping, she let out a long, shrill cry and slumped against my face.

"My my, that was fun," she said breathlessly. It only took a few seconds to catch her breath. "There now, don't you feel better?"

"Yes, I think I do," I said. "Thank you. Though I think my hands are starting to go numb."

"Ah, yes. Let's get you out of all that." She flew over me and suddenly I was free. The ropes fell away.

I sat back and shook the blood back into my hands, and checked my body for marks. There were distinct impressions on my wrists, and somewhat lighter ones on my shoulders and thighs. They stung a little, but it was more of a nice memory than anything unpleasant.

I stood and shut off the computer. There was a bit of a wet spot on the carpet, but it wasn't anything that hadn't happened before. I knew how to clean it up. The thing I wanted to clean first was myself. "I'm going to take a shower," I said. "Care to wash my back?"

In legend, fairies are known to be fickle creatures, easily distracted and fond of leaving humans puzzled whenever we think we've figured them out. This proved to be true for my visitor as well. I never saw her again after that night. I missed her for a while, but when I realized she wasn't coming back, I put myself together, and posted a message on my favorite social fetish site.

"Lesbian bondage slut seeks top. Age, weight, height unimportant."

If you enjoyed this story, you can discuss it with other readers
and the author at the *Elf Esteem* story page at
http://forbiddenfiction.com/library/story/NR1-1.000118.

The Three Wives of Bluebeard

Annabeth Leong

The cruel captain Bluebeard marries Mollena moments after her father's burial, only to brutalize her and abandon her in his isolated mansion. Her only consolations are dream visits from two beautiful, seductive women and her explorations through her husband's mysterious house. But Bluebeard forbade Mollena from the door locked with the small, gold key — and that's the one place her dream lovers want her to go.

Chapter 1
Taken to Wife

Bluebeard came to take Mollena to wife moments after she buried her father, the failed merchant Andre du Toussaint. He stepped up beside her in the church graveyard and gripped her upper arm with one of his big hands, rough and scarred from working the sails of ships in his youth. Ignoring her tears, he pulled her away from the fresh mound of earth atop her father's coffin and led her to the priest.

"Father Arsenault," Bluebeard said in his flat and gravelly voice. "I'm sure you're busy today, but I wondered if you would accept some coin in exchange for a quick wedding ceremony. I'm afraid there's a bit of a rush. I sail tomorrow, but I promised my bride's father that I would provide for her after his death."

The priest glanced from Bluebeard to Mollena. The girl tried not to let her terror show. She had begged her father not to promise her to the burly ship's captain, whose previous two wives had disappeared under mysterious circumstances. She had sworn that she could spin or take in laundry or serve in some family's house as a governess. But the dying old man had insisted that she become a respectable married woman, and Mollena knew she was poor and plain, with hair like a soiled dishrag, a hooked nose, long and awkward limbs, and close-set eyes. None but Bluebeard would have her.

She met the priest's eyes bravely and nodded. Bluebeard displayed an embarrassing quantity of coin. The priest pressed his lips together and took the money.

Two of her father's pallbearers served as witnesses, all but her new husband still dressed in black for mourning. The captain's midnight blue hair and beard shone, he rose two hands above the next tallest man there, and his black eyes were cold with secrets. He wore a tailored suit that must have cost more than Mollena's father had made in a year. The ring he shoved onto the third finger of her left hand might have been made of iron the way its weight pulled upon her arm and heart.

Then Bluebeard took her home. Mollena craned her neck, stunned by high ceilings, the scent of fine wood and exotic spices, and a multitude of doors. Bluebeard jerked her closer to him, wrapping one meaty arm around the back of her neck. "You'll have time to see the house later," he said, undoing his belt buckle.

A thin, dry servant came to take the leather strap, fixing Mollena with a lascivious, appraising glare in the process.

"She isn't much," the servant said.

"No," Bluebeard agreed. Mollena waited for him to soften the statement, but he did not. He squinted at her. "Let's get this over with."

They left the servant behind, Bluebeard dragging Mollena up the stairs to his bed chamber at a pace just faster than she could comfortably walk. She stumbled and strained to keep up. Fine baubles displayed in the hallways blurred together. She saw only Bluebeard's broad shoulders, his purposeful stride. He shouldered his bed chamber door open and thrust her inside.

"Strip, girl," he commanded, freeing himself of his own clothing. Bewildered, she began to undo buttons. "You're not making much of a show of it, are you?" Bluebeard grabbed her hands away from her collar and pinned them beside her hips.

He leaned in close. His bitter breath clogged the air around her face. Bluebeard gripped her right hand and guided it to the mass of flesh between his legs. She had tried not to look at it. It felt far softer than she expected, the skin downy, two balls flopping loosely in their sack, and his tool dangling between, limp and slightly hot.

Mollena choked at the thought of herself, mere hours after her father's death, naked in a strange man's room, caressing him intimately. Blood rose to her cheeks.

Bluebeard shook her right hand impatiently. He wrapped it around his soft member. "Listen, girl," he said. "You're no joy to behold. You've no money to speak of. You're no pleasant companion.

You'll live easily here and want for nothing. This is your only duty. Learn to do it well."

Mollena blinked up at him. She attempted to move her hand over his flaccid shaft, but her nerves turned her gestures into weird jerks. Bluebeard glared and slapped her hand aside, replacing her uncertain grip with his own well-practiced fingers.

"I'm sorry," she tried. "I don't know anything about–"

"You can end your sentence there," Bluebeard said, gasping a little and humping against his hand. "You don't know anything." His shaft had grown a great deal in a short time. It now sprouted alarmingly thick and long from his lower belly, barely covered by his large hands. Mollena stared at it, biting her lip. "Lie down on the bed and spread."

She hesitated, glancing from the bed to his bulky body and back.

"Now!" Bluebeard roared, releasing himself in order to grasp her and throw her down. He forced her legs apart and hooked them over his shoulders. Mollena gasped at the discomfort of the unnatural position and struggled to move them down. Bluebeard growled and held one foot in place with one hand. With the other, he probed her sex, spreading her and lining up his club of a member.

"Hold still and take it, wife," Bluebeard said between gritted teeth. He forced himself inside her. Mollena could not help but sob, shocked by his manner as much as by the intrusion. Bluebeard grunted and adjusted his grip, fastening both her ankles to his shoulders and driving into her hard.

"Stop crying," he snarled. "That face is ugly enough without your pathetic expression. I've bedded whores old enough to be your grandmother who were prettier than you, not to mention wetter between the legs."

Mollena could bear neither the pain in her body nor the pain of his words. Bluebeard pounded into her, his flesh slapping against hers, his wild motions catching and pinching the dry skin between her legs. She grunted and cried out as he stabbed into her depth, beating and bruising her on the inside.

She turned her face toward her arm to hide from him, silent tears dripping from her cheeks onto the bed. Bluebeard increased his pace, finally grinding hard against her with a roar. His seed pumped into her, dribbling out around his member and pooling between the cheeks of her buttocks.

Bluebeard released Mollena, wiped himself with the corner of the bedclothes, and flopped onto the bed beside her, clasping her tight against his hot, hairy chest. She lay awake after it was over, imprisoned by his big arms, trembling with grief and fear, and shocked by all that had changed.

A great clock in the hall outside the bedroom struck every hour with dour precision. At midnight – the witching hour – she began to hear footsteps, sighs, and weeping in addition to the clock.

"Hello?" Mollena whispered, wondering if she should wake the man who had married her.

The door swung open, and in stepped two achingly beautiful women, one like night and the other like day. They clasped each other's hands tightly, and tears streamed down both their faces.

Pearls and opals dripped from the dark woman's throat and wrists. She wore white, and her long, black hair wound about her head and ears in complicated braids. Big green eyes opened wide at the sight of Mollena and she gestured to her companion, the smell of lilies wafting from her slender wrists as she moved.

The light woman wore a daisy chain in curly red hair, and her yellow dress clung tightly to her ample curves. She was round as the earth, with thick thighs and a soft belly. Her skin ruddy with freckles, laugh lines warmed the corners of her blue eyes despite her tears. She smelled like sun-warmed linen. She smiled sadly at Mollena.

"Who are you?" Mollena said.

Both women glanced at Bluebeard and shook their heads. Each pressed a finger to her lips. Mollena and the women stared at each other until the new wife drifted off to sleep.

Birds began tentative songs as morning broke, sunlight tapping its fingers against the sky, testing. Bluebeard snored in Mollena's ear.

She twitched a stiff leg, her body sore from Bluebeard's attentions. Seeing the door to the room closed, she decided she must have dreamt the two women.

Growing pressure in her bladder forced her to attempt escape from Bluebeard's grasp. Barely daring to breathe, Mollena pressed at the meaty forearms to make enough space for her to wriggle out.

She had nearly gotten free when he woke and gripped her tighter. His member pressed against her belly, threatening her with his desire.

"Just a minute," she whispered. "I'll be right back."

Blushing, she slipped out of bed to relieve herself. Fluids from the night before caked her inner thighs. The lips of her sex burned when they rubbed together, irritated by the ferocity of her new husband's attentions. Mollena made a tentative attempt to wash herself, half hoping that Bluebeard would fall back to sleep if she took her time before returning to him.

"How long will you keep me waiting?" Bluebeard muttered roughly from the bed. Mollena jumped and ran to him. He pulled her under the covers and opened her legs unceremoniously. Still tender from the night before, his ministrations hurt more this second time. Mollena bit her lip and tried to endure it.

He rolled out of bed as soon as he had finished with her. "I hope you feel like a woman now," he said, "because I don't have time to do any more." He turned his back and began to dress. "I'll be away for a few months. This is your home; enjoy it and keep it warm and ready for my return. My servant's not much for talking, but perhaps you can convince him to listen to your woman's prattle."

He paused heavily in the doorframe before leaving. He looked over his shoulder at her. She could not resist pulling the blanket higher to cover herself.

He smirked. "In the nightstand, you'll find the keys to every room in this house. You can use any of them and go wherever you like. With one exception: if you use the small gold key we'll both be sorry."

He placed his broad black hat over his blue-black hair and slammed the carved oak door shut behind him.

Chapter 2
The Ladies of the House

Abandoned for the present by her husband, Mollena tried to enter social life as a married woman. She sent invitations into town, but received polite excuses and complaints about the distance of the journey. Only after she'd been rebuffed by everyone from childhood friends to desperately lonely spinsters did Mollena realize the truth: no one would come to visit Bluebeard's house. The stories about his first two wives had done their damage.

Mollena screwed up her courage and went to the old servant, who was polishing fine, filigreed silverware in the kitchen. "I want you to take me to town."

"The master said to watch you here," the old man replied. His thin, frail body bent nearly double, but the malice in his voice made her fall back a pace.

"Just to visit a friend," she pleaded. "Would you trap me in my own home?"

The servant laughed. "Did the master tell you it was yours?" He narrowed his eyes. "He didn't mean it. You don't want to make him angry like the others did, do you?" He tapped the piece of silverware in his hand with a gnarled finger. The sharp blade of the knife glimmered when it moved.

Mollena swallowed. "What are you saying?"

"Questions," the servant sighed, running his cloth lovingly over the blade. "Questions make him angry. Be a good girl and run along."

Mollena wasted no time escaping him. She did her best to accept being alone in the house with the old man. She locked the door to the bed chamber at night and stayed out of his way as much as possible, doing her own cooking and cleaning and washing whenever she could. She entertained herself by singing old songs and playing what little she could on the piano in the main hall.

If Bluebeard had not behaved so cruelly, Mollena might have believed she had married well. The house was well-appointed. She found he had left her a closet full of fine dresses and, through the servant, access to accounts in town that allowed her to order any food she desired.

After her encounter with the servant, she feared the keys. But finally the day came when she had scrubbed even the imagined spots on the windowsills in the bedroom, kitchen, and hall. Her throat ached from singing. She sat on the bed and opened the nightstand.

Dozens of keys of all colors, shapes, sizes, and materials testified to the size of the house. Awed, she poked at them with her finger. The mass of metal and wood shifted to reveal a tiny golden key, tarnished and dirty.

A wail rose from the passage outside the room, followed by a woman's sob that cut off abruptly. Mollena gasped and slammed the drawer shut. She sat absolutely still, heart pounding. Mollena found the courage to extricate herself from the drawer and investigate the source of the sounds.

She searched a long time and found nothing. Shaken, Mollena ran downstairs and out onto the lawn, feeling the house and its secrets hulking behind her all the while.

The two women opened the bedroom door again. This time, instead of weeping, they giggled. The dark woman stepped boldly into the bedroom and flung herself down beside Mollena. The bed creaked under her weight.

Nervously, Mollena dragged herself up onto her elbows. "Who are you?" she demanded of the dark woman. The light woman still lingered in the doorway. "Am I dreaming?" Mollena asked.

"It depends," the dark woman said with a smirk. She laid her hand delicately on Mollena's wrist. "If you decide you're dreaming, will you let me do this?" She leaned in and pressed her lips to Mollena's.

The startled sound Mollena made transformed into something throatier. She had endured Bluebeard with no understanding of the heat he seemed to feel. This woman's touch freshened the very air in the room. Mollena trembled, breathing in the smell of a garden in spring just before a lightning storm.

The woman's lips caressed Mollena until she opened beneath them. A soft, warm tongue slipped into Mollena's mouth, stroking gently. The woman's smooth black hair trapped the sweet fragrance of her breath and the heat of her skin against Mollena's cheek. Mollena tried, tentatively, to return the kiss, bringing her own tongue to meet the woman's. She ran through the limited knowledge she had gained during her night with Bluebeard. Feeling uncertain, she reached up and gripped the black-haired woman's dress at the upper arms, trying to get up the courage to reach into it or unfasten something.

Before long, all thought slipped out of her mind. That maddening, patient tongue possessed her. Its movement inside Mollena's mouth telegraphed to every part of her body. Finally, the woman released Mollena, who lay flat on her back and panting.

"Am I dreaming?" Mollena asked again.

"A little bit yes and a little bit no," the woman said.

Mollena had forgotten about the light woman until she laughed. "Cecily is so enjoying being mysterious with you," the light woman said. She, too, settled on the bed beside Mollena. The soft warmth from the two women's bodies set off a fierce longing in Mollena. "I'm Francine. You are dreaming, but this is a true dream, and we are not figments of your imagination."

"You live in this house?" Mollena asked.

"We used to," Francine said.

"Now who's being coy?" Cecily said. She flopped away from the group, rolling her eyes. "We still live here, in every way that matters." Cecily's delicate black eyebrow arched. "We live here body and soul."

"Why don't I see you when I'm awake?"

Francine stopped Cecily from answering and shushed Mollena with a soft, sweet kiss on the lips. She stroked her, slipping her hands into Mollena's nightgown and caressing her breasts and sides. After a moment, Mollena surrendered to the sensation, letting her head press deep into the pillow and arching her back. "You want something, don't you?" Francine said, giggling.

"Yes," Mollena managed.

Francine's fingers began to move along her belly, tickling and teasing as they went. But Cecily sighed loudly and trapped Francine's wrist before the light woman could satisfy the desire that had begun to bud in Mollena. "Don't distract her," Cecily said. "Let her ask her question." She turned to Mollena, easing Francine's hands away in the process. "What was it you wanted to know, dear heart?"

"Do you live in some other part of the house?" Mollena said, looking from one to the other. "Why haven't I seen you during the day?"

"You could look for us," Cecily offered. "With all those keys, you'll certainly find something."

Francine scowled at the dark-haired woman. "Don't tell her to do that. Why don't you ask Bluebeard about us?"

"That idea's no better," Cecily said. "If you don't want her to look for us, then I suppose you should just go on distracting her."

Mollena shook her head. She couldn't think clearly through the haze of the dream and the intoxicating presence of the two women. "I don't understand," she said. "Who are you?"

Francine smiled sadly at Mollena. "There's no distracting her," she told Cecily.

"Well, of course not," Cecily said. "And you don't really want her distracted. You want her to look for us, you just don't want to admit it." Cecily patted Mollena's cheek. "You won't have any trouble finding us if you want to, my sweet."

Mollena tried to protest and ask more questions, but both women settled close to her, undoing her nightgown completely. Cecily nibbled Mollena's left nipple, while Francine suckled at the right. Thought fled Mollena completely as the clarity of the dream dissolved into a sensual swirl.

Mollena woke with her hand between her legs and an aching in her head. The set of keys gleamed dully from the nightstand drawer beside the bed, which she didn't remember opening. Mollena moved slowly. She sniffed the pillows on the bed and couldn't decide whether she imagined the scents of sun and lilies that she detected there.

She sat upright and steeled herself. Holding her breath, she snatched up the keys.

The small gold key came into her fingers without her having to look for it. She worried at it with her thumb and forefinger as she stepped out into the passage. A door opposite the bedroom led out onto the widow's walk, a thin balcony that spanned the outside of the second floor and looked down on the cliffs and water below the isolated house.

The master bedroom was on the second floor of Bluebeard's mansion, and Mollena hadn't explored the rest of that level at all. The corridor extended the length of a large ship. In the dim light from the widow's walk, Mollena could make out dozens of doorknobs, to both left and right.

She crept to the nearest, a round red door, not able to explain why her heart pounded so. Goosebumps rose on her skin as she ran her fingers along the painted wood and pressed her cheek to listen for noises from the other side. She heard nothing.

After a long pause, Mollena turned her attention to the ring of keys, trying one then another until at last she found one made of brass, fitted with an engraved, heart-shaped handle. She screamed a little when the door's lock turned over under her hands. Slowly, she swung the door open, half expecting to find Cecily and Francine waiting on the other side.

The women weren't there, but Mollena's eyes adjusted to the darkness to reveal a room outfitted to rival the finest, most fashionable theaters. She couldn't stop herself from smiling. Her father's fortunes had been good when she was very small, but she'd been too young at the time to appreciate fine fabrics and she hadn't had a woman's shape or the desire to flatter it.

Mollena took a step inside.

"Looking for something?" She jumped at the dry voice behind her. She hadn't been face to face with the servant since the day in the kitchen.

Bluebeard had given her permission to explore the house. He had given her the keys she held. Still, she could not prevent a guilty expression from forming on her face.

"Give me the keys," the servant commanded.

Mollena handed them over before she could think to question his tone. The old man sorted through them, singling out the small gold key and holding it close to his eyes to inspect it. "What are you doing?" she managed finally.

"Watching you for the master."

"He said not to use that key."

"He did indeed."

"Then why–"

The servant tossed the keys on the floor before her feet. "Women," he said, "do not always obey."

Only after she watched him plod heavily away down the hall did she lean over to pick up the keys. Her delight in the room had vanished. She closed the door and locked it behind her.

Mollena folded back the covers of Bluebeard's big bed with a sigh. Life had always been lonely, but never so much as this. Even her father in his illness had been better company than this gloomy house and the single, menacing servant.

She closed her eyes and prayed for her soul, but in her heart, she wished for another visit from Cecily and Francine. Sleep came grudgingly, in fits and starts, and at uncomfortable angles.

Noises in the hall reached her ears.

"She doesn't care for us," Cecily's voice said. "She's not really searching."

Mollena tried to turn her head toward the sound, but could not.

"Let her be," Francine replied. "Let her have what peace she can."

"You want to let her die without ever learning the truth? You want us to continue to rot unwept, with no hope of rest?"

Mollena struggled to rise from the bed. Her limbs would not obey.

"Perhaps it will not be so," said Francine.

Cecily snorted. "You think he cares for her? He will return to the house soon. She does not have much time to act."

Finally, Mollena managed to lift herself and turn. She saw nothing. She stepped out into the hall. She waited, shivering in the cold corridor, but the only sound was of the house settling deeper into its perch on the cliff.

Mollena stood in the hallway outside the bed chamber, holding the ring of keys. She would go mad without companionship. She needed to appease Cecily and Francine. And yet, the servant's observation and innuendo chilled her.

"You won't have any trouble finding us if you want to, my sweet," Cecily had said. Mollena traced the lines of the small gold key in her hand. But her mind did not wish to know what her fingers did.

There would be no harm, she reasoned, in trying the doors. If they opened with any other than the forbidden key, Bluebeard could not blame her for looking inside. Cecily and Francine would see her honestly searching, and might return to her bed. As for the door unlocked by the small gold key – when she found it, she could decide.

With plodding resolution, Mollena worked her way down the hall, opening one door at a time. Under different circumstances, she would have felt delighted. Rich things from Bluebeard's travels stuffed each room from floor to ceiling – exotic wooden statues from the other side of the world, aromatic stores of spices, books bound in animal skin, erotic paintings.

Without the memory of his cold, dark eyes, Mollena could imagine the wonders stored in this house persuading her to fall in love with the man who had collected them. But she thought of the way he had used and abandoned her along with the rest of his treasures, and the things in the rooms took on an air of mourning. Bluebeard knew how to collect things, she thought, but he didn't know how to care for them. Dust covered all his splendid prizes, hiding their rich colors and eating their softer parts into disrepair.

The servant lurked often in the upper corridors these days, sometimes just watching her, and sometimes demanding, "Keys." He seemed disappointed whenever he peered at the small gold key.

Bluebeard might have meant the second floor alone to occupy Mollena for months – perhaps even until his return. Her search for Francine and Cecily, however, pressed her to explore more quickly than she otherwise would, spending days investigating rooms where she would have spent weeks.

When Mollena's explorations descended to the first floor, the old servant seemed ever at her elbow. He took to calling her, "Mistress of the House," the sarcasm dripping from his nearly nonexistent lips.

Mollena gritted her teeth through it and continued to explore. The first floor rooms seemed richer and better kept – perhaps present-ing the trophies of the adventures of Bluebeard's younger days. One room was bare except for a large, stuffed tiger, the knife wound that had killed it still visible across its throat despite the taxidermist's skill. Another room held a full suit of primitive armor from a warrior chief-tain, the breastplate and helmet covered with brilliant orange and yel-low feathers arranged in swirling patterns. She gazed upon it briefly and backed away.

"The master will be sorry to hear how little of his collection ex-cites your fascination," the servant said from far too close behind her. Mollena restrained her scream and turned with as much dignity as she could muster.

"It's all very lovely," she said sincerely.

"How can you know? You spend so little time in each room." His tongue darted from his mouth. "Unless you are looking for some-thing?"

Mollena let the question hang, stepping around him and continu-ing down the hall.

She found stores of money and jewels, vivid dyes, precious metals, and bills of sale from seaports around the world. She'd known her husband was a rich man, but the weight of all that treasure brought it home to her in a way she hadn't realized before.

The weeks wore on. Cecily and Francine did not come to her bed. Even the servant seemed weary of tormenting her. The rooms went on endlessly. The memories of her night with Bluebeard softened. Could she truly not enjoy her time in the house? Would she let a dream take over her days, turning them urgent and fitful?

Mollena woke one morning and picked up her key ring. She searched for the brass key with the heart-shaped handle. Wonder budded in her breast as she opened the round, red door. A Paris stage! It might be childish, but she could pretend.

She darted in and hunted through the bits of satin, fur, and velvet, rubbing them against her skin and dressing herself in scandalous outfits. It made her giggle to see her simple body dressed in such fine things. She played in the room until long after dark, then slipped back to bed still wearing black lace underthings.

"I see you've finished exploring, beautiful." Cecily's lips brushed Mollena's ear as she spoke. "Have you forgotten us?" Mollena struggled up and opened her eyes. Francine sheltered a candle in a flower-covered dish, providing dim light to the room.

The women were both dressed as if they'd played in the dressing room with Mollena earlier that day. Cecily wore a dark green silk corset that pressed her small breasts up into full white globes, and an elegant waistcoat. Francine's bright pink nipples peeked through her short, sheer white shift.

Francine set down the candle and came over to straddle Mollena on the bed. Mollena reached up to hold the other woman around the waist, but Francine swatted her hands away and peered at her face. "She never searched for us in the first place."

"I did! I tried, but I didn't find you," Mollena said. She reached out now for Cecily, wanting to feel the comfort of flesh from at least one of the women.

Cecily obliged, taking Mollena's hand and idly stroking her neck and shoulders with it, guiding Mollena's fingers toward her cleavage.

"Listen," Cecily said. "We love you. Can you believe that?"

Mollena pulled her hand away from Cecily and tried to concentrate. "No one's ever touched me the way the two of you do."

"Not even your husband," Francine said in a satisfied tone.

"Of course he didn't," Cecily said. "He was interested only in his own pleasure. Making you learn the 'duties of a wife.'"

"Don't sound so bitter," Francine said. "Those aren't so bad."

"Hmmph," Cecily said. "I prefer when these things aren't done out of duty." She trailed a finger up Mollena's outer thigh. Her tongue followed her finger, licking first Mollena's thigh then Francine's. Mollena nearly went mad. Involuntarily, her hand went to the back of Cecily's head and her back arched, lifting Francine. The light woman laughed and pushed Cecily's head away. "Please concentrate."

Cecily rolled her eyes, then looked back at Mollena. "We love you," she said again, and the words sent a thrill through Mollena's body that ricocheted back and forth between her heart and the groove between her legs. "If you love us, too, you won't give up. And when you find us, you might learn about the terrible fate that awaits you in this house."

"Don't tell her to–"

"I'm warning her, Francine. I'm being fair."

"She shouldn't look for us," Francine said.

"Do you really think she's safer if she doesn't?"

Mollena sat all the way up, pushing both women off her. "Please don't fight. In the morning, I will continue. I promise."

Cecily smiled. "I know you will." She took Mollena's hand again, this time guiding it under her waistcoat. Mollena slid her hand in deeper, feeling the soft fur between Cecily's legs, and the warm, wet slit it covered. Cecily thrust her hips forward to open herself to Mollena. Her flesh parted, and Mollena blushed as her finger slipped inside the tight passage into her body. Cecily's flesh was almost uncomfortably hot. Despite her nervousness, Mollena could not help but probe Cecily, and the other woman gasped with every movement of Mollena's hand.

Idly, Francine reached under Mollena's lacy black petticoat and began to swirl her finger against the bare skin there, working her way between Mollena's legs. Francine mirrored the motions that Mollena took up with Cecily, trailing kisses up Mollena's neck as she did.

Mollena reached for Francine with her other hand. The red-haired woman pulled up her shift so that Mollena could reach her between her legs as well. Mollena pressed two fingers into the tight sheath there.

Cecily raised a sly eyebrow as Mollena began to move her hands rhythmically inside both of the women. Cecily crawled her hand across Mollena's belly and pulled her garments entirely out of the way. She tweaked Mollena's nipples and pushed her fingers into her mouth. Then, she brought her hand down to join Francine's at Mollena's entrance, working her fingers in beside the red-haired woman's and stretching Mollena wider than Bluebeard had done.

The stimulation made it impossible for Mollena to keep her fingers moving, but Francine and Cecily took over, rearranging themselves sinuously so they could rub themselves on Mollena's hands while retaining access to her body.

Cecily's hand moved sharply inside Mollena, her fingers thrusting in deep and hard. Francine was softer, cupping her mound gently, pressing against her inner wall with her fingers, and rubbing her thumb over the bud between her legs.

Mollena almost choked on her moans. Every muscle in her body tensed until it almost hurt. She forced her eyes open so she could see the two beautiful creatures that shared the bed with her. Cecily's black hair had come loose from her braids, tendrils sticking to her sweaty, pale forehead. Francine's blue eyes narrowed to slits as she rolled her hips on Mollena's hand at the same pace she used to stroke between Mollena's legs.

A long, low cry burst from Mollena's throat and coaxed the rest of her body to follow it. She felt herself rising above her body. Then her awareness snapped to the throbbing between her legs. She would have flailed, but the weight of the other women on her hands held her in place. Mollena screamed as the throbbing spread into a beautiful ache across her entire body.

And she understood when Cecily and Francine held her wrists firmly and brought themselves to join her in that state. They were all together there, safe in the pleasure of the dream. Mollena would have been perfectly content except for the lingering thought of her search, and fear of what secrets it would uncover.

Chapter 3

The Small Gold Key

Mollena slept almost until noon the next day, waking with a foul taste in her mouth and a foggy head. It had been a long time since her last meal and she was starving, but she rolled up and immediately reached for the key ring that Bluebeard had given her.

She sat cross-legged, sorting through the keys. She could avoid the truth no longer. The small gold key seemed sullen in her palm.

Mollena's heart pounded urgently. She could not be bold enough without help.

She put on a floor-length blue silk gown, arrayed her hair in an appealing cascade, and added a string of pearls and a pearl ring. She pretended to have Cecily's fire and Francine's sense of calm. She hung the keys at her waist and went downstairs for a quick meal.

As she ate, Mollena lifted the gold key and looked at it closely. The grooves along its sides held old, rust-colored stains. She recalled Bluebeard's voice, as clearly as if he stood beside her now: "If you use the small gold key, we'll both be sorry."

Mollena hardened her heart to her awe of Bluebeard's trove. She worked her way through the house faster now and more methodically, opening every door in case it hid further rooms or closets, sorting the keys she'd used from the ones she hadn't. She soon finished exploring every wing, nook, and alcove of the first and second floors. She hadn't found Francine and Cecily, but three unused keys remained on the ring Bluebeard had given her. There had to be three more doors somewhere in the house.

Mollena hesitated. There was no sign of the old servant. She heard nothing but her own breathing. The basement promised the only additional doors. She gathered her courage and descended.

She doubted anyone had disturbed it for years. She lifted her candle high and almost choked at the sight of the passage before her, clogged with gloom and spiderwebs.

Mollena stepped forward, waving her hand around her face and compulsively brushing filth off her hair and fine dress. The first door she tried opened onto darkness so thick that the candle's frail light didn't penetrate it. Mollena swallowed a nervous scream and stepped deeper into the room.

She tripped and scrabbled for something to hold, her hand finding and grasping a rusted iron bar. She forced herself to calm down and turned slowly, letting her eyes adjust to the dim light that began to penetrate the room's dark corridors. It was a wine cellar. Mollena almost cried with relief.

She returned to the passage. Her pulse didn't speed at all as she calmly opened the door to a storage space crammed with tools and broken furniture. This was simple, she thought. One door to go.

She continued down the passageway, looking for the final lock. Bluebeard couldn't possibly know that she had used this last key, she told herself. The servant, for all his threats, wouldn't be able to say for sure either. She could open that door, tell Francine and Cecily that she had looked for them without finding anything, then accept that they were figments of her imagination. She could enjoy the eroticism of the dreams, and set about accepting the realities of life with her husband. Perhaps things would be all right. He'd been cold and unsympathetic about the death of her father, but he was very rich and seemed resolved to leave her mostly to her own devices.

The floor of the passage changed from stone to dirt. Every trace of finish disappeared, and it turned and slanted deeper. The air chilled. Mollena began to wonder if the tunnel could collapse on her, or worse, behind her. She touched the golden key and could have sworn it felt hot in her hand.

The passage ended abruptly in a flimsy wooden door that didn't close all the way. A thick chain and a tiny padlock secured it. She didn't have to look at the key in her hand to know that it would fit.

Mollena glanced at her candle. She wasn't sure if she would be able to make it back to the stairs before it ran out. Her heart thudded in her chest.

Tentatively, she reached out to the door and tried to pull it open without opening the lock. She succeeded in getting a sliver of a view into whatever was beyond, but couldn't see into the darkness. A strange, sweet smell wafted from the door.

Mollena turned away and started back up the passage, but only made it a few steps before she stopped.

Deliberately, Mollena set the candle down in the earthen floor near the door and fitted the golden key into the padlock. It sprang open so violently it almost hit her in the face. She unwound the chain and pulled on the door.

She smelled sweet rot and iron. Mollena pulled her dress up to keep it from trailing on the ground and ducked a little to step inside the room. She recognized Francine and Cecily immediately, even considering their current state. Propped up against the opposite wall, their hair – one head black, one red – spread around their partially decomposed bodies. Francine seemed to have been there longer than Cecily, but the corpses had been stored the same way, well-preserved in the cool of the basement. Bluebeard must have killed them in this room – blood covered the floor.

Mollena jumped at a sound that turned out to be her own voice sobbing. She fell to her knees and heaved. She was light-headed. Mollena passed out on the gruesome floor.

"Now she knows," Francine said grimly.

Mollena still lay on the floor of the basement room, but the redhaired woman smelled like sun again, and her flesh was whole and glowed with health. Mollena stood, wobbling a little, and reached for Francine's throat, feeling the unbroken skin there.

"What's going on?" Mollena said.

Two thin, strong hands gripped her shoulders and steadied her. Cecily.

"When you're unconscious, you see us as spirits, not bodies," Cecily said. "But there isn't time to be unconscious now. That old servant sees more than you think he does, and the signs that you've been here are all over you. You need to get up, go upstairs, and figure out how to escape this place."

"I can't leave the two of you like this," Mollena said. "You deserve a Christian burial, at the very least."

"Cecily's right," Francine said. "You should save yourself."

Mollena laughed in disbelief. "If that's how you feel, why did you bring me here in the first place? Why did you visit me at all?"

The other two looked ashamed. "We needed you to open the door," Francine said finally. "We wish to take our revenge."

"You are the only one who understands us," Cecily added. "We've shared pleasures with you that we never felt in life. You've shared our mortal peril."

"We love you," Francine whispered. "You are so alive."

"We mean to keep you that way," Cecily said firmly. "Listen to me now and get up. We'll be all right where we are."

Mollena felt hysterical. "No!" she said. "I swear to you, I'm not leaving without you. I promise I will make sure you both get a chance to rest in peace."

Francine cursed. "Bluebeard will be home soon, and his servant is watching you!"

Cecily's pale skin turned almost translucent. "Get up now, girl! Run upstairs! Run all the way up, to the widow's walk! At the very least, don't let him murder you in the darkness below. Fling yourself into the sea before he does!"

Francine slapped Cecily. "Don't tell her to throw herself into the sea! Run, Mollena, but we'll be with you. We'll help you escape. Don't let him take your life."

Francine's last word ended in a scream that shook the foundations of the house and shocked Mollena out of the dream.

Mollena jerked to a sitting position as if someone had pulled her up. The candle had gone out, and she was alone in the blackness with the corpses. The room's sour smell made her retch again. She felt around the filthy floor until she found the keys. Horribly, impossibly, the blood that stained it felt wet and sticky against her skin.

Putting out a hand, Mollena found the wall and guided herself to her feet and back to the passage. Once there, she walked as fast as she could without tripping in the dark. The stairs seemed farther than she remembered.

Mollena stopped at the base of the stairs to listen. She could catch no hint of what might be waiting for her above. As silently as she could, she crept to the top of the stairs and listened again at the door. Still hearing nothing, she pulled to ease the door open a crack. It wouldn't move.

She forced herself to stay calm and tried a second time. The door was shut and locked from the outside.

Harsh laughter reached her ears from the other side of the door. "You foolish girl," the servant said. "Did you think I had neglected my duty? You can wait there until the master returns."

Mollena gasped. "What? No! I'll die in here."

"Nonsense. You probably won't starve before his ship puts in."

Mollena pounded and screamed, but the door did not give way, and neither did he.

Mollena could not guess how long she sat huddled at the foot of the basement stairs, the corpses of her dream lovers decaying slowly just a short walk from her position. Without light or food, she lost all sense of time.

The light that flooded down the staircase could have been a hallucination, and so she did not lift her head when it touched her.

But with the light came a shadow. "Hello, wife," Bluebeard said. "My servant tells me you have been very much enjoying the run of the house."

Mollena tried not to whimper as she straightened up. She felt like a child before him, so much shorter and smaller and weaker. "Hello," she said. Her voice cracked.

"You look dusty and a bit the worse for wear," Bluebeard said. Mollena looked down and saw cobwebs and dust clinging to her arms and palms. She had been sick on her dress, and it was dirty and stained. "May I see the keys I gave you?" Bluebeard's tone rang sweeter than she had heard from him.

Mollena climbed the stairs to stand before him. Her hand trembled as she handed them over. She thought she could hear Cecily and Francine screaming about escape in her mind, but his big body blocked her way, and she couldn't think where or how to run.

Bluebeard gave a little cry and lifted the golden key apart from the rest. Sticky blood dulled its entire length. "I said we would both be sorry if you used this key," he murmured. He dropped the keys and settled his arms on the doorframe to either side of Mollena, stepping in so that his body pressed tight against hers. His member rose hard between them. Bluebeard kissed her neck. Mollena flinched. "I find I'm not sorry at all," he murmured into her hair. "Though I daresay you will be."

"What are you talking about?" Mollena said.

"You know now, my love. You know everything. We can have one last night together, and you can get to know me as I really am. No longer any reason to hide the truth." His rough hand cupped her throat gently but completely.

Mollena stiffened. Her mind raced. She could shove him, but he was stronger and well-placed to resist her. Desperately, Mollena tried the opposite. She pulled him toward her as hard as she could, winning a surprised grunt from him and upsetting his balance.

He grabbed a fistful of her dress and the fabric separated as neatly as if it had been cut. Mollena didn't stop to watch him fall. She broke free and darted toward the staircase. There was a thud behind her, and she ran for all she was worth.

She took the stairs two at a time, fear making her faster than she'd thought possible. Before long, she heard Bluebeard's heavy footsteps behind her. Mollena followed Cecily's instructions and made for the widow's walk.

She burst out onto it, shrieking as she grabbed at the outside of the house to stabilize herself. The sharp tang of the sea stung her nose as she fought for breath. The widow's walk stretched along the cliff side of the house, ending across from Mollena under a forgotten, tattered flag, where the structure faded into disrepair.

She looked over her shoulder. Bluebeard ran at her heels.

She darted away, but her foot slipped on a patch of damp, rotting wood and she caught at the side of the house for a dizzying second. The world spun, and the house seemed to stretch even higher above the cliffs. Mollena forced herself to keep moving, to edge out along the treacherous, narrow walk. The wood creaked beneath her feet. She was afraid to wait for Bluebeard, but also terrified to test the walkway any further.

"Run!" She heard Cecily and Francine shouting. She obeyed, forcing herself to trust her feet on the precarious surface.

"You won't get away, woman!" Bluebeard called. "There's nowhere to go!"

Looking ahead, Mollena couldn't help but agree. She was running out of walkway already, and as she approached the end, the structure grew even more rotten and unstable. Just behind her, it splintered under Bluebeard's heavy weight.

Soon, Mollena could go no further. She glanced at the foamy waves below. Cecily had said to fling herself onto the cliffs rather than allow Bluebeard to get her. Francine had said to throw him down instead. Mollena couldn't do either one. She held herself as tall as she could and turned to face Bluebeard.

He stopped his forward charge and stared at her. "Francine, Cecily, and Mollena. My three wives will all be together."

"You killed Francine and Cecily," she said, finding her voice.

He produced a knife from his coat. Mollena shuddered, recalling the tiger and the bodies in the basement. Bluebeard shook his head. "I didn't kill them," he whispered furiously. "They chose to die. All of you chose not to obey me, as a good wife should. But I have been a faithful husband. I take time to visit them whenever I am at home. And I will keep you, too. I will provide a home for you so long as I live." He stepped closer, the walkway complaining beneath him.

Mollena didn't want to die. The ragged flag snapped above her head, and she glanced up at it. Bluebeard took another step, and the joins holding the widow's walk to the side of the house creaked loudly. She scrambled up onto the banister and grabbed the flagpole with both hands.

Clinging to the metal, she stomped as hard as she could on the rotten wood, hanging on for dear life when the walkway gave way beneath her feet.

Bluebeard fell with it, cursing her all the way down. The cliffs waited below, beaten by the violent ocean. Mollena swallowed hard.

It was a long time before Mollena got the courage to unwrap herself from the pole and ease her way back across what was left of the widow's walk. When she got back inside the house, she went straight to the bedroom, locked herself in, and collapsed under a weight of fear and exhaustion.

Cecily and Francine waited in the dream, sitting on the bed as if they'd been there all evening. Mollena blinked wearily, tired even in that other place. "I promise I will come to you just as soon as I can. I'm sorry I didn't have the strength to do it right away."

Cecily and Francine held hands. They both wore wedding gowns, Francine's light and frilly and Cecily's fitted and shimmering like a pearl. "We have special instructions," Cecily said. "Please don't bury us."

"What?"

"Throw our bodies into the sea," Francine said. "Our spirits can't find peace until we break our ties to Bluebeard. We want to go in after him, meet him underwater, and make him answer for his crimes."

Mollena felt a chill at the fierce expression on Francine's normally serene face. She put her hand on top of the other women's hands. "I will," she said. "I'll make sure to do it exactly as you wish."

The three looked at each other for a long time, and Mollena burst into tears.

Francine stroked her back. "What's the matter?"

"The two of you are the only friends I've had in so long," Mollena sobbed. "I'm so sorry for what happened to you, and I'm glad that you're going to find peace now, but I'm going to miss you so much. I don't know what I'll do without seeing you."

Francine pulled Mollena's face into her bosom, its sun-kissed scent igniting intense desire in her lover. Mollena reached around her back and tore open the buttons of her gown, pushing it down off Francine's shoulders and revealing her round, full breasts. Mollena threw herself on them, kissing, licking, stroking, and squeezing. She pinched both nipples and Francine gasped.

Cecily's full, throaty laugh filled the air behind Mollena. "You're not shy tonight, my dear heart," she said. "I'm glad." Cecily undid Mollena's nightgown and slipped it off without making her pull away from Francine for even a moment. Francine had begun to moan urgently under Mollena's attention to her breasts. Her hips bucked wildly, still tangled in the lower half of her nightgown. Cecily reached over and slid that off, too.

As soon as she did, Francine guided one of Mollena's hands down between her legs. Mollena couldn't believe how slick she was. She let her hand explore Francine idly, smiling at the desperation with which the red-haired woman ground and gyrated her hips.

Out of the corner of her eye, Mollena saw Cecily stand and peel off her own gown, tossing it on the floor. When she returned to the bed, her pale skin was so soft that Mollena groaned. "Let me show you something," Cecily murmured, the usual hint of ironic amusement in her voice.

She grasped the back of Mollena's head and guided her away from Francine's breasts and down to her belly. Francine panted and murmured incoherent words. "Don't stop yet, my sweet," Cecily said. She pushed Mollena's head down further, to the cleft between Francine's legs.

"Lick her," Cecily whispered.

Francine's moan had a sob in it the first time Mollena put out her tongue. She lapped tentatively against the other woman's sex, her hand still moving inside her. Between Francine's legs, Mollena tasted tang of summer ocean. She breathed deep, finding herself almost overwhelmingly aroused by the flavor. She licked up the slick wetness that covered every bit of the soft pink skin between Francine's nether lips.

"You're going to drive her mad," Cecily said. She pushed Mollena's head again, centering her on the hard bud of flesh at the top of Francine's cleft. "Suck on that."

Mollena did. Above her, Cecily kissed Francine, so that the sharp, desperate moans that Mollena unleashed from the red-haired woman were muffled by Cecily's mouth and tongue.

Francine's body tensed and bucked hard. Mollena slid a hand

around to her bottom and held tight, not letting up on sucking that bud of flesh. Mollena thrust her fingers in and out, sharply the way Cecily had done to her, then she and Cecily were both holding Francine as the red-haired woman writhed and wept in their grasp.

When Francine finally relaxed, Mollena let go and sat up, grinning at Cecily. The dark-haired woman kissed Mollena, her lips soft and lingering. Her rough tongue darted out to lick Francine's juices off Mollena's face.

Mollena moaned and pushed Cecily onto the bed on her back, spreading her legs around Cecily's thigh.

"You two look beautiful together," Francine said.

Mollena had never felt so beautiful. Her lifelong ideas of being plain disappeared in Cecily's arms. She buried herself in a kiss that felt as smooth as silver, rubbing against Cecily's thigh as she did. Soon, she felt Francine's hands, too, pinching her nipples, smoothing her hair, teasing her sex.

Mollena gasped and pressed harder against Cecily's thigh. "Wait," Francine whispered. She pulled Mollena away from Cecily a little and worked her way beneath her. Mollena shrieked as Francine arranged Mollena's thighs to either side of her head reached inside her with a soft, hot tongue.

Cecily smiled against Mollena's mouth and pulled away from their kiss, sliding her body up so that Mollena's mouth could easily reach her own slit. She pulled Mollena's head into her lap, murmuring, "You know what to do now, love."

Cecily petted Mollena's hair, spreading her legs and leaning back against the headboard.

At first, Mollena couldn't move her tongue. She was too caught in the pleasure of what Francine was doing between her legs. Then she forced her tongue out and tasted Cecily, sharper and sweeter than Francine had been. She closed her eyes and felt herself enveloped by the two women. She mimicked the movements of Francine's tongue and fingers, and soon they were all moaning.

Cecily grabbed the back of Mollena's head and pulled her in tight, groaning and thrusting her hips up. The feeling of Cecily shuddering against her face overwhelmed Mollena, who ground against Francine's face. Francine nipped her softly, and Mollena gasped into

Cecily's body and shuddered with her. She couldn't have said where the pleasure started or ended, all she knew was that it passed so freely between them all.

Francine kept her tongue moving until Mollena was sobbing, her cheek resting against Cecily's thigh.

They eased away from each other, all breathing hard. Mollena studied the others, their shapes so dear and yet still so mysterious.

Cecily started to kiss her again, but Mollena stopped her. "I have to know what's going on."

"Well," Cecily said dryly. "For one thing, you're going to be very rich. I imagine you'll inherit Bluebeard's house and everything in it."

"Considering what he did to you, don't you think his wealth was ill-gotten? How could I keep it?"

Cecily's face hardened. "I paid with my blood," she said, "as did Francine. If there is any benefit to be had from his crimes, I demand that it go to you."

Mollena nodded slowly, trying to put on a brave face. Francine pressed her cheek against Mollena's stomach. "Do not worry," she said. "Do as we asked. Leave Bluebeard to us."

Francine and Cecily held her close until her exhausted mind slipped into a black sleep.

When Mollena woke, she went at once to the basement to take Francine and Cecily out of that horrible room.

She did this herself, despite how she struggled and retched, loading their corpses onto a cart and rolling them up to the staircase, then hauling each up the staircase, then loading them back onto the cart. It was noisy, rough work, and the old servant came in while she did this and stood watching her, his mouth working. "You can't unleash those demons on the world," he said finally.

Mollena could not help laughing. "Demons? Your master was the demon. These were victims."

"Hungry spirits. No revenge can satisfy them. They should be left where they lie, locked in forever."

"If you wanted me to believe you," Mollena grunted, resuming her work, "perhaps you should not have trapped me in the basement."

The servant dropped to his knees.

"What are you doing?" Mollena asked.

"I feared the master," the servant whimpered. "But do not let the spirits free."

"Are you afraid they'll take revenge on you, too?" Mollena stared him down, feeling powerful and pitiless. "Women," she said, "do not always obey." She pushed past him, calling over her shoulder, "You will need to find other employment, of course."

Mollena dragged the cart with the corpses out of the house and to the cliffs. She tried not to look at the bodies as she rolled them off the edge to fall a long way into the cold, green water. She wanted to remember Francine and Cecily as beautiful, warm, desirable women, not as these broken, brutalized shells.

She sat on the slimy rocks, looking out over the water. She wondered how many things it held in its unknown depths. She searched her memory for a prayer she could say to ease Francine and Cecily on their way, but words escaped her. At last, she made the sign of the cross and went inside.

It was her house now, and it was empty. She didn't like the idea of being alone here, without even Bluebeard's ghost wives for company. Mollena laid plans in her mind, resolving to send to town to hire on several servants to help her clean and put things in order.

That night, Mollena dreamed of Francine and Cecily, but their presence didn't feel real. Mollena's mind simply produced memories of their stroking hands and soft skin and warm mouths.

She pushed the visions away and searched for something true.

If you enjoyed this story, you can discuss it with other readers and the author at *The Three Wives of Bluebeard* story page at http://forbiddenfiction.com/library/story/AL1-1.000075.

Do Virgins Taste Better?

R.W. Whitefield

When the dragon kidnaps a princess, he find himself wondering if a cow would have been a better idea after all. Who knew a princess was so demanding, or so kinky?

Do Virgins Taste Better?

When the dragon slithered down from the ice-blue sky, the princess was the only one who didn't scream. She leaned over the rail of her balcony, chin propped on fist, watching the peasants below wave their pitchforks and torches at the scaly beast.

The dragon, who had really just come to see if the cows grazing in the meadows were fat enough to eat, was surprised at her apparent boredom, as a great flying lizard breathing fire ought to be a fairly noteworthy aspect of a princess's landscape. He blew a little gout of flame in her direction, just to see her jump.

She merely lifted her head, and a slow, cattish smile grew on her face. Her dainty hand rose to her cherry-red lips, and she blew a kiss back into the dragon's fire.

Cows suddenly seemed far too common a dish for the dragon. He ducked his head, rippled his neck sinuously, and dove towards the princess. She didn't scream as he enclosed her in his scaly claws, but laughed and tossed her head back, as though she were on a carriage ride. Her laughter grew wilder and turned into cackling as the dragon flew, a sound that should come out of no princess's mouth, and she kicked her shapely legs in delight. The dragon began to fear that he had inadvertently kidnapped a witch.

As soon as he got to his cave, the dragon set the princess down on a rock outside. She stumbled a little, but quickly drew herself up and arranged the tatters of her gown; the gauzy pink fabric had snagged on the dragon's scaly claws during his flight. "So sweet of you to rescue me."

The dragon settled himself on the ground and folded his wings. "Rescue you? I mean to eat you." He let a little jet of flame escape his mouth.

"Eat me? I know dragons. If you wanted a meal, you would have stolen some of the peasants' cows."

"A princess's flesh is sweeter and softer than that of some peasant's cow." The dragon licked his chops, letting his tongue wander slowly over his dagger-sharp teeth.

"Oh," the princess sighed, "and I'm sure that virgins taste even better, don't they?"

The dragon nodded. "Virgins melt like honey on the tongue," he told her. "Their bones crunch better, their blood is sweeter..."

"Hmph." The princess smirked at him. The dragon fidgeted. In truth, he had never eaten a human, much less a virgin princess.

"Particularly the princesses," he bluffed, hoping to scare her. "Their skin is so soft and silky, what with the... baths they're always taking." As he spoke, he hooked the tip of a single huge claw into the princess's bodice. "Delicate, untouched by any man." With a twitch of his claw, he ripped the tattered dress off her body.

To his surprise, the princess didn't shriek and cover herself, as he'd heard human girls were apt to do. She stretched like a cat, shaking out her red-gold curls and rolling her shoulders. "That dress was terribly itchy. Anyway," she added, "if virgins are so sweet, I'm sure I'd taste like old hay, I've let so many knights sneak into my bedroom over the years."

"That won't stop me from eating you, you know. I'm very hungry." The dragon ran his tongue over his teeth again, hoping she'd get the point this time.

The princess laughed. "Why do you think I let you capture me in the first place?" She ran her hands down her body. "Look at my skin! Look at how pale and flawless it is!" Her skin was indeed pale and flawless, like a bowl of cream, and the dragon thought that she must not be allowed to walk in the sun very often.

"It's certainly very pretty," the dragon agreed.

"I'm sick of it. All of my knights treat me like a delicate, little flower," the princess complained. "They're afraid to do anything that would leave even the slightest mark on a princess's skin. They leave in the morning, and there's nothing to remind me that they ever touched me. No raspberry marks on my neck, no teeth marks on my thigh for me to run my hands over in secret during a state dinner and smile." She sighed, and stroked her thigh absently. "Skin this soft was just meant to be marked."

The dragon blushed green and inspected his claws. "And where do I fit into this?"

"Why, your teeth! Don't you see? Dragons have the sharpest teeth of any beast in the world," the princess explained, "and I know they aren't afraid to use them."

"Oh, that's it?" The dragon threw his head back and laughed, waving his tail so that the emerald scales glittered in the sunlight. "I hate to disappoint you, princess, but my jaws are a thousand times more powerful than those of the strongest man. If I gave you even the lightest nip, it'd take your arm off."

"I don't believe you." The princess crossed her arms and glared at the dragon. The gesture pushed up her breasts, and where her skin was as pale as milk, her nipples were as pink as flower petals.

The dragon lowered his head down to the princess's level, and stared into her bright green eyes. "Do you want me to show you?"

The princess held out her arm. "Go ahead. I'm not afraid."

The dragon inhaled. If he was really going to eat this princess, he was going to savor her, not just gulp her down like another cow. A salty-sweet scent hit his nostrils. "Hmm."

"I asked you to bite me," the princess informed him crossly, "not sniff me."

It was really quite a nice scent, better than the mud stink that the cows he usually ate gave off. He gave her neck an experimental lick.

"Oh, that's better." The princess arched her neck. "I bathed in rose water this morning," she informed him. "So I should be quite sweet."

The taste was oddly addictive. The dragon flicked his tongue over her breasts, where the taste grew stronger and saltier.

"Oooh," the princess sighed. He dipped his tongue into the hollow between her breasts, the tips of his forked tongue dancing across her skin and lapping up the little droplets of sweat. So this was why his ancestors had demanded princesses, this salt-rose taste! Peasant girls, even the virginal ones, would be covered in grime, and taste no different from cows. The royal ones could afford to bathe in rose water every day, to be sweet for the dragons.

The taste grew saltier, and he moved his tongue down to her smooth, taut belly, tracing circles and spirals on her skin to tantalize her. The princess moaned. "Lower," she insisted, "lower." She sank down to her knees, as though obeying her own command. "Here..." She leaned back and stroked the patch of red-gold hair between her legs.

"Hair tastes nasty," the dragon said. "It's the texture. I can barely stand cow hair as it is."

The princess let her fingers disappear between her legs. "Here." She spread her legs further, dipping her fingers into the cleft there, settling on the nub between her folds.

The dragon licked a stripe down her inner thigh. More rose taste, and something else, dank and a little spicy, that he couldn't quite name. It grew stronger as he dragged the tip of his tongue up her thigh, and the rose taste almost disappeared as he dipped his tongue into the folds of skin between her legs.

The princess gasped. "Oh, you dear sweet dra... dra... wyrm... oh, teeth, teeth..." She threw back her head and sighed. The dragon imagined he must be doing something right. The princess's folds were beginning to taste different, the moisture becoming thicker, tasting of something mammalian.

Flicking his tongue back and forth to catch the other taste, not quite as delicious as the rose-sweat mixture but still quite nice, the dragon wondered whether he really should bite her. On one hand, she would be a very tasty snack, and he was getting very hungry. On the other hand... well, his cave wasn't very far away from the village, and while a few cows here and there hadn't been enough to make the king send out the guards in the past, he knew enough about human society to know that a missing princess would certainly be enough to raise the whole army.

In fact, they could very well be heading this way already.

He glanced down at the princess, who was writhing on the rock like an earthworm after it rains. She was touching her breasts, circling

one nipple with the tips of her fingers while pinching the other between her forefinger and thumb. "Your tongue," she moaned, "is the best thing I've ever felt. I'll never be able to go back to a man— oh—
"

The dragon withdrew his tongue from between the princess's legs and gave the nub between her legs one last flick. The princess stopped touching herself and looked up at him, her eyes narrowing. "What are you doing? I didn't tell you to stop."

Princesses, the dragon thought, could indeed be haughty. They were bred to be. "I want to taste something else," he said, and flicked his tongue at her nipples. The princess shrieked and covered her breasts with her hands.

When the dragon licked her fingers, she smiled. "Well," she said, "if you're so interested..." And she uncovered her breasts, spreading her arms. "I'd like to see what else you can do."

The dragon licked her breasts, tracing circles around her nipples the way that she had been doing with her own fingers. The princess laughed and giggled. "That tickles!"

"Good?" the dragon asked, rolling his tongue back into his mouth, so it came out sounding more like "Gmmph?" Once the princess was satisfied, he thought it might be much easier to deal with the threat of the king's army.

The princess grinned at the dragon. "You've got the best tongue in the kingdom." She sighed in satisfaction. "If you weren't so big and scary, I'd keep you for a pet and have you tongue me every day. No, twice a day."

The dragon snorted a jet of fire at the ceiling. "I'd make an awful pet. I eat more in a day than your kingdom could produce in a month."

"Then you'd better finish me off quick," the princess said, and her hands went down to the inside of her thighs.

"All right," the dragon said, and flicked his tongue out again, but the princess shook her head.

"I need more than a tongue," she said severely. "What else have you got?"

The dragon looked at his claws doubtfully. Each one was two feet long and ended in a wicked point. "Well," he said, "I don't know.

How do you please yourself?"

"You don't know?" the princess asked, her lovely forehead creasing.

The dragon shrugged. "I don't usually please princesses," he said. "I eat things."

"Well," the princess asked, "how are dragons pleased?"

"By curling up on a big pile of gold," the dragon said. He thought of plates and chunks and chains of gold sliding against his scales, the cold smoothness of the metal sensuous against the rough, glittering plates on his body. "Sometimes we lay eggs, and we make nests for them in our gold. It makes our babies very comfortable."

The princess frowned. "That's certainly not how humans work. Although I do like gold," she added. "But I'll show you."

She moved her hand down between her legs, making a V with her fingers, rubbing the nub between her legs. "This is the spot you've got to hit," she informed the dragon. "Now, keep doing that thing with your tongue, and I'll show you what else we do."

The dragon began to lick at the nub again, swirling his tongue around it. The princess pushed two of her own fingers inside herself and began to move them in and out. "Move your tongue like that," she instructed the dragon.

Eager to let the princess finish being pleased, the dragon began to move as she told him, flicking his tongue rapidly up and down her nub. The princess began to writhe again, her fingers moving faster, the dragon keeping up with her pace.

She moaned wordlessly, and soon she was shoving her fingers inside of herself and keeping them there. The dragon licked long stripes up and down her nub to match until the princess reached up with her free hand and grabbed the base of his horn. "Faster," she said. "I want your tongue to be a blur."

The dragon flicked his tongue as hard as he could. Surely, he thought, the friction would be hurting her delicate body by now—but the princess showed no sign of pain. Indeed, the next thing out of her mouth was, "Oh god, dragon! Dragon! Bite me! I can't come if you won't bite me!"

It would have been impossible, of course. The dragon's jaws were far too big and strong to do anything but rip her in two if he had tried.

But the princess wanted what she wanted, and if she wanted marks, she would very well get marks. Perhaps he could fly her back quickly, before the king's soldiers were halfway to his cave. He cupped his claws so they made a semicircle of points, and gently, ever so gently, pressed them into the princess's chest, hoping and praying that he wouldn't miscalculate the pressure and impale her.

He saw red blood start to well up around his claws, and hastily withdrew them, wiping them on the grass beside him. The princess jerked twice and shrieked, then lay still with a half-smile on her face.

"Perfect." She let her hands wander up to her chest, and touched the wet blood. "Oh... you dear thing. You did bite me!" She gazed at the tiny spot of blood on her hand.

"Of course. Took all my willpower to keep from crunching you up, too." The dragon scooped up the rags that were left of her dress, and dropped them on her chest. "Here, put this on. I'm taking you back to the castle."

"Mmm. That's all right." The princess let the dragon scoop her up in his claw. "I want to stay here with you."

"Here?" The dragon looked around his tiny domain, a sparse, rocky cave surrounded by sparse grass. "Why?"

"At least for a little while." The princess smiled and stroked his scales. "And you can do that again."

"Do you want to get me killed?" The dragon raised her to his eye level. "I just kidnapped you, princess. Everyone saw. The soldiers are going to be here any second, and it's been too long since I fought even a single knight for me to stand a chance. If I can get you back to your castle, I might be allowed to live." He sighed. "Especially with those... tooth marks on you."

"Fine." The princess held the bundle of rags to her chest, covering the marks. "I'll tell Daddy not to kill you." She gazed up at him. "And if you do want to come back and get me, just every so often... I think I can convince him to give you some extra rose water. And maybe some cows."

The dragon's mouth watered at the thought of the rose taste. "I could get used to that." He launched himself into the air, towards the castle.

If you enjoyed this story, you can discuss it with other readers and the author at the *Do Virgins Taste Better?* story page. at http://forbiddenfiction.com/library/story/RWW-1.000077.

Red and the Wolf

Kailin Morgan

Aidan is content. He's got a good job, nice house and is comfortable in the small town—far away from anyone who knows his secrets. Yet, he feels the prickle of something stalking him. It doesn't help when a stranger starts insinuating his way into Aidan's life. Newcomer Seth is attractive in a way that stirs something in Aidan he had thought long buried. Can he keep his secret and continue in his solitary life or will events conspire against him to drag the truth into the light and change everything?

Chapter 1

Watcher in the Woods

Aidan sighed as he made his way to the showers. It had been a long day and he just wanted to clean up, go home and slob out on the couch with a beer and a pizza. He knew he wasn't going to, but the thought was nice. Opening his locker he pulled out his towel, dropping it on the bench beside him as he shed his sweaty tank top.

Pulling off his shorts and underwear, he shoved them gracelessly into his rucksack before he grabbed his soap and padded into the shower room. He let the warm water pummel the muscles of his shoulders and back, the ache fading into something more pleasant. Aidan loved his job as a physical therapist and trainer, but some days were definitely harder than others.

He soaped up, running the lather through his close-cropped dark hair before turning his face up to the spray, letting the suds run down his back. Blinking water from the long curl of his lashes, he washed the rest of his body, working his fingers into his biceps and triceps, the hard curves of his thighs, easing out the stress.

After rinsing off, he shut off the water and ran his palms over the swell of his pectorals, the firm planes of his abdomen, sluicing away the beading droplets. He collected his towel, rubbing it over his head and face, before drying the rest. He dressed swiftly, briefs, jeans, shirt, socks and boots, then shoved his towel and the rest of his belongings into his rucksack.

He picked up his hooded sweatshirt from where it lay crumpled at the bottom of his locker, shaking out the fabric as he made his way out of the staff locker room. He stopped at the reception desk, smiling at Anita. The perky brunette was well suited to her job, her smile almost permanently affixed to her face, her sympathetic nature letting her settle the most difficult of clients.

"That you away, honey?" she flicked a glance to the clock up on the wall behind him. "Putting in extra hours again?"

"Yeah. Had the Ellis kid in. He was just doing so well, I mean the way he's come on since he first arrived here. Couldn't say no to him, you know?"

Aidan thought back to his first meeting with Richie Ellis; the kid sitting in his wheelchair, scowling blackly at the ground, ignoring everyone. Then today, after doing their usual set of stretching and flexibility exercises, Richie had asked to try walking again.

Aidan had helped him over to the bars, supporting him from behind as he wobbled, muscles still weak. Richie had shrugged him off, gripping tight, taking a couple of shaky steps. Aidan had moved around in front of him, giving him something to aim for and Richie had taken another step, lifting one arm away from the support, then another and another until suddenly Aidan was backing into the wall and Richie had walked half the length of the room, unsupported.

He collapsed, shaking but jubilant into Aidan's arms before pushing himself back up, legs trembling like a newborn colt's, mouth curved into the widest smile, eyes sparkling and damp with tears of pain and excitement, as he walked back across the room. Those were the moments that Aidan worked for.

He came back to the present as Anita laughed and said, "Yeah, I saw him when he came out, boy couldn't have been happier. If he smiled any more, I thought the top of his head would flip right off."

Aidan laughed too. "I told the kid that if he can do that he should have no problems asking a girl to the prom. Shoulda seen the way he blushed, but he said he's gonna ask Sophie on Tuesday, so we have another day to practise the whole standing thing first. Apparently, she's even prettier than you."

Aidan shot Anita an extravagant wink before he pulled his red sweatshirt over his head and slid his arms through the straps of his rucksack. He dodged the slap she aimed at his arm, laughing and made his way through the doors into the cool evening air.

It was just a fifteen minute walk from the office to his house. Aidan slipped his earbuds into his ears, turning on his music player.

He cued up a playlist and let his stride lengthen into a steady pace, keeping his muscles loose and relaxed. He enjoyed the journey home, letting his body just walk, all the parts working together in a harmony of movement.

He'd made the trip so often it was now almost automatic, turning off into the woods, cutting through a corner of the parkland that spread out to the west of the town. The trail wound into the trees, the sun's low rays barely making it through the canopy above, shimmering between the trunks, illuminating the swirling clouds of gnats, occasionally cut through by the darting form of an early rising bat as they chased the erratic flutters of moths.

Aidan glanced about him, noticing the way the leaves were beginning to change, colour ripening from greens to orange and russet, the wide maple leaves gleaming vivid reds and coppers. A rabbit broke from cover ten feet up the path and Aidan went still, attention focused as he watched it pause, nose and ears twitching frantically before it seemed to spot Aidan and continued its mad dash away into the undergrowth. He looked for what could have spooked it, but saw nothing.

Eventually the trees began to thin again and Aidan shifted back onto tarmac, moving along Maple Avenue towards the corner of Pine. His house came into view and he switched off the music, slowing his pace, swinging out his arms a little more, rolling shoulders and neck. As he bent to pick up the mail, he froze, sure someone was behind him. Goosebumps tracked up his spine, sweat prickling under his arms, in between his shoulder blades.

Aidan turned, slow and steady, but there was no one there, the wide street empty on both sides. Backing through his door, he kept scanning the street until it was blocked from his view by the white wood of his closing door. He locked the door and toed off his shoes, tucking them away, before he removed his hoody, draping it over the end of the banister. A soft sigh of relief gusted out of him.

After a meal of grilled chicken and salad, Aidan finally let himself relax in front of the TV, queuing up the latest episodes of Leverage. He jolted awake to the sound of Eliot Spencer throwing someone against a wall and rubbed at his eyes, fumbling for the remote control and stopping the playback. A wide yawn had his jaw creaking and

Aidan pushed himself up from the couch, padding barefoot through the house to check the locks and windows.

He paused in front of the wide kitchen window, staring out into the garden. Again he had the strangest feeling that he was being watched but there was nothing visible in the soft, orange glow of the street light. Aidan thought about heading outside, triggering the security light, actually had his fingers on the handle of the back door before he laughed softly at himself.

"Man, just go to bed. Too much bad TV has you paranoid," he told himself. Switching off the lights he went upstairs, brushing his teeth and slipping into soft pyjama bottoms before he collapsed in a lazy sprawl on his bed. He slid under the quilt, muffling another yawn in his pillow, sleep dragging him down into its quiet embrace.

He waited outside for another minute or so, waiting to see if the light came back on inside the man's den. The building — house — remained in darkness, so he backed up before bunching his muscles and launching himself up and over the wall that surrounded the man's territory.

He tracked around the outside of the building, lifting his leg at the corner to mark the territory as well, to warn off any others that might be interested in the tall human. He sucked in air through his sensitive nose, sorting out the many scents that filled the night air.

On top of everything was his own scent, warm and musky, familiar as sunlight and breathing. Underlying that was the man's; softer, saltier, edged with juniper and the bitter sting of lime that made his upper lip curl. A faint part of his mind tried to insist that the man's scent should be stronger, but he ignored the wrongness. Another male scent that tracked all over the neighbourhood was under that but he knew he had nothing to fear from that smell, the human was older, not so virile, his scent only ever approached the door, did not linger anywhere else in the man's territory.

Keeping to the shadows, he huffed happily before he moved back towards the tree-line, following in reverse the path the man had taken earlier. He disappeared back amongst the trees, shifting through the shadows of the trunks, feet making little sound on the soft-packed needles, the newly fallen leaves that had not yet had time to dry and curl, to blow in drifts that begged to be pounced upon.

He thought back a couple of days to that morning when he had first scented his mate. It had been the first morning with a bit of chill in the air, the first sign that the season was changing, fading from the balmy heat of summer to the cooling breezes of autumn. He'd been out walking, checking on his territory when he'd stopped, entranced by the delicious scent of heat, of mate.

A Were's mating instinct was somewhat different to that of both humans and normal wolves. It was stricter, designed to stop them breeding indiscriminately. Both wolves and humans could mate quite happily with as many others as they liked, although in wolves (and sometimes in humans) the alpha tended to guard the females quite strongly. Weaker males had to resort to trickery or subterfuge.

Weres could have sex with humans if they so desired, and in fact some humans were known to seek them out, looking for the thrill, the risk, but there would never be progeny, the relationships proving sterile. Mating kept the gene pool diverse and strong. The instinct helped the Packs to prevent interbreeding by encouraging them to search outside their home territory for their mate. To this end, the Packs held gatherings throughout the year to allow different packs to meet and exchange news and let the members of each pack mingle and socialise. It also gave each Were child two parents that generally had a stronger attachment than many human relationships. A strong pack or family base was something vital for a child that could shift into a ferocious creature.

Attending so many of these gatherings as a younger adult, he had never come across the scent that called to him, that made his blood sing in his veins. After several years he'd given up, left his pack and moved out on his own. His friends and family had tried to dissuade him, a solitary life was not something most Weres sought, but he had been adamant, sure that there was something out there for him, if only he could find it. Now, finally, here in this small town he'd found him. He'd spun on his heel, moving towards the path that cut through the edge of his territory, catching a glimpse of red fabric. He followed the tempting aroma, watching as the man moved out of the trees and back onto the road, heading towards the down-town area, the office buildings and shops.

He'd stared after him, taking in the way his jeans moulded to the firm muscles of his thighs, the high curve of his ass. His upper body was hidden by the thick folds of the red sweatshirt but he had no doubt that his mate would be as strong and well-muscled there as the rest of the body appeared to be.

He'd thought about him all day at work, barely able to concentrate, pulse thudding heavily as heat pooled in his stomach. It had been so long that he was beginning to think that he was destined to be a lone wolf, to be one of the few who lived alone, without pack or family, descending into madness and frenzy as loneliness ate away at their soul.

But here he was, strong and virile and smelling delectably of juniper and cut grass and warm male. He'd changed that night, as soon as the sun had hidden its glowing red eye, letting his fur pour over him, bones twisting and reshaping, teeth lengthening. The bright artist's palette his human eyes saw faded into shades of black and grey, with dull splashes of colour, but his mind could name each distinct hue.

The change took one sense but gave back twofold, his environment erupting in a swirl of scent and noise. He could pick out each particular element of his mate's distinctive aroma, the faint mix of basil and mint in his aftershave, the juniper in his shampoo, the warm, musky scent underlying it all that was purely male. He would be able to find him anywhere now.

A flurry of sound, a muffled growl and a squeak brought him back to the present. The odour of warm iron and copper flooded his nose, the acrid stink of dog fox and rabbit. Life and death surrounded him. The noises of the town faded as he moved further into the trees. He'd marked his mate's house, claimed it, and now all he needed to do was claim his mate. He tipped his muzzle up to the moon's pale face, letting amber eyes close against her lambent glow and howled his joy to the night.

Friday came with a flurry of new placements — one referred from St

Barts, another coming in from the local football team. Aidan would have preferred the football player, something easy for a change. It was always easier working with someone that wanted to be there, that was willing to put in the same amount of effort as Aidan did.

Instead he got the referral, a sulky young man barely into his twenties, convinced his life was over now that he was going to be left with a permanent limp and scarring from the drunk driving accident that had put him in St Barts. It was Aidan's job to try and convince him that a permanent limp was better than the wheelchair; that if he worked hard and paid attention they could make it nearly unnoticeable.

It was a difficult morning, his client angry and hurt and scared but despite the swearing and the coffee that now decorated Aidan's office wall, he thought that they had made some progress. By the time it got to lunch, Aidan just needed to get out of the office. He grabbed his sandwich and a bottle of water from the small fridge in the staff room and wandered out to the small square in front of building.

All the businesses that fronted onto the square had worked together to add benches and plantings and it was a nice place to sit and talk with colleagues or just find one of the smaller seats and enjoy your lunch in the late summer sun. He was halfway through his sandwich when, once again, he had the feeling he was being watched.

He settled his sunglasses better on his nose, using the movement to hide the way he glanced around the open space. He could see Lisa and Meggie from the veterinary office across the way, but they were engrossed in dissecting last night's America's Next Top Model. Aidan shifted in his seat, reaching for his water and that's when he saw him.

It wasn't that he was stunningly attractive; although the broad shoulders that narrowed down to a slender waist and long muscled legs were certainly hot enough; it was more his stance, the complete and utter focus in his gaze, in his movements. Aidan very rarely saw people so aware of their place in their surroundings.

Aidan studied him discreetly from behind the screen of his sunglasses, tipping his head back to take a drink from his water as he did so. Thick brown hair fell around his face, the ends lightened to a tawny colour. Sunglasses hid his eyes, but drew attention to the strong line of his jaw shaded slightly with stubble, the sensual curve of his mouth beneath the dark frames.

Aidan could almost feel the man's gaze on him, the connection heating the air between them. He pulled his eyes away, concentrating on folding the wrapper his sandwich had come in, brushing away imaginary crumbs from his thighs. He felt it when the stranger left the square, the weight of his stare obvious in its absence.

All afternoon, the image of the man lingered in Aidan's mind. He buried himself in paperwork, trying to catch up on his patient notes until Anita knocked on the door and told him, "Honey, it's Friday. Go home!"

After shoving everything back into his bulging 'In' tray, Aidan locked up his office and, waving goodbye to Anita, headed out the door and home. He took the long way to his house, stopping at the store to buy beer and some groceries so that he wouldn't be forced to have cheese on toast for his dinner. Thinking about it, he probably didn't even have the fixings for toast.

As he walked along Maple Avenue, again he had the feeling that he was being watched. He paused, adjusting the groceries in his arms, but the street was empty apart from Mrs Lawrenson out on her porch. She was engrossed in her crochet work, so Aidan doubted it was her making the hairs on the back of his neck rise, his pulse stutter.

He let his pale green eyes flicker over to the other side of the road, knew he would see nothing, the undergrowth thick where the canopy fell away, letting sunlight reach the forest floor. He started walking again, gaze shifting nervously from side-to-side. Then, out of the corner of his eye, movement in the trees had his head swinging back round. A laugh burst out of him as the branches of a small bush parted to reveal the delicate head of a small deer, its ears twitching nervously as it nibbled at the green leaves.

It was probably just the strains of the day getting to him, maybe a lingering memory of that strange moment in the courtyard outside the office. Perhaps if Aidan were a shade braver, he might have had the nerve to have gone over, made a small comment on the weather or something, judged if the interest he had felt was returned.

But a bad incident in Aidan's past had left him wary about exposing himself in that way. Just the chance that the other man had noticed him, was interested, had his fight or flight instinct kicking in. Although the physical wounds had faded, the memories still lingered, buried deep in his mind. He pushed the thought away, along with the image of slim hips and long fingers, a plush mouth curved in a slight smile. He had his new start here, no one knew about his past, knew what he was, and things were going to stay that way, temptation be damned.

Saturday morning dawned bright and sunny, but with a nip in the air that had Aidan pulling on his red sweatshirt. He opened the garage and patted the trunk of his Buick lovingly. Some folk said she was an ugly car, not suited for these modern, more eco-friendly times, but Aidan loved her. He'd rebuilt her engine and she ran, smooth as silk, purring like a kitten, and she had never let him down.

He drove to the large store outside of town, pushing a trolley round as he stocked up, almost automatically. The only things that changed in his diet were the fruits as they went in and out of season. This Saturday though, he bought extra beer as well as a couple of packets of nacho chips and the ingredients for fresh guacamole and chicken fajitas. Packing the bags into the trunk he drove home, enjoying the way the road disappeared under his baby's tires.

He tucked her safely away in the garage again, promising her a wax and polish on Sunday afternoon. Once back in the house, he put most of the groceries away, leaving out the ingredients for the fajitas and the beer. Those went into a rucksack and Aidan set about making up the fresh guacamole, mashing avocado and lemon and peppers together. He sealed it in a plastic tub and placed that in the rucksack too.

Making a last round to check the house was secure, he grabbed his phone and wallet, pulling on his sneakers and sweatshirt and left the house. Aidan settled into a steady jog as he crossed the road and started making his way along the path that led deeper into the forest. He still wasn't sure how it had become a routine, wasn't even really certain of how it had all started but now, every other Saturday during football season, Aidan made his way into the woods to visit Jeffrey.

Chapter 2
An Unexpected Guest

Jeffrey was a Forest Ranger, living out in a clearing in a wooden house he claimed to have built himself, somewhere in the middle of the forest. He had a barn next door, in which he kept all his monitoring equipment. He also had a couple of cages in there for animals that he'd found in traps or those that had been injured.

That was how they had met. Jeffrey had brought a young fox into the clinic next door to Aidan's work after it had gotten some discarded tent rope trapped around its neck and leg. The vet had managed to sedate the animal enough to allow Jeffrey to remove it and had then cleaned out the wounds. Whilst the fox was recuperating Jeffrey had come out into the square and had just started talking to Aidan.

It was odd, they didn't have that much in common, but they bonded; the irascible older man, living happily on his own out in the woods and the younger man, looking for something he needed but unsure as to what it was. Jeffrey had turned up one afternoon at Aidan's work with a case of beer, two packs of sausages and an invite to watch the local football team get beat on the sixty-two inch flat-screen TV he had. Aidan couldn't think of a reason to say no.

So now it was a thing. Aidan had offered to bring food, mainly in an attempt to avoid food poisoning or an overdose of protein. He enjoyed cooking and Jeff seemed to enjoy eating it so everyone was happy. The trees started to thin out and Aidan stepped out from under the branches into a clearing. A log cabin sat in the middle of the open space, a simple two storey structure with a wide porch that sat under the overhanging roof. The shutters were thrown wide open, the white-painted inner sides contrasting with the soft tones of the aged wood of the walls.

The barn, which was really rather more of a shack, sat off to one side, door padlocked shut, a quad bike parked outside. Aidan made his way across the open space, stepping up onto the porch, almost silent in his sneakers. He knocked briefly at the door before pushing it open and making his way inside.

The door opened straight into the main living space, a large room that took up more than half of the ground floor. To Aidan's right was a small dining table, surrounded by four chairs, the door to the kitchen half open behind it. Aidan had already toed one sneaker off before he noticed that Jeffrey wasn't alone. He paused, awkwardly balanced, his socked foot hovering for a moment before it thudded to the polished wooden floor.

"Aidan, there you are, man. Just take the stuff on through to the kitchen. There's beer in the fridge already if you want a cold one." Jeffrey's voice was gruff, his bearded face cracking in a smile as he waved a hand at Aidan. He was sprawled in his usual position, the old leather recliner creaking beneath him every time he moved.

Aidan stared, mute with surprise, as the unexpected guest met his green gaze and smiled, wide and slow. Aidan's gaze dropped to the other man's mouth, watched his lips curve and part, exposing white teeth, the faintest flicker of a pink tongue. He swallowed and dropped his attention to his feet, carefully pushing off his other sneaker before he made his way to the kitchen, avoiding that wide, tempting smile.

He tucked his beer to the back of the fridge, pulling out three bottles from the front. He removed the rest of the food from his backpack, piling it up on the counter, adding the guacamole to the fridge. He pulled in another slow breath, searching for his centre, that point of relaxation and calmness that existed within and turned to head back out into the main room.

"Jeffrey, you didn't tell me you had another guest," he mock scolded, adding, "I don't know if I've got enough food."

"Ah. It's not like I knew he was coming, you know. But it would be rude to turn away a neighbour, 'specially on game day. Oh, I should introduce you guys. Aidan, this is Seth. He just moved up here, bumped into him out in the woods. 'Parently he's studying for some kind of wildlife degree or something."

Jeff turned to Seth, "This here is Aidan, works at the PT clinic in town, next to the vets office; that's how I met him."

Seth held out a hand and Aidan blinked at the long fingers, desperate to discover how they felt wrapped around his own, stroking his overheating flesh, but also sure that it was a very bad idea. Instead, he thrust one of the bottles he was carrying towards the extended hand.

"Nice to meet you, Seth." Aidan coughed and tried not to blush at the squeak in his words. He'd never been this instantly attracted to another man. He coughed again and continued in a lower register, "Didn't I see you before? The other day?"

"Yeah, in town, just trying to find my way around." Seth's voice was deep, drawling, and Aidan shifted from foot to foot. Jeff only had the recliner and the long couch Seth was currently sprawled out on. Seth patted at the other end of the couch.

"Sit down, man. I don't bite. Well, not unless you ask real nice." He grinned again, dark and dangerous and Aidan had the sudden feeling that he should really just turn around and leave. He shrugged off the disturbing thought and made his way around the coffee table Jeff had carved from a fallen tree a couple of years back, perching on the edge of the cushion at the other end of the couch.

Jeff stared at him, eyebrows raising in slight confusion before he shrugged, appearing to dismiss Aidan's odd behaviour. Aidan knew he needed to relax before Jeff decided to open his big mouth. The man lived out on his own, with only trees and birds to talk to; tact was not his strong suit. So he edged back further, resting his elbows on his knees, fingers wrapped around the chilled glass neck of his beer bottle. He stared with unseeing eyes at the pre-game show, searching his mind desperately for something to say.

Luckily he was saved by Jeff, who waved his beer expansively as he said, "Aidan here and me, we got a deal. He cooks — and he does it well by the way — and I supply the entertainment. I'm sure there'll be more than enough for us all. I got a freezer full of venison from the last deer I had to shoot. Daft thing broke its leg. What you making this time anyway?"

Aidan looked up at Jeff's question, meeting his curious brown eyes. "Thought I'd make chicken fajitas. Brought some fresh guacamole, was hoping you still had some of those tomatoes left for the salsa?"

Jeff was trying to live a sustainable life out in the forest and had been experimenting with growing different vegetables. This year conditions had been just right and Aidan had been going home laden down with tomatoes, green beans and peas as well as handfuls of salad leaves. So much in fact that he'd been taking them into work. Jeff nodded and pushed himself to his feet.

"I'll just head out and bring some in, got some late salad leaves too." Jeff placed his half-empty bottle onto a coaster and made his way to the sliding doors that led out to the back of the building.

That left Aidan alone with Seth. He picked at the label on his bottle before hauling in a deep breath, berating himself internally for being such an idiot. What was he, a twelve year old girl? He really didn't know why he was so unsettled. There wasn't any reason for it. Internal pep talk over, Aidan shifted round on the sofa until he was facing Seth, looking up from his bottle to meet that curious stare.

Aidan's breath wanted to stall in his throat as that warm, amber gaze locked on his. He'd never seen eyes quite that colour, a rich golden honey, the pupils widening slightly as Aidan continued to stare. He blinked and swallowed, lashes fluttering down to break the connection.

"So, you just moved into town? How're you finding it?" That should be a safe enough conversation starter, Aidan thought as he glanced up again. Seth was still watching him, mouth curled into a small smile.

"It's nice, getting better by the day actually." Seth smiled wider, all sharp, white teeth and flash of dimple. Aidan's stomach flip-flopped.

"Jeff said something about a degree?" Aidan continued to unconsciously pick at the label, small curls of paper falling and sticking to the leg of his jeans. Seth leant over and picked one off, raising an eyebrow in mocking enquiry.

"Oh, yeah. You know, nervous habit. Not that you make me nervous," Aidan lied quickly. "Just thinking about food and that. I should probably go get started on the chicken." He pushed himself up, socked feet silent on the wooden floor as he crossed to the kitchen door.

He had to swallow a small squeak — of surprise or dismay, he's not quite sure — when Seth followed him into the kitchen. Aidan moved to the sink and washed his hands, turning to find Seth standing there, holding out a towel. Aidan reached gingerly for it, drying his hands quickly and passing it back.

"You don't need to keep me company, you know. You should go watch the game."

"No, it's okay. If you're going to feed us, the least I can do is offer to help. Maybe chop veggies or something?" Seth widened those intriguing tawny eyes, pushing his hair away from his face. How was Aidan supposed to say no?

"Sure. Okay. You know how to make salsa?" Aidan smiled at Seth's shake of the head. "Yeah, guess it was too much to hope that you would be a great cook as well as..." Aidan cut himself off before he blurted out anything incriminating.

"When Jeff brings in the tomatoes, just rinse them off and quarter them, then just kinda chop the quarters into three. Don't want the bits too small you know? You can chop an onion too, if you like, nice and fine."

Aidan brought out the chicken strips and coated them in dressing and marinade before he put them to one side and began to carefully chop the chillies he'd bought. Jeff came in with the tomatoes and Seth washed and chopped them, piling them in the bowl Aidan passed to him. Jeff leant against the far counter, drinking his beer and talking with Seth about some insect indicator or some such thing. Aidan finally relaxed.

The fajitas were a success, even if the game was not, their team losing in the final five minutes. The beer has being going down rather too well and Aidan found himself slumped further into the cushions, beer bottle resting on his thigh as he listened to Jeff retell a story about finding a bear out in the trees a couple of years ago.

He ignored the way his gaze would keep flickering to Seth, tracing the line of his throat, the swell of his biceps as he brought his bottle to that soft-looking mouth. He found himself wondering what that mouth would feel like pressed against his own, wondered if it would taste of beer and spices or if it would be more distinctive. He swallowed hard and pushed himself off the sofa.

"Bathroom," he muttered gracelessly, just managing not to run.

He pissed and flushed and washed his hands, splashing the cool water over his heated cheeks. It was just biology, he told himself. It'd been a long time since he had anything but his own hand for company, so that's all it was, a little animal lust. Once he got home it would all be fine. There was nothing more to it than that.

Taking a deep breath he left the bathroom and went to the kitchen, bypassing the two men still sprawled in front of the TV. The sun had long since set and the night air was growing chill as Aidan packed up his bowls and spices, adding the extra tomatoes and salad Jeff had given him. He fastened up his bag and took it through to drop it by the door.

"I should probably head home, Jeff. Thanks for the beer and the veggies." Aidan smiled at the older man when he waved his hand dismissively.

"No, I should thank you. Food and company. Save me from becoming a crackpot hermit out here all by myself. You watch out on your way home, think we might have wolves moved down from up north a bit. Heard them howling couple of nights ago. Could be ordinary timbers or could be Pack."

Aidan nodded and pulled his red sweatshirt back on, the hood shadowing his face and his expression as he swallowed nervously, eyes clenching closed at the thought of Weres moving in. He folded it back around his neck and blinked at the look on Seth's face; for a brief moment he had looked hungry, almost feral, his amber eyes seeming to glow above the strong cheekbones. But when he looked back, Seth just smiled amiably at him.

"You mind if I walk back a bit with you? Still new to this whole place, don't want to get myself turned around and end up in the river, you know." He laughed, the low sound doing odd things to Aidan's pulse. Maybe he was coming down with something.

Seth pushed up from the sofa, rubbing his hands over the strong muscles of his thighs, smoothing out the denim. He turned to Jeff and Aidan did not find himself admiring the firm curve of ass, nu-uh, not at all. He flushed guiltily when Seth turned around, glad that the lighting in Jeff's place was dim, and made a fuss of checking for his phone and keys.

Jeff rose to his feet as well, walking both men to the door, clapping Seth on the back and pulling Aidan into a brief hug.

"Thanks again, fellas. Nice to have the company. You drop by any time, Seth, if you need help with that project of yours. I'll see you next time, Aidan. Oh and bring extra, just in case."

The two men moved outside, listening to Jeff lock up before they stepped off the porch and into the shadows of the trees. The moon was just past full, still casting enough light for them to find the start of the path back towards the town.

Seth smiled to himself as they stepped onto the path. Of course it wasn't just co-incidence that had led him to be at Jeff's house. Seth had found the house shortly after he had moved into the new territory, curiosity leading him to investigate. Even though Aidan wasn't a frequent visitor, his scent had lingered from the last time he was here.

He had engineered the meeting in the woods, had already known what Jeff was and had tailored his reasons for being in the forest to something Jeff would approve of. It was hard to act as a subservient beta to appease Jeff's more gruff and dominant alpha tendencies but Seth had managed it, drawing the man into conversation, securing that invite to 'drop round any time'.

Even though Weres and humans mostly kept to themselves, Seth knew enough about humans to understand their passion for sport. It was their version of the rough and tumble play of Were cubs, the modified thrill of the chase, of the hunt, even if all they were chasing was a little pigskin ball. It appeased their need for pack, for belonging as well.

His eyes sharpened as they moved into the dark beneath the trees, head tilting to compensate for the human inability to twitch his ears as he picked out the small night sounds. He was aware of Aidan next to him, body moving gracefully through the dark. He could hear the soft exhales of breath, the shift of fabric over skin, the chafe of the rougher fabric of the backpack against that red hooded top.

He wondered if Aidan would run if he flashed his fangs or would he stand and fight? Perhaps the chase was something they could do once they were mated, once Aidan was his. The thought of hunting down his mate, chasing the increasing heat of his body as muscles flexed and bunched, lungs pumping air, heart speeding to send that rich, warm blood flushing through his limbs, had Seth's fangs pushing from his gums, his cock beginning to swell.

His mind took the scenario further, had him catching Aidan, tackling his mate to the ground, rolling over and over the carpet of fallen leaves. He could almost feel the hard knob of bone at the top of Aidan's spine between his teeth, taste the warm salty flesh on his tongue. He swallowed the growl that threatened to edge between his teeth, fangs catching on the sensitive inner lip.

"Sorry, you say something, Seth?" Aidan's voice came out of the dark from farther down the path. Seth hadn't even realised that he had stopped walking. He jogged briefly to catch up, shaking his head before he realised that Aidan would barely see it in the dark.

"Nah. Just thought I heard something out in the trees."

"What, you afraid of the big, bad wolf?" Aidan giggled, slightly drunk, defences down in the sheltering dark. "My, my, what big eyes you have," he cranked his voice up into a squeaky falsetto.

"All the better to see you hiding in the trees." This time his voice came out in a low growl that went straight to Seth's libido. He barely bit back his own growl as Aidan continued through his laughter, pushing his voice high again.

"My, my, what big teeth you have."

"All the better to bite you with." Seth closed his eyes at the sound of his own voice, dark and full of promise. He heard the spike of Aidan's pulse as he reacted to the threat, backing away from Seth. Seth kept his eyes closed, knew they would be glowing slightly as the Were inside him rose to the surface. It didn't matter that he couldn't see Aidan; he knew exactly where he was.

"I should go home." Aidan's voice was soft, giggles long gone as he swallowed, sobriety returning on a rush of adrenaline. Seth held his breath, listening for the sound of footsteps fading into the distance.

When they didn't come he opened his eyes, blinking at the face in front of him, Aidan's eyes wide and wary but also determined.

"You should come with me." It was barely a whisper, Aidan's breath ghosting across Seth's skin. His tongue flickered out to moisten his lips and Seth couldn't drag his gaze away from the soft curve that now glimmered faintly in the pale glow of the moon. He reached out and dragged the pad of his thumb over the ripe swell, before sucking it into his own mouth, getting the faintest taste of Aidan.

He heard Aidan swallow, saw his tongue dart out again, blood pulsing heavy in his veins as the scent of arousal deepened around them.

"No, I really shouldn't. You don't know — there are things I should tell you first..." He fought back the urge to deny the words, to reach out and take what had been offered, instead he let the soft look of confusion and disappointment fade from Aidan's face, replaced by realisation and something that looked like relief.

"No, you're right. I should go home, sleep it off. I'll — I'll see you around, I guess?"

Aidan raised a hand in a brief salute and turned and disappeared into the darkness. Seth watched him go, dropping to his knees, hands fisting in the dirt as he swallowed against the need to claim his mate, to hunt and capture and take what was his. Yes, he was part beast, but he was also part man and he wanted his mate to come to him sober and aware.

But he had made the first move, now he just had to court him, to show that he was a good provider, able to take care of his mate. The faint scent of Aidan still lingered, something slightly unusual about it, and Seth sucked in a slow breath, savouring the cool air before he made his own way home.

Chapter 3

Losing Control

Aidan let his lashes fall as the mouth moved lower, tracking over the burning flesh of his chest. A tongue flickered over a raised nipple before it was sucked into the warm cavern of a mouth and Aidan moaned softly as teeth nipped gently at the sensitive flesh. The hot, open-mouthed kisses moved lower, trailing down over the ridges of his abdominals, nipping and sucking at the thin skin over his hips.

He groaned, reaching for the waves of dark hair that tickled against his abdomen, wanting to push the teasing mouth lower, to get it to where he wanted it, needed it. A gentle laugh echoed in the still of the room and there was a harder suck right over the arch of his hipbone, bringing blood flushing to the surface.

Aidan's hips jerked and twitched and he sighed and began to plead softly, his cries interrupted by a clatter and a dull thud. The taunting hands, the pleasing mouth pulled away and Aidan reached out, desperately wanting them back. A low rumbling noise covered his pleas and Aidan surfaced from his dream to the sound of next door mowing their lawn.

He buried his face in his pillow, cock hard and aching beneath him and he ground down against the bed, jamming his hand into his pyjama bottoms, fingers clenching and tugging. It wasn't what he wanted, what he needed, but he tightened his grip, jerked harder, faster, until he came in hot spasms over his hand and the sheets crumpled beneath him.

Sighing, he pushed up from the sticky sheets and pulled off his pyjamas, dumping them on top of the bed. He went and showered, letting the warm spray clear the rest of the fog from his head. Picking up the damp towels as well as the bed linens, he wandered downstairs, starting the washing machine before he made himself coffee.

He sipped it slowly, trying to ignore the urge to go out for a run in the trees, just in case he bumped into a certain amber-eyed man. He had no wish to encourage the attraction any further. In fact it was probably better if he tried to avoid Seth altogether. He had a feeling that there was more to Seth than most people knew; something in the way he stood, his awareness. If anyone would be able to discover Aidan's secret it would be someone like Seth and that was the last thing he wanted.

Aidan traipsed back up to the bathroom and picked up a bottle of sunscreen. Unscrewing the lid, he tipped out a plastic bag. He unsealed the top and fished inside, fingers reaching for one of the tablets. He pulled one out and swallowed it, taking a couple of mouthfuls of water from the tap to help wash it down. He counted the rest of the pills; only five left. He'd need to make a trip out of state to get more. He cursed under his breath. It was unusual for him to let his stash get this small.

He'd email Jordan now; see if they could work something out about getting some delivered instead. It was riskier, but better than running out. He tucked the remaining pills back in their hiding place and stowed the bottle back on the shelf.

It was shameful, but Aidan hid out in his house for the rest of the day, only going out to collect his Sunday newspapers and some fresh rolls from the bakery. At least his house was a lot tidier now than it had been. He thought about phoning in sick but knew that he couldn't let his clients down, and he needed the money. Especially now he had to pay Jordan again.

His phone beeped late on Monday afternoon. An anonymous caller left a message that read: 'J out of town. Supp stock low. Can get u 10 on Fri, more nxt wk.' Aidan sucked his bottom lip between his teeth. It would mean he would be without for two days, but it was probably the best deal he could get. He sent a message back with his acceptance and thanks.

Ten minutes later another message came through. 'Meet Fri, 8.30. SG. Bring cash.' Aidan noted the time and place and deleted the texts. He'd need to get to the bank. Work kept him busy but by Wednesday afternoon, he was beginning to feel the effects of the suppressants wearing off. Everything was beginning to smell stronger. After being muffled for so long it was almost overwhelming. His sense of smell was heightened anyway but now he could scent what people had had for breakfast, whether they'd been with someone else the night before. Seemed like Anita had a new boyfriend.

By Thursday he could hear the therapist in the next room, could hear the faint hum of the water filtration system for the hydrotherapy pool. He tried his best to ignore the growing thrum of his senses coming back online. It was like his whole body had been muffled in cotton wool and suddenly something had torn it all away, exposing him to a loud, bright kaleidoscope of feelings. He didn't like it all.

He wrapped up his last session abruptly, forgoing his normal shower; instead just shoving his street clothes into his rucksack and pulling sweatpants and his red fleecy top on over his shorts and t-shirt. He just needed to get back to his house, lock himself away for the night. He would call in sick tomorrow; it wasn't like he didn't have sick days coming. One perk of his condition was that he seldom caught the viruses that seemed to fly around.

He smelt Seth as soon as he went out into the Reception area and his eyes went wide, gaze darting madly around the small room, relief rushing through him when he realised Seth wasn't there. Anita beamed at him from behind her desk and rolled her eyes at the large wicker basket sitting on the corner of her desk.

"You are a naughty, naughty boy, Aidan McCormack! Keeping secrets from me." Anita beckoned him closer to the desk and, against his better judgement, Aidan sat himself down on the spare corner. "Why are you keeping him a secret? Oh my lord, he's gorgeous. Where did you meet him? And more importantly, does he have a straight twin brother?"

Anita turned her brown eyes up to his, rested her chin on her hand and circled with the other hand, her signal to him to spill all his dirty, little secrets. Aidan raised a hand and uncurled his thumb, pushing against it as he counted of his first point.

"One, I'm not keeping him a secret. I've only really met him once, he's probably more Jeff's friend than mine." He raised his index finger.

"Two, why would you even assume that Seth is that way inclined or would be interested in me? And three, no I don't think he has a twin and did he really bring me a basket? What's in it?"

Anita grinned at his curiosity and stood up, grabbing at Aidan's raised fingers. She folded one away and said, smirking. "Oh, I can tell. Take a look at what I'm wearing."

Aidan looked at her, taking in the red, v-necked, short-sleeved knit top that clung lovingly to her curves, revealing the soft swell of her breasts, hinting at the lacy cups of her bra as she leant forward on the desk. His gaze tracked down to a tiny waist and the viola curve of hip, emphasised by the tight, black pencil skirt she was wearing.

"Yeah, that was the look I got off him. Look over at Steve." Aidan glanced sideways and caught the heated look that Steve was giving Anita as she bent over the desk towards the basket. She smiled fondly at Aidan and folded down another of his fingers.

"Why wouldn't he be interested in you? You're cute enough in your own, weird way. Okay, you seem a little too attached to that red hooded top, but you've got that kind of buff, military look down, and those gorgeous green eyes. You're funny, dedicated, kind—you're a total catch, honey."

She tucked away the last of his fingers and handed him the basket. "Three, I have no idea what's in there, but it smells good, so I'd take it home and find out. Go on, get." Anita shooed him towards the door and Aidan gave her a faint smile.

"You know I'm right. I'll be expecting a proper introduction next time!" Aidan just raised his hand in acknowledgement and farewell, pushing the door open and heading out into the chill evening air.

He felt kind of strange walking home with a wicker basket held in his hand. At least the cloth was a dark blue stripe, rather than a pink gingham check or something equally girly. He placed it on the counter in his kitchen, stepping back into the hall to remove his shoes and top, checking the locks on the door.

He'd been able to tell some of what was in the basket as soon as he had picked it up, his nose twitching at the scent of cooked chicken, the sharp aroma of rocket leaves. He padded back into the kitchen and opened it up. A small folded note lay on top and Aidan lifted it off, looking at the array of foodstuffs inside.

There was chicken; a cooked one from the deli across town, its skin crispy and brown, still slightly warm from the oven. Next to the chicken was a ziploc bag full of salad leaves from Jeff's garden; tangy rocket, the small ovals of baby spinach leaves, the curled edges of lettuce. There were tomatoes too and a cardboard box that opened to reveal a rich, dark chocolate brownie, the bitter scent of chocolate and hazelnuts making Aidan's mouth water.

Hunger curled in his gut and he pulled out the chicken, sinking his teeth into the warm flesh, tearing at the meat, swallowing down the savoury flesh with a low moan of pleasure. He was on his third mouthful when a slight noise from outside had his head jerking up. He paused, staring at his reflection in the window, aghast. He had the whole chicken cradled in his palms, fingers curled tight around the carcass, juices dripping down his chin. His eyes glowed softly. He dropped the bird with a soft cry of dismay, backing away from the counter until his back hit the wall.

His legs folded beneath him until he was sitting on the floor, knees up in front of him, a protective barrier. He could still taste the chicken, his tongue slipping out to glide over his lips, seeking the remaining traces. Dropping his head to his knees, Aidan sucked in several slow breaths, fighting for control.

Eventually he pulled himself back to his feet, giving himself a stern pep talk. It was only one more day. So what if he had a little lapse in control, it wasn't like anyone could have seen him. He just had to make it through tonight and tomorrow, then he'd get his meds and everything would go back to normal.

He pulled out a plate and mixed up a small amount of salad, slicing some meat from the chicken and placing it on the plate which he took to the table and ate carefully with a knife and fork, not like a ravening animal. He allowed himself a small piece of chocolate brownie, closing his eyes as the gooey, bitter-sweet cake melted on his tongue.

He carefully washed and put away the crockery, wiping down the counter top. It was then that he remembered the note. He reached out for the piece of paper, unfolding it with only the slightest shake to his fingers as the warm scent of brambles and forest that was distinctively Seth rose from the paper.

Just to say thank you for the meal the other day. I really enjoyed meeting you and would like to get together again sometime. Hope you like brownies. Seth.

Aidan blinked at the nondescript message. He'd been expecting something more... just more he supposed. He lifted the paper closer to his nose, inhaling the faint traces of Seth that still lingered, his cock thickening slightly, body warming and loosening. A soft groan slipped from between lips that were unconsciously curving in a smile.

Tucking the paper away safely, Aidan took himself upstairs for a shower; a nice, cold one was probably appropriate.

He woke up in the small dark hours of the night, sheets wrapped around his calves and thighs, the cotton damp with sweat. His skin was flushed, burning, cock standing up proudly from the trimmed nest of curls at his groin.

Aidan fought with the fabric tangled round his limbs, ripping it away and almost falling from the bed. He staggered to his feet, cock bobbing in front of him. He palmed it, pressing the hard length of it up against his stomach, hips jerking forward slightly as his body sought the welcome friction.

He gasped for breath, a welter of scents confusing his hind brain; the musk of his arousal, sharp mint of his toothpaste and underneath that bramble and growing things. That! That was what he needed. Seth would help him. He was so hot — why was he so hot? Outside — get outside, cooler there. A small part of himself cried out in denial, realising what the burning flush, the desperate ache between his thighs meant. But after being suppressed for so long, his hormones were in control.

Aidan barely remembered to grab the pair of pyjama pants that he had thrown over the back of the chair earlier. He jerked them swiftly up over his hips, moaning at the feel of the brushed cotton against his aroused dick. Rubbing it gently with the palm of his hand, he stumbled downstairs.

Hand automatically reaching for his red hooded sweatshirt that hung in the hall, he made his way through the kitchen, heading for the back door and the relief of the cool night air. Locking the door behind him he stared up at the night sky and the three quarter moon that hung there, pregnant with promise.

The fresh air brought relief and Aidan sighed softly as the burning need abated somewhat. He moved farther into the garden, shoving his keys into the front pocket of his top. Perhaps a quick walk, some mindless exercise to relax his muscles, to ease away the spiral of tension in the pit of his stomach; then he could go back home, try to sleep until he could get his meds.

Seth jerked back into the shelter of the trees as Aidan walked through his back gate, heading straight towards him. His eyes flared amber as he took in the other man's appearance. That stupid red hooded top, the one that caught Seth's eye in the first place, bright and garish to both wolf and human side, clashed with a pair of blue striped pyjama pants.

His feet were bare, moving soundlessly across the stretch of grass that separated the row of gardens from the trees. Seth moved further back into the darkness under the trees, gaze fixed on the man walking towards him.

The slight breeze shifted slightly, blowing from behind Aidan, carrying his scent towards Seth. Seth could barely swallow down the growl that curled up from his stomach as he scented the arousal surging off his mate. The tinge of *wrongness* that had marked his smell previously was gone, now Aidan smelt purely of Were and arousal and *need*. Seth's fangs pushed against his gums, breaking through as his cock began to swell.

Seth moved silently through the trees, keeping downwind of Aidan as he began to jog slowly along the path that wound deeper into the forest. Seth watched the long legs, the high curve of Aidan's ass and another growl trickled out between the sharp points of his canines. The temptation could not be ignored.

He sped up, almost noiseless on the soft carpet of pine needles and last year's decayed leaf matter. As he moved closer his Were side began to pick up on the signals oozing from Aidan's pores and everything clicked into place in Seth's mind. The way that Aidan's scent had been almost muffled before, the fact that it was now so strong, almost overpoweringly so; Seth wanted to both groan with despair and leap on his mate at the same time.

Aidan was Were. Not only was he Were but he was a beta, a submissive; a submissive that had been suppressing his nature with chemicals, chemicals that were wearing off rapidly, allowing him to come into heat. Seth growled again, his dominant side rising, lips curling back to reveal the sharp curve of his canines. This time Aidan must have heard him, his head twitching round, eyes shining in the faint shafts of moonlight that made it through the branches spreading above them.

Seth stepped out onto the path, showing himself. He was a dominant, he had no need to hide his nature, aware of his needs, his desires. He inhaled deeply, pulling more of Aidan's warm scent into his lungs, across his tongue, until he could almost taste the salty skin, the heated flesh. A low rumble worked its way up through his chest, spilling out into the still air between the two men. A soft whimper left Aidan's mouth, eyes widening further. Seth would put good money on the bet that if he were closer he would be able to see Aidan's pupils wide and dilated, the irises a glowing green ring around that deep, dark core.

He stalked forward, gait loose and rolling, cock hardening in his jeans. He ran a hand down the centre line of his chest, fingers trailing over the glint of belt buckle, stopping just before the hard line that was beginning to push up against the denim at his crotch.

Aidan's eyes dropped to follow Seth's hand, and Seth grinned, all teeth and dark promise. Time seemed to freeze around them as Seth took another step forward, almost within reach. The small nocturnal animals had already gone quite around them, sensing the threat, but not sure whether it was aimed at them.

A tongue flicked out, wetting Aidan's lips, saliva gleaming on the soft bow. His hand rose slowly up, almost as if he were reaching out towards Seth. Seth gave a satisfied rumble, taking another step forward, his mate now within reach. He reached out, and at the point his fingers made contact with Aidan's wrist, Aidan flinched, darkness fluttering in the depths of those green eyes.

"No, can't... hurt me..." The words were barely a breath, if Seth hadn't been a Were he never would have made them out. Aidan blinked and suddenly turned and ran. Seth hesitated for a long moment, bewildered and angry at the denial. Instinct roared through him and, unable to deny it, he gave chase.

Sprinting after Aidan, he slowed his pace once he drew closer, driving Aidan through the trees, pushing him subtly towards Seth's house. Aidan may have been Were, but he had been suppressing it for so long he didn't have the same control over his body, over his nature. All too soon, the stress of the chase, the hormones racing around his body had him slowing, the all out run turning into a long lope.

Seth steered him towards the clearing that held the modest cottage he was renting, moving up on his left side, making Aidan veer right. Aidan hit the clearing and paused, taking a moment to examine the house, wondering if it would offer sanctuary.

Taking full advantage of his mate's distraction, Seth pounced, catching his submissive around the waist, pulling him down onto the soft carpet of grass and herbs that surrounded the small building. They rolled over and over, Aidan bucking and twisting beneath him, breath heaving out in wild gusts and soft whimpers.

Eventually, Seth's greater strength and control won out and he pinned Aidan, hands above his head, one thigh thrust up between Aidan's parted legs. Seth dipped his head, fastening his teeth around the soft arch of Aidan's neck, worrying gently at the sensitive skin, tongue fluttering out to taste the salty sweetness.

Aidan submitted as soon as the teeth closed on his throat, neck arching in invitation, his Were nature winning out over his frightened human side. Seth took advantage, licking at the expanse of skin, trailing kisses up along the line of Aidan's jaw, down over his cheek, searching out that pink bow of a mouth that has been starring in some of his dreams.

Aidan opened his mouth to Seth on a soft sigh, head tilting to allow Seth to sink in deep, his tongue sliding past the soft swell of lip, the edge of emergent fangs to tangle around the heated slickness of Aidan's. Seth kept the kiss slow and gentle, allowing Aidan's pulse to slow a little after the chase. He could sense his mate's nervousness, the tension that fought against the rising burn of arousal.

Seth slid off of Aidan, keeping one hand wrapped around Aidan's wrist as he pulled them both up. He leant into Aidan, peppering his swollen mouth with soft biting kisses as he steered them both towards the cottage. Pulling Aidan in against his side, Seth snuggled his mate close as he unlocked the door and ushered him inside.

Chapter 4

Secrets Revealed

"What are we... where... you...?"

Seth smiled and turned, closing the door before he turned back to Aidan, pushing him back up against the wall in the small entrance way, nuzzling up under his neck until Aidan mewled softly and arched his hips up and away from the wall, seeking the pressure of Seth's pelvis against his.

"This is my place. You'll be safe here. Let me take care of you. Gonna treat you so good, baby. Gonna make you howl my name."

Seth toed off his shoes and placed another kiss on Aidan's softly pouted mouth. He smiled and rubbed a thumb along the arch of Aidan's cheekbone, feeling the soft flutter of lashes as Aidan's eyes fell closed.

"Stay here. I'll be right back." Aidan heard his footsteps move through the house, followed by the sound of a tap turning on, water gushing into a sink. Seth came back quickly, bringing a cloth that he had soaked in some warm water. He dropped to his knees in front of Aidan, smirking at the low groan and the twitch of hips that Aidan couldn't hide. He lifted one of Aidan's feet and carefully wiped away the dirt and crushed leaves that stuck to the bare skin. He repeated his actions with the other foot and rose back up, dropping the cloth carelessly to the floor.

Senses finally working fully, Aidan got a noseful of Seth's scent as his body unfolded and Aidan stared at him, pupils wide, breath coming in slight pants. "You're a... you're like... oh gods you..."

"Yes, I'm Were, like you. I knew there was something about you, something that drew me to you. But you didn't smell right, not like you do now — all ripe and hot and ready for me." Seth licked at Aidan's mouth, seeking entrance, pressing his mouth hard against Aidan's before easing back, sucking at his lower lip, nibbling at the top one. He swallowed the low noises that leaked from Aidan's lips, until the hall filled with the warm aroma of arousal.

Pulling back, he tugged Aidan after him, moving along the hall to his bedroom. Aidan froze momentarily in the doorway until Seth brought the captured wrist up to his mouth, scraping his fangs against the tender inner wrist, feeling Aidan's pulse race against his mouth. Something seemed to snap in Aidan at this point and he pushed forward, knocking Seth backwards on to the bed, following him down.

Bodies connected chest to thigh, Aidan shifting to allow his legs to fall on either side of Seth's hips, aligning his pelvis with Seth's, grinding down with a soft cry of pleasure. Seth let Aidan take control for a moment, opening his mouth to allow Aidan's tongue in, caressing it with his own, sucking gently at the tip.

A short burst of involuntary laughter brushed over Aidan's face as he pushed his hands up under Seth's shirt, tickling the sensitive skin above his waist. Aidan pulled back from the kiss and repeated the motion, mouth curving in a smile as he discovered Seth's weakness.

Seth growled and flipped them over, taking control of the situation again. Leaning back on his heels a little, he pushed the red sweatshirt up, baring an impressively ridged abdomen, the dimple of bellybutton and the small trickle of hair that ran down from it, disappearing beneath the waistband of Aidan's pyjama bottoms.

Seth pushed the top all the way off, swooping back down to take Aidan's mouth in another heated kiss, hips rubbing down against the increasing swell of Aidan's cock. He pulled his mouth away from those lushly swollen, dark pink lips to pay attention to the long line of Aidan's throat, placing small kisses down the length of it, scraping teeth over the ridge of collarbone, sucking his mark into the heated flesh just beneath.

He wanted to take his time exploring his mate's body, wanted to suck and lick at each dark peak of a nipple until they were swollen and flush with blood, wanted to trail his tongue down the ridges of Aidan's stomach, nibble at the tight skin around his navel, feel the hard length of his cock bob and strain against him, begging for attention.

He also wanted to be buried deep in Aidan's body, shoved in hard up to the hilt, tied to him, filling him up until he screamed with pleasure.

Aidan writhed on the bed beneath Seth as he tormented his flesh with nips and sucks. He could feel his heart pounding in his chest, his cock straining against the soft flannel of his pyjama bottoms, hips trying to push up towards Seth, desperately seeking friction. He edged Seth's shirt higher, wanting it off, wanting to feel the heat of the other man's skin against his own. The way the other man held him down, had just flipped him over and taken control, had Aidan's submissive side rolling over, belly up.

His heat flared through him, blanking his mind, any semblance of rational thought flaring and blowing away like ashes, consumed by the fire burning inside him. He shivered as the warm body above him pulled away slightly, moaning happily as it returned, bare to the waist, skin sliding smooth over his sweat-slicked torso. He pulled Seth's mouth back down to his, lapping at the curve of lip, seeking the damp interior, the ridges of teeth, the firm muscle of Seth's tongue as it tangled with his own.

He continued to grind his hips upwards; slow, teasing movements that brought him closer and closer to the edge. His mind fogged with desire, he allowed Seth to ease his pyjamas down over his hips, his cock bobbing up towards his stomach, head damp and glistening in the low light.

Seth pulled away to remove the last of his clothing and Aidan gave a soft cry as he slid back over him, his hard length brushing up against the smooth line of Aidan's cock. The heady aroma of dominant male, the salty taste of his skin, the delicious heat and pressure of the other body against his own made Aidan moan again, rubbing himself hard against the velvet skin that covered the hard curve of Seth's pelvis. Close, so close, just... just...

His body froze and stiffened as Seth's fingers slid down between

them, over the tight, drawn-up skin of his balls, tickling the skin behind, moving towards Aidan's tight furl. He pulled away from the
memory, body still desperately needing release even as that small
scared part of his mind tried to make him move away. Aidan twisted his hips, trying to push them down into the bed, to avoid Seth's
seeking fingers, whilst maintaining that delicious pressure against his
dick. He wrapped his hand around the length of Seth's cock, tugging
upwards in a slight twisting movement, hoping to distract the other
man.

Seth groaned into his neck, and his teeth scraped against him; that
faint reminder of his dominant nature pushing the human side of him
away again. Seth thrust into Aidan's hand and Aidan relaxed further
still, the tension that had suddenly rushed through him ebbing away
again as he palmed the head of Seth's cock, the semi-hard shaft, feeling the loose skin at the base start to swell slightly as Seth drew closer
to orgasm. He just needed a few more moments, but then Seth was
pulling away from his neck, sliding down his body, mouth closing
over the small, hard nub of a nipple, tongue flicking at it as his teeth
grazed the skin around it, stoking Aidan's arousal higher again.

Seth paid equal attention to the other side of Aidan's chest and
Aidan felt his nerves recede, overcome once more by the rising tide
of pleasure. Seth moved lower still and Aidan felt warm, wet heat
close over the head of his dick. He pushed himself up slightly, looking
down the length of his body to watch the damp head of his cock re-
emerge from between Seth's plush lips, chased by the pink flutter of
his tongue as it lapped up from root to head, curling around the small
pearl of pre-come that leaked from the tip.

Aidan's head fell back as a low moan echoed around the room,
followed by a soft hum from Seth as he swallowed down the length
of Aidan's shaft. Seth bobbed his head up and down the silken shaft,
sucking hard, swirling his tongue around the tip. Aidan couldn't hold
back the low growls that spilled from his lips, the soft pleas for more,
murmured blasphemies and wordless sounds.

He could feel his balls draw up harder, his orgasm spiralling
tighter and tighter, ready to flood through him, he was just... right on
the edge...

Then Seth slipped his fingers back behind Aidan's testicles, tracing across the velvet soft skin, pressing gently against the hidden pucker and Aidan froze. Past memories overrode his need to submit, to orgasm, and panic flared through him, instant and unstoppable. He jerked away, falling off the bed in his frenzy, legs clamping together, hard-on wilting away, eyes and mouth wide.

"No, no, please... please..." His body fought with his mind; the Were side of him wanting to complete the mating so suddenly denied it, his mind urging him to fight or flee, to escape. His legs scrabbled on the floor, pushing his body into the corner, half behind the small bedside cabinet. His gaze flickered around the room, taking it in in a flood of images.

A soft comforter, in shades of dark blue, spilled onto the floor from the end of the maple framed bed. The cabinet beside him was maple as well, the pale golden wood contrasting with the darker wood of the floor. A door on the wall beside him was just cracked open, the tile of the floor indicating its purpose. The door to the hall was on the far wall, on the other side of the bed. The bed on which Seth was kneeling, eyes wide with surprise and worry.

Aidan could only curl further into the corner, away from the more dominant Were. He could feel his head still shaking back and forth in negation even as Seth remained on the bed. He could hear a small, angry growl rumbling up from the broad chest, but Seth's gaze was on the rumpled sheets, his emotions hidden from Aidan. He braced himself for Seth's attack, but nothing happened. Aidan stared, wide-eyed, as Seth backed away, amber light fading from his gaze, reaching for the grey pyjama bottoms that had fallen to the floor.

Seth pulled them on, hiding the fading evidence of his arousal, and circled round the base of the bed, pulling the comforter with him. He draped it over Aidan's legs, wrapping it round him and Aidan could only stare at him, confused, his flip-flopping emotions beginning to take their toll.

"You're not... you won't...?"

Seth tucked the material around him some more, a hurt expression flickering across his face. He looked away from Aidan for a moment, pulling in a slow breath. "No. Come on. Why don't we get up off the floor? I'll bring you some tea. I've some camomile, or maybe peppermint? Or hot chocolate?" Seth rose to his feet, and Aidan struggled to make sense of the emotions that flickered across his features, before Seth settled on a blank, faint smile.

Feeling vaguely ashamed and very confused, Aidan gave a small nod to the last suggestion and Seth disappeared through the door. Aidan pushed himself up, finding his discarded pyjama bottoms, pulling them back on before he wrapped the comforter around himself, edging slowly out the door. He padded down the hall, almost silent apart from the soft shush of the comforter trailing along the floor behind him. Seth looked up from the pan he was using to warm the milk.

"You could have stayed in the room, but I can see why you'd feel more comfortable out here. Go sit down and you can tell me why you nearly hit the roof back there." Seth's tone was calm, his smile a little more genuine this time and Aidan fought the urge to just give in to his Were nature, to let the more dominant male take care of everything.

"I don't..." Aidan tried to demur, really not wanting to talk about it all, just wanting to go home and forget that any of this had happened. His body fought against him though, stomach curling at the soft look Seth gave him, pulse speeding at the glimpse of chest as Seth turned round to fetch cups, the stretch of muscles in his back as he moved to pull down the jar of cocoa.

The warm smells of Seth's home assaulted his sensitive nose. The lingering aroma of coffee from that morning, the chicken from Seth's dinner, and over that, layered again and again, the scent of Seth himself. The Were in him reacted to the strong smell of the dominant's lair. It made Aidan want to tip his head back, expose the length of his throat, his vulnerable belly, but his human side was firmly in the driving seat now, the fear overriding everything, making him hunch up to the safety of the table.

Seth finished making the drinks and brought the two mugs over to the table, setting one in front of Aidan and sitting himself kitty corner. It means that he has a good view of Aidan, without being opposed to him. He took a sip and nodded towards Aidan's cup. Aidan cupped his hands around the warm ceramic and took a slow drink. It's good and the heat and comfort of the drink relaxed him a little.

"So, when did it happen?" Seth's question was quiet but cutting, straight to the issue that lies between them.

"A while... years ago... how did you...?" Aidan blinked at his inability to complete a sentence, staring at the smooth liquid in front of him.

"I'm an Alpha. Occasionally, you hear about these things happening, sometimes you get to see the after effects. I never thought it was right, never thought the beta was asking for it just because of their hormones. Did you start the suppressants then? What did your pack say?"

Aidan's gaze shot up, green eyes wide and almost guilty.

"Oh no! Don't tell me that was your first time. You didn't know?"

Aidan stared down at the table, memory rushing through him. It was just over eight years ago, but now it feels like it was yesterday.

"We weren't part of a pack," he started gently, words faint, pushed from him. "My dad's job took him off for weeks at a time so I never had a male Were to explain things. My mother had died when I was little so I never had a beta either to learn from. We never really mixed with Weres actually, kinda off the radar. I guess my dad had issues." Aidan swallowed hard and took another slow sip of cocoa, cradling the mug to his chest, a fragile barrier against the memories.

"It was late summer. I'd been feeling off for a couple of days; everything was just too much, too noisy, too smelly. I couldn't sleep properly, the sheets itched against my skin, I was always tossing and turning. Then I had these hot flushes whenever a cute guy would walk past. I already knew I was gay, but this was much more than just being... you know... interested."

Aidan placed his cup on the table and wrapped his arms around himself. "Nobody had told me what to expect. I had no idea what was happening to me, why I felt the way I did." He turned large green eyes up to Seth, meeting his gaze briefly before he stared back at the edge of the quilt, twisted in between his fingers.

"I don't know how they found out. They weren't from town, maybe they were just driving through. Anyway, this truck pulled up next to me when I was walking home. Had two guys in it. And they just—just the way they looked at me—like they wanted to eat me up. Had my skin burning and my cock rubbing up against the front of my shorts."

A slow tear trickled down the side of Aidan's face and he turned away from Seth, ashamed. Seth reached out slowly, making sure that Aidan could see the movement before he made contact.

"It's okay. You don't have to go on if you don't want to." Seth's thumb rubbed slow circles on the back of Aidan's arm.

"I didn't want to, but it was like my body didn't care. I climbed into that truck and they drove out to this cheap motel somewhere. By the time we got there, the guy who wasn't driving had his hand down my shorts. My skin was so hot and I kept grinding up against him, like some kind of cheap whore. He kept telling me what a good bitch I was, how he was gonna make me take his knot and then he'd pass me over to his friend. I wanted to say no, I really did."

Aidan turned green eyes round to Seth, lashes spiked beneath the glitter of unshed tears.

"That was my first time." The words are so faint, just a whisper against the rim of the mug. Anger flared hard and fast in Seth, Aidan could smell it, could sense his pulse speeding, hear the tiny growl that trickled from between his lips.

"That's when I looked for some way of getting rid of it. I knew no-one could make me not Were, but they gave me pills that could suppress it, that would suppress everything. I've been taking them ever since. I've had boyfriends since then, but they've always been human and I've never–" Aidan looked around the room and continued in a rush, "It's only ever been handjobs or blowjobs."

Seth sat back in his chair, his thumb still rubbing slow circles on Aidan's arm. Aidan could feel the heat radiating from that small point of contact, sending slow sparks of pleasure up his arm, into his chest. Aidan studied him from under his lashes, the anger in Seth feeding some small needy part deep inside.

"Did they tell you what had happened? When you asked for suppressants?" Aidan blinked at the question and then shook his head. "No, it was pretty much an 'Ask me no questions' deal. I didn't ask how they got them, they didn't ask why I wanted them. As long as I paid up and kept it discreet. So no. You know what it is? Why it's happening again?"

Seth nodded and curled his fingers around Aidan's hand, thumb rubbing into the curled palm, easing out some of the tension. "It's called heat. Even though it's not strictly a heat like female animals go through. I mean you're not suddenly going to get pregnant or anything." Seth grinned and Aidan relaxed a little more, untangling his hand to take another sip of cocoa.

"It's more a kind of signal, that the betas send out to attract their mates. It shows us that you're receptive to being courted. Once a beta is mated the females will continue to have a less intense version of it when they're most fertile. Males tend to grow out of it. I guess since you hid yourself and never mated, it's been kinda building up inside you. And then I turned up and things kinda spiralled from there."

Seth's brow creased in a frown, and his lip pulled in between his teeth. Aidan waited, gaze flickering up and down until Seth continued.

"I'm sorry I'm going to ask this. You don't have to answer but did they... did they injure you?" Aidan could hear the pain in Seth's voice, pain that was for him and he turned slightly in his seat, placing his near empty cup on the table. He traced the grain with his finger, eyes fixed on the wood as he answered.

"No. I guess I was lucky they'd been drinking most of the afternoon. The first one came real quick and he was kinda small." An inadvertent laugh followed that statement. "By the time he could pull out the other guy was so worked up he couldn't get his knot in. He tried with his fingers but I think he was too drunk and too frustrated. He made me jerk him off and then they left me there. I was injured sure, they smacked me around a little when they couldn't get off properly, and they didn't prep me and it did hurt, but nothing, you know, permanent."

Aidan felt a little lighter for finally having told someone, someone who wasn't judging him, who was on his side. A small yawn escaped and he blinked slowly, drained.

"Come on, you should sleep. You can stay here. There aren't that many Weres around but your scent is pretty strong. My scent should throw them off if they come looking." Aidan pushed from the table, another yawn cracking his jaw as he followed behind Seth, confused and enervated.

Seth must have seen his puzzled look because he continued, "You know you're in heat again? Quite frankly you smell delicious, edible, hot, wet, ripe..." He cut himself off with a sheepish grin. "Yeah, so, I'm sure I can control myself enough not to rape you in the middle of the night, especially now that I know what happened. I'm sorry about earlier, really really sorry. If I'd known... I thought you were just playing but still, that's not an excuse."

Aidan stopped in the bedroom doorway, turned to Seth and placed a hand gently on his shoulder. "You're right, you didn't know. How could you? But you did stop when I said no. That makes you different. And you're still respecting my decision even though I can see your body wants to ignore it." Aidan's eyes tracked the still emergent fangs, just hidden by the full curve of Seth's lip, the firm line in his pyjamas.

"Thank you." Aidan slipped through the door, still wrapped in the comforter and curled up on the bed. Seth pushed the door closed and slumped against it, swallowing the low moan that rose out of his chest.

Chapter 5

Heat

Maybe if he went and stood next to the open freezer. Seth tried not to touch the long line of his cock where it curved up, pushing out the front of his pyjamas in an obscene tent. He'd told Aidan he was safe here, and he had been Alpha long enough to have control over his actions.

He pulled a spare blanket from the cupboard in the hall and prepared for an uncomfortable night spent on the sofa. Switching off the lights and checking the door, he rearranged the cushions and curled up, draping the blanket over his legs. He sucked in a deep breath, running the mix of scents over his tongue, through his nose. It smelt right, the mix of Aidan's and his aromas, brambles and fresh grass. His eyes drifted closed, a soft smile curving his lips.

The scent of juniper was stronger, mixed with the warm, heavy scent of heat, of lust. Seth fought his way out of sleep, shifting against the weight against his legs, the hands trailing up over the planes of his chest. He moaned as a soft, wet mouth pressed against his lips, tongue flickering over the dry skin, seeking a way in. He let his lips part, allowing the hot muscle to slide in, to trail over the inner surfaces. He twined his tongue around it, sucking at the faint taste of cocoa, chasing it back behind the sharp ridges of teeth, the hard points of distended canines.

The hands pressed harder against his chest, fingers curling and nails scratching gently, teasingly at his skin. One set of fingers shifted, found the hardening nub of a nipple, circled it, rubbed over the pebbling skin until Seth arched into the touch, gasping into the mouth that was still pressed against his own.

He rose further out of sleep as hips ground down against the soft line of his cock, stirring his interest. The mouth pulled away from his, lips trailing over the line of his jaw, up to the tender, thin skin behind his ear where it sucked at the flesh until Seth tilted his head. He wrapped his arms around the warm body hovering over his, feeling heat and naked skin. He forced his eyes open, squinting almost cross-eyed at the close-cropped dark hair of the man currently fastening his extremely talented mouth around the peak of his right nipple.

Fangs scraped and tongue tip flickered and Seth arched and moaned before he managed to pull himself together enough to murmur, "Aidan?"

The other man nuzzled into his chest, trailing wet, open-mouthed kisses across the centre of his ribs, towards the other nipple. He hummed an affirmation but didn't look up from his task. Seth groaned inwardly and wrapped a hand around the curve of Aidan's throat and jaw, tugging his head upwards so that Seth could see him. Aidan's eyes were dark with heat and lust, irises a thin band of almost emerald green around the blown pupils.

"Aidan, do you want this? You have to be sure. Oh god–" Aidan turned his head and licked over Seth's palm, suckling at the base of his thumb. "Oh god, you have to be sure, because I don't think I can hold out much longer. Tell me you want this."

Aidan curled his tongue around the end of Seth's thumb, sucked the digit into his mouth, laved it carefully before he pulled back, hips grinding down against Seth's, eyes fixated on Seth's parted lips.

"Want this. Want *you!*" The words are almost a growl, distorted by the canines pushing against the swell of Aidan's lower lip. Seth groaned, eyes closing for a long moment, picturing the image of temptation rising above him. He wrapped strong arms around Aidan's torso, before he jack-knifed up from the sofa, pushing to his feet, taking Aidan with him.

Aidan wrapped his long legs around Seth's hips, their erections rubbing together in a most interesting way. Seth staggered slightly, but gathered his focus and stepped quickly towards the bedroom. Aidan nipped gently at Seth's throat before trying to seek out his mouth again. They crashed into a wall, and Seth took advantage of its support to ravage Aidan's mouth, tongue dipping deep and hard, exploring the delicious warmth until Aidan was pushing up against him, keening low in his throat.

Seth adjusted his grip and wobbled the final few steps into the bedroom, dropping Aidan's weight to the thick mattress, chasing him down. He fastened his mouth over the long line of Aidan's neck, sucking a raspberry stain up to the skin's surface, making sure that everyone would know he belonged to Seth, before he followed Aidan's earlier actions, searching out the hard pebbles of the other man's nipples.

He circled them with his tongue, laving the flesh until it glistened in the faint moonlight, sucking at each one until it darkened and tightened further, soft pleas falling from Aidan's mouth.

"Don't worry, I'll make it good for you, gonna get you so open and wet, until you can't bear the thought that I'm not inside you. Gonna make you come and come, make you so wet and sticky, you're never gonna think about anyone other than me."

Seth trailed his mouth down the centre of Aidan's body, nipping at the point of his sternum, sucking another mark into the soft flesh at the top of his belly. He dipped lower, his tongue circling Aidan's bellybutton, teeth scraping at the skin as he mouthed at it, swirling his tongue into the small indentation, a prelude to other things to come.

He moved lower still, hands tracing the elasticated edge of Aidan's pyjamas, pushing at the fabric, working it slowly downwards, kissing each strip of exposed skin.

"Take them off. Yours too." The words are low, husky, and Seth glanced up the long line of Aidan's body to find him resting, pushed up on his elbows, watching intently. Letting Aidan have these small moments of control, of choice, Seth stripped the clothing from Aidan's body, pulling away briefly to remove his own as well. He swore he could hear a soft growl coming from the head of the bed.

He moved back, kneeling between Aidan's legs as the other man wriggled back up the bed, pushing the pillows up behind him. Seth reached up an arm.

"Give me one of those." Aidan blinked but passed him a pillow, his skin flushing a deeper rose with realisation as Seth tucked it under his hips. A small smirk curved the edges of Seth's lips as he moved back down, this time placing a soft kiss to the curve of Aidan's hip bone, pushing his face into the cut of muscle, licking up with a long rasp of tongue.

Aidan sighed out a long breath, hips jerking slightly and Seth smiled against the skin pressed to his face as the scent of arousal deepened. Aidan's cock lay in a long line against his stomach, the shaft thick and smooth and Seth took his time, admiring it until Aidan groaned and tried to hide his face. Seth trailed a finger through the soft fuzz of hair around the base, then up the shaft, following the line of the vein, before following his fingers with his tongue.

He lapped at the smooth skin, pressed soft kisses to the shaft, curled his tongue around the tip, chasing the small pearl of liquid. Aidan's cock looked mostly human, maybe thinner, with less of a defined head. Seth slowly swallowed it down, hands firm on Aidan's hips, sucking lightly as he pulled back up. But he knew that, nice though it probably felt, this wasn't what Aidan needed.

Seth shuffled back a little more, mouth moving lower over the velvet soft skin of Aidan's sac. He mouthed at the small globes, sucking gently at the extremely sensitive skin, letting his fangs re-emerge to tease carefully. He felt the small tremor as Aidan's head collapsed back against the bed, his arms no longer able to hold him up, hips twisting and pushing against Seth's grip.

He licked at the small patch of skin behind Aidan's balls. His scent was strong here, deep and musky and Seth moaned against the skin, making Aidan shudder and cry out softly. Seth let his hands trail down, moving from the prominence of Aidan's hipbones, through the valley of his inner thighs, rotating his wrists so that he could cup Aidan's buttocks, tilting him upwards.

Aidan assisted by pulling his legs up, toes curling against the mattress, thighs spreading wide. Seth stared at the wanton display in front of him. He grinned slowly and dipped his head down again, licking a quick stripe up the length of Aidan's shaft before he moved lower again.

Burying his nose in Aidan's balls Seth inhaled deeply of his scent before he flickered his tongue against the small circle of muscle below. A gasp of surprise that devolved into a soft moan came from the head of the bed.

"What are... you can't... oh that's..."

Seth smiled against Aidan's skin and lapped up again, flattening his tongue this time, pressing harder as he licked all the way up to Aidan's sac. Using his fingers, he gently eased Aidan's cheeks apart, exposing him more clearly to his avid gaze. He rolled his tongue in his mouth, building up saliva and dipped in again, painting the furled muscle with tiny dabs and licks until it glistened and began to flush a soft pink.

Aidan continued to sigh above him, hips twitching in tiny circles, fingers clutching at the crumpled sheet below him. Seth pointed his tongue and licked harder at Aidan's entrance, working the tip into the small hole. Slowly it started to warm and flush a deeper rose, the muscle easing around his tongue. Seth groaned deeply against Aidan's body as he finally eased inside, savouring Aidan's hot, musky flavour.

"Oh god, Seth. You..."

"Mmmm, taste so good baby. Gonna try a finger now, you ready?"

Seth groped around on the bed for the lube he had dropped there, squeezing a small puddle of the almost translucent liquid into his palm. He slicked up a forefinger and trailed it around the small pucker before pushing slow and easy. Aidan opened up around him and Seth slipped just the tip inside, teasing the rim with tiny wriggles. He dipped his finger into the lube again and this time worked his finger in to the second knuckle, spreading the thick liquid liberally over the heated inner flesh.

Aidan mewled above him, hips pushing down, trying to get Seth's finger deeper inside. He obliged, gliding it all the way in, corkscrewing it around to coat Aidan's insides. Seth reluctantly eased his finger from the warm clench of Aidan's body, covering it with more lube before thrusting it back inside. It slipped in quickly and easily, Aidan's pucker opening up for it.

Seth tilted his finger, working at the rim, opening Aidan up before he pulled out, lubing up two fingers this time. He pushed slowly at the small opening, a low moan pulled up from his stomach as Aidan pushed against him and sucked him in, soft inarticulate cries spilling from him. Seth built up his speed and thrust in deep, curling his fingers, searching the velvet warmth for that small spot.

Aidan's muscles fluttered around his fingers, his cock jerking against his belly, precome spilling onto the flat muscles as Seth rubbed over his prostate. Seth leant in, lapping at the twitching plane of Aidan's belly, the head of his cock, determined to drive his lover crazy. The taste of salt and bitter-sweet precome exploded across his tongue. He continued to work the two fingers in and out, easing them apart as he pulled out, occasionally hitting that small inner spot.

Seth dropped down again, staring entranced at the way Aidan's body was opening up for him, the muscle smoothing out around his fingers. He ducked down, holding his fingers just inside, opening Aidan up for his tongue as he thrust inside, fluttering the muscle against the heat of Aidan's inner walls, sucking gently at the rim.

"Seth! *Need you, please...*"

"Just one more first. Gonna take another finger for me, sweetheart?" Seth's warm breath washed over Aidan's skin as he spoke, making the delicate membrane shudder, making Aidan beg.

"*Please!* Just anything, feels so good, didn't know... *Oh fu...ck.*" The last comes out on a long, low moan as Seth worked another finger inside, Aidan's passage now slick with lube and his own faint secretions. Seth twisted his hand, working the knuckles against the flesh that fluttered around them, his other hand slid up Aidan's body, rubbing over the reddened buds of his nipples, feeling the driving pulse of Aidan's heart under the flushed skin of his chest.

Not able to wait any longer, Seth eased up on to his knees and flipped Aidan over, the breath gusting out of him, a mix of surprise and the crush of his chest against the mattress. Aidan pushed himself up onto his hands and knees, tilting the pert curve of his ass up towards Seth, his body begging for him, words drowned in gasps and cries of need and want.

Seth stroked the remaining lube, now body-warm and dripping, along the length of his semi-hard cock. Aligning himself with Aidan's hips, he slowly fed himself inside, the twitches of Aidan's muscles pulling him gradually deeper. Seth dragged out again slowly, working his shaft against Aidan's inner walls, searching for the right angle.

He pushed back in, faster this time, Aidan's body opening up for him, his hips pushing back towards the cradle of Seth's pelvis. Seth could feel himself hardening further and pistoned his hips faster, wanting to push Aidan closer to the edge before they were locked together.

"God, so good for me, baby. So tight, burning me up, gonna knot you, fill you up. You want that, Aidan? Want to be tied to my dick, my spunk filling you up?" Seth moaned as the obscenities continued to spill from him, Aidan's soft pleas and gasps filling up the spaces as Seth thrust into him, hard and deep.

Seth could feel the clenching spiral in his stomach, heat flooding down towards his balls, skin flushing with blood and he wrapped his hands tight around Aidan's hips, hard enough to bruise, as he jerked Aidan back onto his cock, shoving in balls deep.

They both cried out in unison as Seth's knot pushed through the tight ring of muscle, Aidan's body flexing around it, gripping it tight as it began to swell further, pushing against him. Seth dropped forward, draping his body over Aidan's, one hand coming down beside Aidan's, fingers brushing. The other wrapped around Aidan's dick, working up and down, jerking him fast and dirty.

Aidan sucked in a breath as Seth rotated his hips, grinding deep inside him, the bulge of his knot rubbing over and over in all the right places. Another inhale followed and then Aidan arched, hips pushing back, head dropping and then flexing back, mouth opening in a wail of pleasure as he came hard, coating Seth's hand and the sheets below him.

Another two hip-jerking grinds were all Seth could manage before his own orgasm flooded through him, folding him around the body beneath him. Panting through the pleasure, he murmured softly, "Need to... on your side... 'kay?" Aidan blinked at the garble of words, but followed Seth's lead, sinking down onto the mattress, rolling onto their sides, Seth spooned around him. The movement tugged in all kinds of interesting ways at the point where they were joined, and Seth moaned as Aidan's body fluttered around him, pulling more pulses of thick come from his body.

After a long moment of panted breaths and soft moans, Aidan managed to squeeze out two words, "How long?" He wriggled his hips, trying to move out of the damp spot he had created.

"How long?" Seth sounded bemused for a moment before blood

recycling back to his brain caught him up. "Oh, about twenty minutes. More than enough time to get you off again." He grinned against Aidan's shoulder, nipped at the flesh, before placing a smacking, open-mouthed kiss to it.

He raised his come-covered hand and licked at the creamy whiteness, Aidan's eyes widening as he tried to twist to meet Seth's gaze.

"Mmm, taste good, sweetheart, but I think I can put it to better use just now." He twisted so that he could meet Aidan's parted lips, placing a soft, sloppy, salty kiss to them before he wrapped his sticky hand around the soft bulge between Aidan's legs.

He worked the slippery strands of come into Aidan's skin, feeling the almost minute twitches as Aidan's body fought to get hard again. He cupped a hand under Aidan's thigh, lifting it and moving it so that he could reach between them, tracing his fingers over the stretched thin skin between Aidan's legs. He could feel the bulge of his knot just inside, holding them together. He tugged backwards a little, moaning at the pressure, the way Aidan's flesh fluttered under his fingers.

Pushing forward again and back in, easing the strain on Aidan's opening, Seth walked his fingers back up, over Aidan's thigh and back to his semi-hard cock. He traced round the head, rubbing the tip of a finger against the slit, teasing at the small bundle of nerves, catching it with the edge of a nail.

Aidan sighed and pushed backwards before trying to thrust forward as Seth wrapped his hand around the length of his shaft. Seth released Aidan after a couple of strokes, grinning at the disappointed mewl that escaped his mate, before he captured his lover's hand and wrapped it around his cock.

"Pleasure yourself, baby. Wanna see you jerk yourself." Seth wriggled his arm under himself, supporting his weight on his elbow so that he could watch over the curve of Aidan's arm and shoulder as he stripped his cock. He licked and nipped at the bulge of muscle, eyes fixed on the motion of Aidan's hand, as it gripped and flexed, curving up over the head and back down to rub at his balls. Aidan's hips ground in small circles, pushing back into Seth, making him moan into the flesh beneath his mouth. Aidan's hand moved faster, his grip tightening. Seth could feel his inner muscles ripple and shudder around his deflating knot as Aidan came for the second time in a soft wave of pleasure.

Aidan collapsed back against him, head lolling against Seth's shoulder, lashes fluttering against his cheeks. Seth trailed gentle kisses across his shoulder and the curve of his neck, hand slipping in between them to ease himself from Aidan's body. Aidan shivered at the feeling of Seth's come trickling between his cheeks, curling up as Seth pulled away.

Moving quickly to the bathroom, Seth found a washcloth and ran it under the tap until it was warm. Squeezing it out he took it through, gently pushing Aidan onto his back and parting his thighs, cleaning the puffy, tender skin with soft swipes of the cloth. Wiping Aidan's stomach as well, he dropped a kiss to the dimple of Aidan's bellybutton, startling a sleepy laugh out of the other man.

He went and cleaned himself up before collecting the comforter from the floor and draping it over a drowsy Aidan, climbing under it himself, wrapping himself around his mate and inhaling deeply. He drifted off to the soft smell of juniper and brambles, intertwined.

Aidan woke, disoriented. The sun fell at the wrong angle across the bed and his pulse began to pick up speed even as his Were side tried to snuggle deeper into the body behind him. The body behind him? Aidan froze, breath stalling in his lungs. He made a catalogue of his body; he was naked; his body ached in unfamiliar places, but it was a pleasant, warm ache.

An arm curled over his waist, heavy and limp, and soft huffs of breath stirred the tiny hairs on the nape of his neck. The room smelt of sex, a mingled combination of his own spend and another's. Finally, his sleepy brain clicked into gear and a name tracked across his spinning thoughts—Seth. He was in Seth's bed.

Last night's events came back to him, replayed across his mind in hi-def Technicolor and Aidan could feel his cheeks flush red with shame. How could he have been so wanton? Another part of his mind smiled, mostly sated and relaxed, and asked when they would be able to do the whole thing again, perhaps with new positions. An image of Seth laid out beneath him, tawny hair spread across the pillows, lips kissed plush and swollen as Aidan rode him, flashed across his mind. Aidan bit his lip and swallowed down a moan as his cock stirred, twitching against his thigh.

"Good morning, gorgeous," came from behind him, the voice rough and deep with the edges of sleep. "Wanna tell me what you're thinking that's got you heating up like that?"

"No?" Aidan's answer sounded feeble to his own ears, so he wasn't surprised to feel Seth's lips curve in a smile against his shoulder blade. "I should... bathroom..." Aidan mumbled and almost fell out of the bed, staggering slightly as he disappeared into the small en-suite room, cheeks burning.

He leant against the door and pulled in a couple of slow breaths before he managed to control his arousal enough to piss. He flushed and washed his hands, staring at himself in the mirror. His cheeks still bore a flush along the line of bone, his eyes were wide, pupils full and dark with the slow burn of arousal that curled in his gut, surrounded as he was by Seth's distinctive scent.

There was a dark hickey on his neck, another on his stomach, faint bruising on his hips and Aidan groaned as he remembered getting each mark. Heat flared within him again and his hips thrust involuntarily, pushing his hard-on against the cool porcelain of the sink. It wasn't enough to discourage his body though and his hand trailed down, palm sliding over the long line of his shaft. A vague thought that it was wrong to jerk off in another person's bathroom, whilst they lay in bed, tried to cross his mind, but was quickly silenced.

Aidan's eyelids fluttered down as he pressed harder, trapping his cock between his hand and the curve of his lower belly. Another faint noise stuttered out of him, masking the sound of the door opening behind him. Seth stared at the scene in front of him, Aidan leaning against the sink, one hand on the rim, the other working the hard line of his dick. His fangs pushed out, visible in the mirror as his own arousal began to show.

Aidan could feel Seth behind him and his skin shivered in anticipation even as he flushed with the faint shame of being caught. He heard the soft sounds as Seth moved closer, the shift of air as he leant in, mouth pressing against the curve where neck met shoulder, fangs nudging at the skin. Aidan tilted his head in automatic submission and Seth bit down harder, teeth threatening to break the skin.

"You needing a hand in here, sweetheart?"

Aidan smirked at the endearment, lust making him brave as he responded, "Already got one, thanks." He gripped his cock hard and twisted up the length of it, stomach muscles contracting, breath hitching. He could feel Seth press another kiss to his shoulder before he moved in hard and tight behind Aidan, hands wrapping around his hips, cock slipping in between the globes of Aidan's ass.

"Maybe I got something else you want, hmm?"

Aidan's ass pushed backwards in blatant invitation but he kept his eyes closed, hiding from himself. Seth pulled away and turned him around, hands closing around Aidan's head and face, thumbs rubbing over his cheekbones, just barely brushing against the soft curves of his lashes.

"Look at me baby, wanna see you. Want you to see me." Aidan swallowed and opened his eyes, fixing his gaze on the hard swell of pectoral muscle in front of him.

"Up here." The command was soft, but infused with enough dominance to have Aidan's green gaze jerking up to meet Seth's glowing amber eyes. "There you are, baby. That's what I wanted. You okay?"

The sincerity behind the question had Aidan pausing, distracted. He thought for a long moment before he nodded and smiled, the corners of his eyes crinkling as his lips curved softly. "Yeah, I'm getting there. I am. I really am." He leant forward and pressed the smile to Seth's mouth, feeling the answering curve, before a tongue flickered out and brushed across his mouth.

Aidan let himself fall into the kiss, lips parting for Seth's seeking tongue, pulling in the taste of his lover as they explored each other slowly with soft licks and swirling probes, mouths shifting and rubbing as they nipped and sucked. The kiss continued for long minutes, a slow stoke of the simmering arousal between them, until Aidan's head fell back on a pleading moan.

"Need you. Please, Seth." Seth turned him round again, placing his hands on the rim of the basin, dotting kisses down the length of Aidan's spine as he dropped to his knees on the cool tile.

"Spread 'em, let me see you," came the murmured command and Aidan shamelessly parted his legs, although he flushed when he felt

Seth's palms on his cheeks, easing them apart. Seth stared at the small muscle, still slightly pink and puffy from their previous exertions. He lapped up over the skin, flexing his tongue against the opening to Aidan's body. He sucked at the rim and Aidan gasped at the sensations that shot through his body. He didn't know whether to thrust forward and away or back into the teasing licks of Seth's tongue.

He could feel the weight of Seth's gaze as he pulled back again, then the butterfly stroke of a single finger down his cleft, tracing round and round. It tapped gently and Aidan felt his knees buckle slightly, his fingers clutching onto the basin's edge.

"You gonna let me back in here, baby? I bet you'll open up for me real nice." Seth leaned forward and lapped again, once, twice, wriggling the tip of his tongue just inside before he pulled away, placing a firm bite to the left cheek of Aidan's ass. Aidan yelped and twisted round, trying to scowl down at Seth.

"Uh-uh. Face the mirror." Aidan turned back, gaze dropping to the pale ceramic of the sink, unable to meet his own eyes in the mirror tiles that lined the wall. He heard the tiny click of a lid flipping up and then felt the soft push of a finger against his entrance. He widened his stance a little more and pushed back, Seth's finger slipping easily inside. He sighed at the feeling and circled his hips, already needing more.

He twisted round, trying to reach Seth's mouth for another kiss, exchanging a soft caress that was more tongue and breath than anything else. Seth pulled out and came back with two fingers, the slight burn pulling a happy moan from Aidan. He wriggled his hips just as Seth crooked his fingers and sunbursts of pleasure shot through him, his cock thrusting up hard in front of his stomach.

"Mmm, there. That's it. Just keep doing that." Aidan fucked himself back onto Seth's fingers, his arousal drawing tighter. Seth's stare couldn't settle on either watching the way his fingers disappeared inside the heated clench of Aidan's body or watching the two of them in the mirror, Aidan's lashes fluttering against his cheeks as he rolled his hips.

Aidan's eyes shot open, meeting his lover's heated look in the mirror as Seth added a third finger. "Oh shit, I'm gonna—" Aidan pulled a hand from the sink, wrapping it hard around his length, tugging swiftly up. Seth twisted and corkscrewed his fingers, seeking that small bundle of nerves. Aidan felt the moment he found it, Seth's fingers tapping against it as he fucked into his own hand.

"Oh fuck, *oh fuck, oh...*" Aidan's voice degenerated into a low cry of pleasure as his muscles drew taut, balls pulling up as he came over the smooth surface of the basin. Seth wrapped an arm around him, holding him up as Aidan's knees shook with the force of his orgasm. Pleasure rolled through him in soft waves, eventually ebbing away and guilt slid in behind. Aidan turned an apologetic glance on Seth.

"Sorry. I know you didn't... but maybe..." Seth's fingers cut off his words as they pressed against his lips.

"S'okay baby. Didn't want to end up knotting you in the bathroom. It really sucks to be stuck in here. Not to say you can't make it up to me in the shower though?" Seth grinned, wide and dirty and Aidan blushed again, although he had no idea where the blood was coming from, since it felt like it was all pooled happily in his pelvis. His remaining modesty didn't stop him from fully exploring the differences between an Alpha Were's body and his own, with the help of plenty of soapy, slippery bubbles.

Twenty minutes later and cleaner of body if not in mind, the two men made it out of the bathroom and into the kitchen, where Seth made toast and omelets. They ate in companionable silence and Aidan washed up afterwards. It was only then that he realised that the only items of clothing he had with him were his pyjama bottoms and red sweatshirt, both of which were rather the worse for wear.

Seth smirked and lent him a pair of sweatpants and a t-shirt, which hung a little loose, even over Aidan's muscular figure. Aidan pulled them on and swallowed hard at the dark look in Seth's honeyed gaze.

"What?"

"My mate, all marked up and smelling of me, wearing my clothes. It's kinda hot. No, strike that, it's possibly the hottest thing ever. I hope you're not planning on getting out of the house any time soon." Seth's grin was full of dark promise and Aidan swallowed again. Then the first half of Seth's sentence registered.

"Mate?" A tremulous smile fluttered at the edges of Aidan's mouth, there and then gone. How could Seth say such a thing? He barely knew Aidan. He couldn't know that all Aidan had ever wanted was a family to replace the one taken from him by the past, someone to come home to. Did Seth mean what he was offering?

Aidan hadn't realised he had spoken that last thought out loud, until Seth stepped closer, cupping a hand around his jaw, thumb rubbing over the pink lushness of his mouth.

"Yes, I mean it. Knew it the first time I saw that red sweatshirt of yours, standing out so bright against the shadows of the world. My Red Riding Hood, walking so unsuspecting through the forest."

Aidan's vision swam slightly and he gave Seth a watery grin as he asked, "So does that make you the Big Bad Wolf?"

Seth let a low growl rumble up from his chest, the scent of Aidan's heat still warm in the air, as it would be until it abated over the next day or so. Aidan shuddered in response, eyes darkening, lips parting in invitation. Seth's fangs protruded and Aidan's pulse stuttered and jumped.

"Run." The command was low, pushed out and Aidan spun on his heel, dodging round the table and out the door. Red only made it as far as the bedroom before the Wolf caught him, but neither of them had the thought to complain.

If you enjoyed this story, you can discuss it with other readers and the author at the *Red and the Wolf* story page at http://forbiddenfiction.com/library/story/KM1-1.000104.

About the Authors

Claryssa Berg is a Norwegian writer of smutty fairy tales of various kinds, who has been published in English since 2004. When she is not twisting myths and ravaging fairy tales, she lives a quiet life in a smallish city in the middle of Norway, together with her son and her cat.

Mina Kelly lives in one of England's most historic cities. During the day she cooks from Roman recipes and swings medieval swords, trying to convince the tourists that history is more than just a pretty background to a photograph. From this she draws inspiration for her mixed up myths and flirtatious fairy tales, and has an especial fondness for things that go bump in the night.

Annabeth Leong found relief in erotica. Reading others' stories opened up a world of freedom and exploration. Writing it increased the thrill. Since her first published story in 2009, she has written for anthologies by Cleis Press, Ravenous Romance, Coming Together, and Circlet. Her work has appeared online at Every Night Erotica and Oysters and Chocolate. She is pleased to participate in Forbidden Fiction's Special Collections. Besides freedom of speech, Annabeth loves shoes, stockings, cooking, and attending concerts — probably in that order. She lives in Providence, Rhode Island.

Kailin Morgan has always been an avid reader. She discovered goth and industrial music and vampires and werewolves at about the same time. As part of the alternative subculture, she has always been open to different fashions, tattoos and piercings and self-expression. She rediscovered the love of writing through fan-fiction and has since quickly become addicted to the thrill of discovering new characters. Although most of her writing is m/m, she also loves writing strong female characters. Her writing tends towards fantasy, dealing with gods and monsters, but she loves to place them into everyday settings and see what happens. Now a slave to the muse, Kailin looks forward to spending many hours hiding from the Scottish weather, hunched over her laptop, typing feverishly whilst existing solely on caffeine.

Matthew Nadelhaft is originally from New York and now lives in Edinburgh. He graduated from the Napier University Creative Writing MA Program and is the editor for Edinburgh spoken-word/storytelling group Illicit Ink. His short fiction has been published in *An Electric Tragedy, Blood and Lullabies, The Reader's Digest 100-Word Story Competition, Desire* Magazine, and *Zombies Ain't Funny*. He studied anthropology, worked as a freelance journalist, co-edited the book "America Under Construction: Boundaries and Identities in Popular Culture" and published many articles and papers. He is a reviewer for Tangent and TangentOnline and has designed several boardgames, including the internet-hit "Oh No, There Goes Tokyo!" He is now bald after twenty years without a haircut.

A few years ago, **Nobilis Reed** decided to start sharing the naughty little stories he scribbled out in hidden notebooks. To his surprise, people actually liked them! Now, he can't stop. The poor man is addicted. His wife, teenage children, and even the cats just look on this wretch of a man and shake their heads. The best that can be hoped for is to just make him as comfortable as his condition will allow. Symptoms include two novels, several novellas, numerous short stories, and the longest-running erotica podcast on Earth. His website is at www.nobiliserotica.com.

Elizabeth A. Schechter is a stay-at-home-mom who lives in Central Florida, where she enjoys seeing the looks on the faces of the other playgroup moms when she answers the question "What do you do?" by describing herself as a pervy fetish writer. Her first novel, *Princes of Air*, was published in 2011 by Circlet Press, and her second, a steampunk novel entitled *House of the Sable Locks*, is forthcoming. Elizabeth can be found online at http://easchechter.wordpress.com/

R.W. Whitefield loves steampunk, fantasy, horror, and anything escapist. She has been writing since she was three years old, and at 25 years of age, shows no signs of stopping. In her spare time, she runs support groups and organizes activist events for her local LGBT community. She lives with a slightly neurotic cat. She likes long walks in the woods, cheesy movies, and three-piece suits.

About the Publisher

ForbiddenFiction.com is a publisher devoted to writing that breaks the boundaries of original erotic fiction. Our stories combine intense sexuality with quality writing. Stories at Forbidden Fiction.com not only arouse readers through sensations, but also engage them emotionally and mentally through storytelling as well-crafted as the sex is hot.

ForbiddenFiction.com is also designed to be a social reading environment. You'll have fun even if just reading the latest post each day, yet you will have the chance for so much more. Readers and authors can be part of ongoing discussions of specific works and individual authors as well as more general topics.

Sign up for a FREE Membership at **ForbiddenFiction.com**

www.ingramcontent.com/pod-product-compliance
Lightning Source LLC
Chambersburg PA
CBHW061134200626
46817CB00016B/1398